The Day the Streets Stood Still

JaQuavis Coleman

www.urbanbooks.net

Urban Books, LLC
97 N18th Street
Wyandanch, NY 11798

The Day the Streets Stood Still Copyright © 2014
JaQuavis Coleman

ISBN 13: 978-1-60162-539-7
ISBN 10: 1-60162-539-1

First Trade Paperback Printing October 2014
Printed in the United States of America

10 9 8 7 6 5 4 3

*This is a work of fiction. Any references or similarities
to actual events, real people, living or dead, or to real
locales are intended to give the novel a sense of reality.
Any similarity in other names, characters, places, and
incidents is entirely coincidental.*

Distributed by Kensington Publishing Corp.
Submit Wholesale Orders to:
Kensington Publishing Corp.
C/O Penguin Group (USA) Inc.
Attention: Order Processing
405 Murray Hill Parkway
East Rutherford, NJ 07073-2316
Phone: 1-800-526-0275
Fax: 1-800-227-9604

The Day the
Streets Stood Still

Word from the Author

Hello All,

Writing this story was very important to me. I wanted to give a lesson on falling from grace and life ills while holding your attention. I intentionally drop subtle gems for the people like me and came from where I came. There are always two layers to my books; not everyone will get the second layer but the ones who do . . . they feel me. You see, I talk to the readers but I whisper to the streets. The streets being people who grew up in the struggle and love to read books because it closely resembles their current or past lifestyles. My books are conversational or at least that's what my intentions are.

If you ever prayed to God, asking Him to show you the way, but in the same breath ask for forgiveness for the things you may have to do until you see the light . . . this one is for you. I understand. I am you . . . you are me. I am the streets. Love you all. *Raises cigar*

—JaQuavis Coleman

Chapter One

"Oh, yes! That feels so good." The moans and groans coming from behind the door were driving Sean crazy as he sat scratching his arms, legs and crotch like a million bugs were feasting on him. He had that dope itch and he needed a hit real bad, but he was preoccupied with what was happening on the other side of the door. The sound of "Sexual Healing" by Marvin Gaye played from an old CD player sitting next to him and as bad as he wanted to smash the radio to drown out the song, the CD player was the last of his belongings that he hadn't sold.

"Yeah, that's it," Sunny's voice filtered through the makeshift door. "Ahh yeah." Sean curled up his fists and pounded on his knees, silently praying that the music would drown out his sorrow as a lone tear made its way down his face. Images of Sunny's face, twisted with a look of lust and ecstasy flashed in Sean's mind and the music just seemed to make his imagination run wild even worse. That was his and Sunny's song back in the days, when things were right with them. He closed his eyes now, picturing how fine Sunny was when he first met her—her long silky hair, her beautiful face with its delicate features, and her striking green eyes—had all captured him then and never let go of their hold on him.

Now he sat listening to his woman sucking and slurping and moaning with another man. Sean bent over, cradled his head in his hands and hit himself in the head trying to get the visions to stop. What had he done to her? What had he allowed her to do to him?

Finally tired of sitting like a lame duck waiting to be fed, Sean jumped up from the filthy, threadbare couch he had been holding down inside of the drug haven he once owned. It had once been one of his most lucrative traps, but it was far from that now. Now, it was what they called a shooting gallery for fiends from all over the city. The darkened railroad flat had fiends in every corner shooting up, smoking, or sniffing their poison of choice. Sean jumped when he heard a scream coming from behind him. Two fiends were fighting over a pipe, the dude lifted his foot over and over again and stomped the woman mercilessly until her face was covered in blood.

Sean's legs were weak, he needed the package or else he was going to be sick in a minute. He jumped around trying to keep the monkey from crawling up on his back. From the sounds of it, Sunny was going to come out on top with the job she was doing and they would be able to get high. It seemed like an eternity that she had been behind that door with the young dope boy that had agreed to give Sunny two packs of heroin in exchange for sex.

Doubt was setting in on Sean and he was regretting the suggestion he'd made that Sunny get their package this time. He would usually take the lead with scoring, even if he had to stick up a store or snatch a purse or two, but tonight he was too sick to pull it off. Sunny and Sean had run out of scams since everybody knew them as mere fiends looking to score now. Sean had run out of favors on the streets and his name was mud with all the street cats that he used to deal with and even the ones that used to work for him. His reign at the top of the game didn't mean anything anymore.

Sean had to kick away empty beer bottles, empty crack vials and used needles to make a pathway to walk. The stench of garbage, shit, vomit and burning crack didn't bother Sean when he was high, but now, the odors were working his stomach. Either that or the sickness of needing a hit was getting the best of him.

"Ouch! Watch where you goin', nigga!" a butt-naked fiend screeched. Sean stumbled as she pushed him. He looked down at her strangely. She was laid out on the floor, pussy bare trying to feel for a vein on her inner thigh to hit. Her titties were shriveled like prunes and her hair was gone in patches. He remembered when she was a striking beauty that frequented his many establishments back in the days. Sean's eyes were wide and sweat dripped down the sides of his face. He hated when the memories of better times flooded his brain, making it harder for him to forget how much he had lost.

It was surreal how fast things could change. Sean whirled around and looked out on the entire room. The floor could barely be seen; every inch was covered with either a body or garbage or drug paraphernalia. Old food containers were scattered around with mold inches thick growing on them. There were flies buzzing all over because of the random piles of human feces that littered the floor. It wasn't strange for a fiend to pull their pants down and relieve themselves right in the room rather than risk leaving and losing their spot or worse someone stealing their drugs.

Sean averted his eyes to a line of dudes on the wall opposite from where he stood all in different stages of taking a hit—one was sucking the end of a glass pipe; one had the end of a belt in his mouth and a needle jammed in the crack of his arm; and one was sniffing a newly crushed pile of crystal meth. He scanned the room some more and his heart broke when he noticed a pregnant chick lying on a dirty foam mattress letting three dudes take turns having their way with her. Thoughts of Sunny popped into his mind.

Sean turned and went to knock on the door to get Sunny out of the room, but he paused when he heard her giggling and groaning like she was having the time of her life. He felt like someone had stabbed him in the heart as he listened to her.

"Oh, baby. Yeah, fuck me, baby. Yeah, daddy." Sunny moaned, sounding like she was in heaven. Those were words Sean had thought he'd only ever hear her say to him. His chest heaved now, but the aching inside of him for the drugs wouldn't allow him to bust in the room and grab his woman. He put his back up against the raggedy wall and slid down to the floor. With his radio on his lap, he turned up the music and let the tears roll down his face as he waited for Sunny.

After what seemed like an eternity, the graffiti-covered door creaked open. Sean got to his feet swiftly, his jaw was rocking feverishly and he clenched his fists at his side. Sean watched the young dope boy bop out of the room smiling with sweat glistening on his face and chest. His pants were still unbuttoned and halfway off his waist where the butt of his gun peeked out. He eyed Sean up and down with a smirk and then laughed at him. Sean looked at the kid with his thick gold Cuban link chains dangling around his neck and his slick True Religion jeans and Louboutin sneakers fitting him perfectly. Sean remembered when he was on that side of the game, wearing nothing but the best clothes, shoes and jewels. He felt ashamed now, standing there in his dirty, faded jeans, beat-down Nike Air Force Ones and a fitted cap so dirty the team name was barely visible anymore.

"That's a sweet piece of pussy you got there. I can only imagine how much sweeter it was before the whole town ran up in those guts," the young boy said to Sean snidely. Sean lifted his fists, but quickly but them back down when he thought about what would happen to him if he bucked on the young kid. Sean was once one of the most feared men on the streets but that had changed too.

"I guess you ain't king no more, huh? King Sean," the kid taunted, waiting for Sean to react so he could clap on him and make a name for himself.

Sean's chest rose and fell rapidly. His radio went crashing to the floor and he bit down into his jaw. The young boy stopped in front of him and pulled his weapon. He sat it on Sean's shoulder in a bold show of bravado.

"Remember when I worked for you and you beat my ass within a inch of my life that time?" the kid asked, then he lifted his gun and cracked it across Sean's head.

"Ahh." Sean winced crumpling to the floor in a heap. The kid stood over him and laughed.

"Damn, now I got your bitch working her jaws for me and ain't shit you can do . . . fucking fiend-ass nigga. You wasn't never no king in my eyes," the kid said viciously. Then he bopped away, leaving Sean scrambling up off of the floor with his pride and manhood crushed.

Sunny stumbled out of the room with her lipstick smeared, her hair an untamed mess and her cat green eyes wild. She refused to hold eye contact with Sean as she dug into her purse for the tiny bottle of mouthwash she had stolen from the drugstore earlier. Finally locating the bottle, she popped it open, took a swig of the mouthwash, gargled it and spit it right on the floor of the dilapidated house. It was all she could do to wash the taste of another man from her lips.

"You ready? I got a twenty for that and I'm hitting more than half for all of my hard work," Sunny smacked her lips and said with a disrespectful tone. It had been hard for her to maintain her respect for Sean and even harder for her to hide it. Sean got to his feet and pushed her back into the room. He snatched the bundle of heroin from her.

"You ain't doing shit unless I say you doing it," he growled, grabbing her collar forcefully. "You enjoyed that shit right? Right?" Sean barked in Sunny's face.

"Don't do that, Sean! Give it back to me! I worked for that!" Sunny whined like a baby, being real careful with her words. She knew how he could get when it came to sharing the drugs and with his already-bruised ego rearing its ugly head, Sunny knew Sean could be violently unpredictable.

"You get what the fuck I give you," Sean spat, squeezing the packs in his hand like he never wanted to let them go. Sunny burst into tears, something she knew would tug at Sean's heart. She had been working that trick on him since they were kids.

"But since you worked for it like you like to remind me, I'ma let you hit first," he relented, softening his tone.

Sunny hurriedly pulled out her works and with shaky hands she tied the belt around her arm. Sean pulled it for her so she could feel the best vein since the room was too dimly lit to see that well. He tossed one of the little black balls of heroin into the spoon and lit the bottom of it. Sunny was salivating as she watched him cook the drugs with a hawk's eye.

When it was ready Sean loaded Sunny's needle and touched the fattest vein in her arm. She looked at him, her once-flawless face finally showing the signs of her addiction. Sean turned his eyes away from her face, it was too painful to see her looking like she did now.

"Do it, baby, hurry up," Sunny whispered in her deepest sex kitten voice. Sean sniffled back the snot threatening to drip from his nose and plunged the needle into her arm easing the poison into her vein.

"Ssss." Sunny winced, her body relaxing against the chair. Her head fell back and her eyes rolled up into her head until only the whites were visible. Sean pulled the belt loose so the drugs could move through her system with ease.

"That shit must be real good," he said as he watched her head roll back forward and her chin fall to her chest.

"Yo, I'm next so c'mon," he demanded anxiously. Sean started cooking his portion of the heroin as his mouth watered waiting for the hit.

"A'ight you ready to hit me?" he asked without looking at Sunny. All of a sudden Sunny's legs did something funny that startled him.

"What the fuck?" he whispered. "You almost made me drop my shit. Stop the shit and get up and help me hit this shit. Don't be so fucking selfish all of the time," Sean growled at her. Then Sunny's body jerked like she had been hit with a bolt of lightning and she fell off the chair. Sean dropped the drugs, let go of the belt around his arm and fell down at Sunny's side.

"Baby! Sunny! Wake up!" Sean yelled, grabbing her into his arms. Sunny's body began convulsing and her eyes were completely white. Her legs flopped around like she was being electrocuted.

"Sunny! No! C'mon!" he yelled, slapping her face vigorously. White foam was spilling from her mouth and her body bucked so wildly even he couldn't hold on to her.

"Help me! Somebody, help me! Help me!" Sean screamed frantically. But there was no one in that house that would care enough to call an ambulance. No one would dare call 911 and risk having the cops bust up in there and break up their getting high.

"Help me . . . God, help me," Sean whispered through tears as he held Sunny's face up against his. He could feel her starting to get cold.

Finally Sunny's body went still. Sean laid her head down and looked down into her face. He couldn't stop the tears from falling as his body jerked with sobs. He hadn't cried like that since his mother had died.

"Sunny!!" he screamed at the top of his lungs. "You can't leave me! I need you!" he hollered some more. He lay his head on her chest and there was no sound. The heart he had fallen in love with so many years earlier was no longer beating.

"I did this to you. I did this to you," Sean said, his voice trailing off and his mind reeling backward.

Chapter Two

Summer 1992

"You tryin'a play me, nigga? What I look like my name is? Where the fuck is the rest of my money!"

Sean's eyes popped open when he heard his mother screaming. He crept out of his bed and opened his bedroom door a crack. Even over the loud music blasting through their house, he could still hear her yelling.

"Oh, you think because I'm a bitch you can short me? A'ight, I got something for that ass," his mother spat. Suddenly she was storming in Sean's direction. With his heart racing, Sean jumped back into his bed and pretended to be asleep. He knew if his mother caught him watching she would tear him up. When Sean heard her footsteps pass his bedroom again, he got back out the bed and cracked the door open again.

"A'ight . . . I'm a ask you one more time. Where is the rest of my fucking money?" his mother gritted. Sean's eyes grew wide when he saw his mother pointing a black handgun at the man cowering in front of her. His mother looked like one of Charlie's Angels standing there dressed in a pair of sexy cutoff jean shorts, a gold tank top with no bra underneath and a pair of gold stilettos, holding her gun out in front of her with her shoulders locked like a professional.

"C'mon, Mook, don't do me like that. I'm always square with you. I told you, I got robbed," the man pleaded with his hands up in front of him in surrender. Sean could see the muscles in his mother's beautiful, shapely chocolate legs flexing as she cocked her head to the side, something she did when she was angry.

"Nah, I ain't tryin'a hear that. If you got robbed I woulda been the first to hear about it from the streets. That's a bullshit lie and you know it, nigga. If I let it slide with you, I gotta let it slide with everybody," his mother said through her teeth. Bang! Bang! Two shots rang out. Sean jumped so hard he fell backward and a little bit of urine escaped his bladder involuntarily. Sean could hear the man screaming.

"She shot me! This bitch shot me! Y'all seen that . . . this crazy bitch shot me!" the man was hollering. Sean got back to his feet and went back to the door.

"Get him the fuck out of here. Throw him in the street with the trash where he deserves to be," his mother demanded. Sean watched as a group of dudes picked up the wounded man and tossed him right out of their apartment door.

"You ain't seen the last of me, Mook! On my life you ain't seen the last of me!" the man screamed. Sean's mother was unfazed by the man's threats. She strutted her beautiful body back into her living room, turned up her music and returned to all of her party guests.

"Now, anybody else got a problem?" she asked, her gun still hot in her hand. A few mumbles passed over the crowd of partygoers but no one spoke up. Everybody went back to playing spades, bid whist and blackjack like nothing ever happened. Within minutes there was the usual loud laughter, music and drinking again.

"Oww! That's my song!" Sean heard his mother scream out as she danced around. "Pass me my shit," she called to someone. Mook was the life of the party and the boss of a very lucrative heroin operation. Everyone gravitated toward her because she threw a hot party every night; she always had good food, good drinks and good drugs. Mook was beautiful with deep, dark ebony skin that was as smooth as silk. Her hair was a thick, jet-black mane down her back, her eyes were chestnut brown and slanted. Mook had a tiny waist, but big round hips that gave her an hourglass shape. She was an exotic beauty and people often call her the Indian, because she looked like one of those women straight from India. Sean thought his mother was the most beautiful woman in the world.

Sean jumped when he saw someone coming in his direction, but he quickly realized it wasn't his mother. He giggled as he watched an older woman that he called Aunty holding the hand of a man, leading him to one of the back rooms. That wasn't unusual at their house either. Several streetwalkers, who Sean called his aunties, paid Mook for the use of her house for turning tricks rather than risking themselves being on the street or working for a pimp who would only take their money. Sean's aunty was wearing a hot pink corset top, thongs, a garter belt and clear plastic high heel shoes. The man was smiling from ear to ear as he followed her. Sean waited a few minutes and then he snuck out of his room, ran down the hallway and put his eye to the keyhole of the room his aunty had gone into. Sean smiled as he watched his naked aunty bounce up and down on the man.

"Boy! Get away from that door and get yo' ass in the bed. You know I don't play that," Mook scolded playfully when she caught him. Sean giggled and ran back to his room. Just as he was about to close his door and really get in the bed this time, he heard that familiar voice that he looked forward to every day. Excited, Sean cracked his door open again and just like he had suspected, Fox was walking in. Sean watched dreamily as Fox glided his six foot, four inch frame through the door. Fox wore a fresh Pelle Pelle leather jacket, crisp Timberland boots that looked clean enough to eat off of and a diamond pinky ring that could blind you from a distance. Fox was his mother's friend, but Sean would pretend in his mind that Fox was his father. Fox was a basketball legend in their neighborhood and one of the few dudes who had actually made it to the NBA. After two years in the league Fox blew out his knee and was cut from team after team. Finally, Fox gave up trying to get rich the legal way and took the money he'd made in the league and invested in his street business. Being a boss in the streets had made him much more money than he would've ever made in the league. Sean wanted to be just like Fox when he got older. He even practiced how to walk and talk like Fox.

"Mook . . . baby, what's good?" Fox chimed, flashing his sparkling smile as he made his way over to Sean's mother.

"Ain't nothing new, baby." Mook smiled, her cheeks flushing red. She got on her tiptoes and threw her arms around Fox's neck so she could hug him. He patted her on the ass and kissed her on the top of her head. Sean giggled; he had always secretly hoped that one day Fox would marry his mother.

"Let's talk," Fox said to Mook.

"Yeah, baby . . . anything for you," Mook said dreamily. "Nobody touch my bud," Mook warned her party guests before she walked out with Fox. She started down the hallway toward Sean's room with Fox hot on her heels. Mook knew he was watching her ample backside so she smiled to herself and gave him a show.

Sean scrambled to get back into his bed. He knew his mother and Fox would be coming into his room to talk business like they always did. Sean also knew his mother had taken the bottom out of his toy chest and hid her money there.

"Yo, Mook, I'm not gonna lie. You made me a believer, baby girl. You always come through with your ends," Fox complimented. Mook turned her face away; she didn't want Fox to see her blushing. Her palms were getting sweaty and she felt things below her navel thumping. She rushed over to Sean to make sure he was asleep. Sean squeezed his eyes shut tight until he was sure his mother wasn't watching anymore.

"This is half of the re-up money and I'll have the rest in a few days," Mook said as she came up out of Sean's toy chest with the rubber banded stacks of cash.

"Good looking out, Mook. I'm putting my chips up now for a rainy day. I'm thinking about going straight one of these days. My lady is carrying my seed and I need to be setting things up for the future," Fox said, flashing his sparkly, diamond-encrusted smile. Mook's heart dropped and her stomach began doing flips, but she put on a fake smile anyway.

"Congrats, Fox, I'm real happy for you. I hope it's a boy that you can love as much as I love that li'l nigga right there," Mook said trying her best to keep a smile on her face. She was really dying inside though. She had loved Fox from the day she had met him. Mook had to make a choice when it came to Fox—business or pleasure—she had opted for business and now she was secretly regretting it.

"Yeah, this a good li'l man you got here," Fox said as he folded a twenty dollar bill into a paper airplane and placed it on Sean's pillow like he always did. That night, Sean finally drifted off to sleep with a smile on his face.

"Mommy, do you love me?" Sean asked his mother the next day as she walked him to school. That was the one thing about Mook, it didn't matter if she had partied all night into the morning, she always cooked Sean a full-course breakfast and walked him to school herself every day.

"Aww, baby, you don't have to ever question my love for you. I love you more than I love my own life and anything on this planet," Mook said, stopping to bend down in front of her son so she could look him in his little eyes. Sean threw his arms around his mother's long, slender neck and hugged it as tight as his little arms could.

"I love you more than anything on the planet too," he said. His mother laughed.

"You still not going back home with me. You going to school today," she joked as she led him up the steps to his school. Sean giggled too.

Later that afternoon Sean walked home with his usual group of friends after school. He couldn't wait to tell his mother about his day. Sean rushed up the front steps to his house and just as he made his way through the door he ran smack dead into someone.

"Sorry," Sean huffed, out of breath, realizing he had hit someone. When he looked up into the face of the person, his heart jerked in his chest. Sean stumbled backward a little bit as the man he had run into smirked at him evilly.

"Watch where the fuck you going, *orphan,*" the man hissed, his eyes glinting with evil. Then he stepped around Sean and ran into a waiting car. Sean turned around and watched the car screech away from the curb and it wasn't until about two minutes later that he remembered the man's face. *That was the man my mother shot,* Sean's little mind registered. He whirled around on the balls of his feet and scrambled inside the door. Sean raced up the stairs to his apartment. He was going to tell his mother that the man had come back and that she needed to make sure she had her gun close by.

"Mommy! Mommy!" Sean screamed as he pushed in their apartment door. As soon as he crossed the doorsill Sean slipped on something wet and fell so hard he hit his chin on the floor.

"Ahh," he screamed. "Mommy! Mommy!"

The house was silent, which was strange to Sean. From birth, he never remembered his house being quiet. Even if it was he and his mother alone, she always had some sort of music playing. Sean went to pick himself up from the floor, but slipped down again on the same slick, wet stuff. He crinkled his brow and looked down at the wet substance that was making it so hard for him to get his bearings.

Sean's eyes went wide and his mouth dropped open when he looked down and saw both of his hands were covered in deep, dark red blood. He began turning around and around, trying to locate the source of the blood. His little legs were shaking now and his heart was hammering so hard he could barely breathe.

"Mom . . . mmy?" Sean whispered, his teeth chattering as he took a few steps forward. Urine spilled from his bladder involuntarily at the sight. He couldn't scream, cry, run or react. His feet had become cement blocks connected to the floor as he looked down at his mother lying in a pool of her own blood with her throat slashed so far down her head looked like it was almost separated from her body. Sean's entire body shook, his mouth hung open, but he would not leave his mother alone.

"Agggghhhhh!" It was the screams of Mook's best friend and Sean's aunty that finally alerted everyone that Mook was dead. Sean had stood in that one spot for hours, unable to move, unable to scream and unable to get help. Aunty had called 911, but the ambulance wasn't going to move the body; that would be up to the city coroner now.

Fox was the first person to arrive that had set Sean at ease. Fox picked Sean up and carried him away from the crime scene and the throng of detectives and police officers that had swarmed Sean's home. Fox set Sean down on his bed, pulled him close and cried with him.

"I'm not going to let nothing happen to you. I'm always gon' be here for you, little man . . . you hear me?" Fox whispered as Sean was wracked with sobs.

"Look at me," Fox said, pulling Sean away from his chest so he could look into his little eyes. "I don't make promises to nobody . . . but I'ma make you promise today. I will always be here for you," Fox said sincerely. Sean shook his head up and down, signaling his understanding.

"Now tell me what happened when you got home today. Was there somebody here with your mother? Did you see anybody outside? I need to know everything that happened once you got here," Fox probed, his tone serious. Sean shook his head up and down vigorously.

"Okay good . . . It's important that you tell me who it was, but you can't tell nobody else, especially not those cops out there," Fox whispered. Sean leaned into Fox's ear and whispered. Fox's eyes went into slits and he bit down into his jaw.

"That's real good that you were brave enough to say. I'm going to take care of it, little man, but remember what I said . . . police can't be trusted so if they ask you . . . you ain't see nobody here," Fox replied, squeezing Sean's shoulder. Sean shook his head again.

"Now listen, they are going to come here to speak to you and probably take you downtown or something until they can sort out who will take care of you now. They're not going to let you go with me or else you know I would take you home in a heartbeat. Take this, it's my number. As soon as you get to a place, call me. I ain't gon' forget about you. I loved her too," Fox told Sean as he handed him a card with his number on it. Sean put the card in his pocket. Then he rushed over to his toy chest, opened it, dug into the bottom, moved the fake bottom out of it and pulled out his mother's stash. He rushed back over and handed it to Fox.

Fox was almost moved to tears as he accepted the bag. "You already smarter than the average nigga. You knew those pigs would toss this place and find all of what she worked for and steal it didn't you," Fox said to Sean. Sean just shook his head again; he still couldn't find the words to say anything with his mouth.

"This is yours and I will hold it for you. You already all right with me, little man," Fox assured. "Let me get out of here before the pigs start lurking. Remember what I said . . . call me."

Sean touched the card in his pocket and he felt a little more at ease knowing Fox would never let him down.

The day after his mother's funeral, Sean sat on his grandmother's stoop swinging on an old rickety porch swing that he had always loved to play on when he and his mother would visit. Now that he lived there, Sean didn't like the swing as much. As he sat swinging, he heard the creaking of the screen door of the connected house next door. Sean looked up just as a little girl came outside onto the porch of the house.

"Whatchu lookin' at, ugly?" the little girl growled, raising her fist at him. Sean's eyebrows flew up into arches and he stopped the swing from moving. He didn't know if he was more shocked by the little girl's striking beauty or her sassy mouth. Sean stared in awe at the pecan-colored girl with her heart-shaped lips, tiny nose, long jet-black ponytails and her almond-shaped, glistening, green cat eyes.

"You live there now? I heard around that you ain't got no mother," the little girl said cruelly with a smirk.

Sean's eyes went into slits and he jumped up from the swing. "Shut up before I punch you in the face!" he gritted, his fists balled at his sides.

"You ain't gon' do nuthin'," the little girl spat, boldly climbing over the small brick partition that separated her porch from Sean's grandmother's. Before Sean could react, the little girl was standing in his face almost nose to nose. He hadn't expected that. He backed up a few steps, thrown by her beauty up close.

"What's your name anyway, ugly?" the little girl asked, softening her tone a bit.

"It doesn't matter," he said, hanging his head a little bit. The little girl brushed passed him and flopped down on his grandmother's swing. Sean looked at her strangely. He had never met a little girl so bold in his life.

"I'm Sunny," she said as she pushed back with her toes to make the swing move.

"I'm Sean." Sunny gave him the once-over and the mean face she had worn softened a bit. She even almost smiled, which was rare for her.

"How old are you?" she asked.

"Ten."

"Me too!" she said excitedly.

"I'm sorry for what I said about your mother," she said. "Sit down."

Sean walked over tentatively and sat next to her. Sweat was dripping down his back and he balled up his toes in his sneakers. Sunny pushed the swing hard enough to move it for the both of them.

"You gonna be my new best friend," she told him.

"How you know I want to be your new best friend?" Sean asked, looking down at his feet.

"I could tell by the way you look at me. I know when a man wants me," Sunny answered sassily. Sean didn't know it then, but her words would prove to be very powerful later.

"Sunny! Sunny!"

Sunny jumped up from the swing and moved away from Sean like he was suddenly a dangerous animal. Terror danced in her eyes and unnerving fear suddenly played out on her face.

"I gotta go," Sunny whispered, her words coming out almost breathlessly.

"Sunny! What the fuck I tell you about leaving out of this house without permission!" a woman screamed from the doorway of the house next to Sean's grandmother's.

"Sorry, Mommy . . . I . . . I . . . was just . . ." Sunny stammered, her bold and sassy attitude gone, replaced by a voiced filled with fear and apprehension.

"You was just my ass! Get the fuck in this house. I have to go to work and Rodney is babysitting you for the night!" Sunny's mother boomed. Sean looked at the woman's wide, fat face drawn into a scrunched-up scowl and immediately thought Sunny looked nothing like her.

Sunny climbed back over the brick partition and inched slowly toward her mother, who was standing brooding at the front door. When Sunny got to the door, her mother snatched her by the collar and dragged her inside the house.

"Please! Don't!" Sunny screamed. Sean jumped up, but quickly realized there was nothing he could do to save her. He tried to listen, but all he could hear was voices yelling back and forth.

"Agggh! I'm sorry!" Sunny screamed as her mother dragged her down to the floor by her long hair. Sunny felt something in one of her knees crack as it connected with the floor. "Please, Mommy! I'm sorry!"

"You fucking fast and hot! Right? Right?" her mother growled as she winded her hand in Sunny's hair for a good grip. "Anywhere there is a boy or a man with a dick you wanna be there right!" her mother screamed, balling her huge, portly fist and punching Sunny in her back and chest. Sunny instinctively threw her arms up over her head in an attempt to shield her mother's blows, but she was no match for the woman's fury. Sunny's mother screamed, spit, kicked and punched Sunny's frail body until she grew tired. Sunny's lips were busted and bleeding, her nose was throbbing like it was broken, and she had friction burns on her knees from her mother dragging her across the hardwood floors. Just like so many times before, Sunny wished she was dead so she could escape her house . . . escape the beatings and neglect.

"Now, bitch . . . I'm going to work. Stay in your fucking room and stay away from my fucking man! If you try to leave this house, so help me God when I get home you gon' get worse than what I just gave you," her mother wolfed, out of breath from beating Sunny. When she was finished her mother used her foot and kicked Sunny in the ribs for emphasis. Sunny lay there in a heap, rolling around in pain.

"I said get the fuck up from here!"

Sunny slowly dragged herself up from the floor and barely made it to her room. She eased her aching body into her bed as tears flooded down her face. She couldn't believe that confessing to her mother what her stepfather was doing to her would turn out to be so disastrous.

When Sunny heard the door slam she knew her mother was gone; she also knew what would happen next.

Rodney, her stepfather, didn't even give it fifteen minutes before he was turning the doorknob to her bedroom door. Sunny had locked it. She counted in her head . . . *ten, nine, eight, seven, six, five.* She didn't even get a chance to finish before he had retrieved the spare keys and opened the door.

"What we tell you about locking doors around here?" Rodney asked snidely. Sunny pulled her blanket up around her neck and closed her eyes.

"C'mon, don't play hard to get. What happened to you was your fault. I told you your mother wasn't going to believe you if you tried to tell her. I told you it would just make it worse . . . didn't I," Rodney taunted. Sunny could hear his belt buckle jingling as he took it a loose. Tears streamed out of her tightly shut eyes and wet her pillow.

"You should like this by now. You ain't no little girl no more," Rodney said. He sat down on the bed with his erect penis in his hand.

"I do it because I love you and I love your mother. If you didn't do this, I would leave her and then she would take it out on you . . . See it's all a part of being a family," Rodney went on. Sunny bit inside of her cheek until she tasted the metallic taste of her own blood.

"Sit up. I'm gon' show you something new. Something you'll always be able to use in life," he said as if he was a caring father teaching his daughter some necessary life skill. "If you suck a man's dick real good, he will always be good to you. You can't lose learning how to suck dick at a young age," Rodney went on, stroking his erection roughly.

"Now sit up and let me show you," he panted. Sunny didn't budge. She couldn't make herself get up.

"Don't be difficult because I like to be fair. I like for you to want to do it," Rodney wheezed, growing more excited by the minute. Sunny lay stock still, her brain screaming do what he said, but her body saying no more.

"Damn, look what you made me do," Rodney said, as he ejaculated his own body fluid all over his hand.

"Get the fuck up!" he barked, suddenly turning into a different person. He jumped up off the bed, snatched the blanket off of Sunny and grabbed her up roughly.

"Please," she begged through tears. "My mouth is busted."

"Well I guess that will make you work harder and faster," he said, forcing her head into his musty crotch. Sunny gagged as she took his limp manhood between her lips. The salty taste of his leftover cum burned the open cuts on her lips and was bitter on her tongue.

"That's it. Gag on it until it grows in your mouth. I'm going to teach you all of the tricks," Rodney whispered, throwing his head back in ecstasy.

A year after he had been living at his grandmother's house Sean awoke one night to the sound of something hitting his bedroom window. Startled, Sean jumped up and grabbed the baseball bat he always kept next to his bed. In the dark, Sean inched around, his heart hammering wildly against his chest bone.

Tick. Tick. Tick. The sound came again, this time Sean realized it was something like rocks hitting his bedroom window. Breathing shallowly, Sean rushed over to the window to see where the noise was coming from. He immediately put his bat down when he realized the source of the noise. Sean rushed to unlock his window and pushed it up quickly.

"Sunny, what are you doing out here?" Sean whispered harshly, his face folded into a confused frown.

"Just please let me in," Sunny replied, bouncing on her legs like she had to pee. Sean had never heard her sound so scared and vulnerable. They had been friends for an entire year now and Sunny was always like an angry tough girl. She had even fought a few boys in the neighborhood when they tried to bully Sean because he was the new kid.

"I'm coming down. You gonna have to climb into the basement window. You can't get up here," Sean whispered.

"Okay," Sunny said, hurrying to the back of Sean's grandmother's house. Sean crept out of his room and down the steps. His grandmother had super ears and he knew any creaking noises would wake her. It seemed to take forever to make it to the basement but Sean finally did. He pushed up the slats on the small basement windows. He could see Sunny already lying on the ground waiting to slide in.

"I hope you can fit," Sean said, worried that Sunny's growing hips and butt would get stuck. Sean had definitely noticed how his best friend was rounding out with newly formed woman curves. He had often fantasized about them during his adolescent wet dreams.

"C'mon hurry up. If my grandmother wakes up she's gonna flip," Sean urged. Finally her body dropped through the window onto a pile of boxes his grandmother had there. Seeing how easily Sunny was able to drop onto the boxes and climb down into his house, it suddenly occurred to Sean that if Sunny could get through the window and use the boxes to climb down, any burglar could. He quickly took the stacks of boxes from the window and locked it.

"Can I stay here with you tonight?" Sunny pleaded, sweat wetting her hair and the sides of her face. "I really can't go back home right now. If I can't stay here I will have to sleep on the street," Sunny rambled. Sean looked at her confused. He hadn't seen her look so frazzled before.

"Like . . . um . . . a sleepover?" he asked, his eyebrows scrunched low. Sunny and Sean had been friends for over a year, but they had never had a sleepover before. "I . . .

I . . . don't know if Big Mama is gonna allow that," Sean said tentatively.

"Please, Sean . . . just sneak me in your room and I'll sleep under your bed. Please. I can't go back home tonight. My mother ain't there and . . . and . . . I'm begging you," Sunny pleaded, her voice suddenly quivering on the brink of tears. Sunny couldn't stop the flood of tears coming from her eyes. She sunk down on top of a box.

"What's the matter, Sunny?" Sean asked her, sitting down next to her. He was suddenly scared inside but he was trying his best to look strong.

"He . . . he . . . is messing with me. But now, he's going . . . you know . . . all the way in," Sunny stumbled to find the words. She pointed the area below her navel for emphasis. Sean's eyes hooded over and his fists curled up at his sides.

"What you mean all the way in? You mean like he's trying to hump you?" Sean said through clenched teeth as he sprang to his feet. Sunny hung her head and began sobbing. She rushed into Sean and put her head on his chest and cried. Sean stood there helplessly, not knowing if he should hug her or go kill her stepfather.

"C'mon. You can stay in my room tonight. Any night you want," Sean comforted, wrapping his arms around her. Sunny kissed him on the cheek.

"Thank you, best friend." She smiled through her tears.

That night Sean couldn't sleep. His mind raced in a million directions with the information Sunny had given him about her stepfather. Sean allowed her to snuggle her body close to his and he wrapped his arms around her so that she would feel protected. Sean watched as Sunny fell into a fitful sleep. He could only imagine what she was dreaming about.

***

Sunny heard the door to her bedroom creak open and she snapped her eyes shut as tight as she could. Maybe if she pretended to be in a dead sleep he would leave her alone this time. The scent of alcohol entered the room before he did and when she smelled it, Sunny lost all hopes of escaping it tonight. She could hear him breathing like some wild animal in heat. Sunny cracked her eyes and he was jerking his dick to get it hard enough. She swallowed hard because that meant there would be more than touching this time again. After a few minutes, she felt her bed moving under all of his weight. Sunny clutched her blankets in a death grip, but they were ripped away from her anyway.

"Please! Stop!" Sunny yelled out, hoping that her mother would intervene.

"Shut the fuck up," he growled, pointing his gun right in her face. Sunny swallowed her screams back down her throat.

"Open your fucking legs. You love this . . . I know you. You a fast-ass little hot bitch," he panted. Sunny looked down and caught a glimpse of his tiny, slimy, musty dick. She snapped her eyes shut and did as she was told.

"I'm a virgin," she croaked out through tears.

"Even better," he snarled. He leaned down and let a gob of his alcohol-reeking spit fall from his mouth onto Sunny's nearly bald vagina. Sunny let out another belch of sobs.

"I said shut the fuck up or I'll blow your brains out and that bitch of a mother of yours," he said gruffly as he swiped his hands up and down to make sure his spit served as a lubricant.

"Ouch," Sunny cried as he probed her virginal opening with his finger first. "Yes. Nice and tight like I like it." He reared up over her and grabbed his dick in his hand. With his knees he forced her slim, child-like thighs open.

"Please don't," Sunny tried one more plea. Her words seemed to just turn him on.

"Ahh," he grunted as he thrust into her with all his might.

"Ahhhhh!" Sunny belted out. Pain like she had never experienced before shot through her vagina, butt and abdomen.

Sunny jumped out of her sleep so fiercely that she scared Sean. His head immediately began pounding from being snatched out of his own fitful sleep.

"Sunny? You all right?" Sean wolfed as he jumped up. He looked at her strangely. Her eyes were wild, her chest was moving up and down rapidly, and her fists were clenched like she was ready for war.

"It's me, Sean. You are at my house . . . Remember, you came here last night," Sean said, trying his best to help her calm down. Sunny looked at him and immediately the corners of her eyes went soft.

"I'm sorry. I just . . . I had a bad dream," Sunny explained. She closed her eyes for a few minutes because she knew that what she dreamt about was actually her reality.

"One day you won't have to live with all of that, Sunny, I promise. One day I'm going to save you from all of that," Sean said with a sincerity in his voice Sunny had never heard from anyone in her life. Sean meant every word of it, too.

Chapter Three

Fall 1999

"Get the fuck up, nigga!" Sean barked, his favorite Glock extended out in front of him. Fox had given Sean the gun as a gift, followed by the words, *"This is the piece that spilled the brains of the nigga who killed your mother. It's yours now."*

"You like fucking with little girls? Huh! You nasty m'fucker! I've been waiting years for this day, you fucking dog!" Sean snarled, cracking the gun over the sloppy, smelly overweight man's forehead.

"Sean! Don't! Let's just leave!" Sunny screamed, her face a mess as the purple, green, and blue rings around her left eye became filled with a fresh set of blood pooling under her skin.

"I said get up, nigga, and face me like a man! You can put your hands on a seventeen-year-old girl . . . well face a m'fuckin' seventeen-year-old nightmare now, bitch," Sean gritted, this time hitting Sunny's stepfather so hard the white meat became exposed on his forehead. Sunny started bouncing on her legs like she had to pee, her hands flailing in front of her like she had touched something hot.

"Sean, please. Stop! He will kill you or get you arrested!" she pleaded. Sean turned toward her, his face folded so tightly in a frown Sunny hardly recognized her friend standing there.

"You come and tell me this nigga been raping you since you was a little girl . . . your ass just had an abortion with his baby at seventeen and you think I'm gonna stop?" Sean spat so hard small specks of spit flew out of his mouth and sprinkled onto Sunny's battered face.

Her shoulders slumped in defeat and she hung her head low. Sean was right, she had run to him and confessed after the abortion and after her mother had almost beat her to death for sleeping with her stepfather . . . or as her mother had put it, Sunny had seduced her man. Sean flew into an immediate rage. He had been waiting years to get his hands on Sunny's stepfather.

Sunny had been Sean's best friend since the day he'd met her and he loved her from a place so deep inside of him that he sometimes couldn't explain the things he had done and gotten into with her growing up thus far.

"Please, Sean. I just don't want you to do something stupid and end up in prison. I wouldn't be able to live with myself," Sunny sobbed. "Let's just leave. Let karma deal with his sick ass," she urged, shooting an evil eye at her helpless, groveling stepfather.

Seeing Sunny so upset made something inside of Sean soften as usual. He turned back toward Sunny's cowering stepfather and placed the Glock against the man's temple.

"You fucking lucky nigga. If you ever fucking touch her again, you might as well cut your own dick off and swallow it because next time I won't have any mercy on your ass," Sean said through his teeth. He grabbed Sunny and pulled her out of the house. Once they were back on his grandmother's porch next door, Sean turned to Sunny with a look of love in his eyes.

"It's time for us to get a place of our own. You'll be my roommate and I'll take care of you until you can get on your feet," he told her with sincerity. Sean was making enough money now that he was helping his grandmother with her bills, buying his own clothes and practically taking care of Sunny already.

Sunny threw her arms around his neck and hugged him, her tears wetting his neck.

"I love you, best friend," she cried. He couldn't say a word to that.

Something inside of Sean changed that day. He had too much pride to admit that he was in love with Sunny, who all these years had just been his best friend and nothing more. He couldn't see himself telling her he loved her, only for her tough girl to come out and say something smart in return. Sean decided he'd keep that information to himself until the time was right. If the time was ever right.

As they stood there embracing, a long, sleek, smoke gray big-body Mercedes-Benz pulled up in front of the house.

"Aye, lovebirds! What's the word!" Fox called out from the Benz.

Sean quickly unhooked himself from Sunny and stepped away from her like she had a disease. Sunny blushed, waved at Fox and scurried into Sean's grandmother's house. Sean put on his best Fox imitation walk and bopped over to Fox's car. Sean leaned down into the open passenger side front window, trying not to look so flushed from his encounter with Sunny and her stepfather.

"You in love! I see that shit all over your face," Fox joked. Obviously Sean's efforts to hide his emotions hadn't worked on the man who knew him so well.

"Nah, nah. She's just my best friend. She's like my sister, man . . . you know that," Sean replied, his cheeks still burning.

"Yeah, I used to say that same shit about Mook. The chance I never took and never got to take in the end," Fox replied, his voice trailing off a bit.

"Anyway, I guess when you're ready to admit that you love that little fine thing you will. For now, get in. Let's talk," Fox said, flashing his signature sparkly smile. Sean hurriedly got into the Benz. He gave Fox some dap with one hand and dug into his pocket for a knot of money with the other. Sean handed the money to Fox eagerly like he did every time his mentor and boss showed up.

"Dayum, boy . . . you just like Mook. All business, all good, all the time," Fox complimented, flicking through the stack of cash real quick. Sean loved to get compliments from Fox, so he was smirking to keep himself from all out cheesing.

"Listen, you been really putting in that work. I see you out here living your mother's legacy. I'm telling you, she would've been proud," Fox continued. Sean nodded, his stomach feeling funny like it always did whenever Fox reminisced about his mother. He never really knew what to say back to Fox when he gave him compliments or spoke of dreamy memories that Sean most times wanted to put out of his mind. Fox was his idol, most times Sean was so awestruck by the man that he just liked to listen to Fox speak.

"Take a ride with me. I wanna show you something," Fox said, as he pulled away from the curb. After riding in silence for a few minutes, Fox spoke up.

"You know I always think about what it would be like if my son was still around . . . you know . . . you and him, growing up together," Fox started, his tone a little more serious than usual. Sean shifted in his seat as his friend Liam's face showed up in his head.

"I never blamed you for what happened you know. I know you blamed yourself for years, but that was just what was in the cards for him . . . you know, part of some plan that I'll never understand but don't question no more. I just want you to know that I never blamed you . . . never,"

Fox went on. Sean turned his face and stared out of the passenger side window; tears were burning at the backs of his eyes as he tried to fight away a memory.

"Let me show you something," Liam whispered to Sean. It was the middle of the night and one of the many occasions Fox had picked Sean up for a sleepover with Liam after Mook had died.

"I'm 'sleep," Sean had grumbled. Sometimes Liam annoyed him. Sean was already eleven and Liam was just eight so sometimes the younger boy was a little babyish and pesky to Sean.

"C'mon you gonna like it. Everybody is sleeping and I won't be able to show you tomorrow before you go home. I'm telling you . . . c'mon," Liam urged, pushing Sean's body to keep him awake. Sean let out a long exasperated breath, tossed the blanket back and got up from Liam's oversized bottom bunk bed.

"Hurry up," Liam whispered, waving Sean on. Liam opened the door, peeked down the long hallway of his parent's huge mini mansion and crept out into the hallway. Sean followed him, sleep still clouding his brain. Both boys went down into the basement, where Fox had his office, his bar and his private area set up. Liam knew his father's sanctuary was off-limits, but he was too excited about his discovery to care.

He kneeled in front of Fox's large, cherry wood, executive-style desk and called Sean over silently with his hands.

Sean knelt down next to him, his face folded in confusion.

"My father left his drawer opened by mistake," Liam said as he tugged on the large bottom drawer on the side of the desk. "And look what I found in it."

Sean's eyes almost bulged from his head and his heart kick started in his chest.

"You better put that back," Sean whispered harshly.

"It's not loaded," Liam said, picking up the .50-caliber, Desert Eagle Special and pointing it.

Sean jumped out of the way and pushed Liam on his arm.

"Don't point that! Put it back!" Sean whispered harshly again.

"Man, we could play cops and robbers. This ain't got no bullets in it," Liam said. "Watch," he said, quickly turning the gun into his chest. Sean's eyes shot into huge circles, but before he could snatch the gun from his friend, Liam had already put his finger through the trigger guard.

"Don't . . ." Sean started. Bang! His words were clipped short by the gun going off. Sean threw his hands up to his ears because the loud boom had instantly deafened him. He fell backward because he had been so close the Liam that the power from the shot had even knocked Sean on his ass.

Sean opened his mouth to scream, but no sound would come out. He lay rocking back and forth covering his ears when Liam's mother and Fox raced into the room.

"No!" Liam's mother screeched. It was the last thing Sean remembered from that night before the shock of the situation had caused him to slip into darkness.

"Yo, we here. Where ya mind at, man? You daydreaming about that girl, huh?" Fox said, snapping Sean out of his memory.

"Nah . . . nah," Sean replied, swiping his hands over his face to shake off the painful memories of his friend Liam.

Sean looked out the window and then looked back at Fox with his eyebrows up.

"That's right. We here for you. Good work deserves to be rewarded. You know who used to always say that to me right? Mook, that's who. Man, I'm telling you I should've made her my lady back then," Fox said dreamily. "Let's go inside. Pick out what you want. It's only right."

Sean couldn't open Fox's car door fast enough. He had been dreaming about getting a car for months since he'd gotten his license early, but he knew he would be saving forever to get the car he really wanted.

"Make sure niggas know who took you to your first dealership and made a all-cash transaction. Hear me," Fox told Sean, putting his hand on his shoulder like a father would a son. Sean shook his head up and down vigorously. He wasn't really even listening to Fox anymore.

Sean was in awe of all the Mercedes-Benz cars and trucks lined up on the lot. He rushed up and down the aisles, smiling all goofy like. Fox walked up behind Sean as Sean used his hands to shield the sun so he would peek into the window of an all-black E-class.

"Hey, man, let me rap with you for a minute," Fox said, interrupting Sean's excitement. Sean stood up straight and looked at Fox expectantly.

"When you walk into a place like this . . . one that screams class and wealth, you don't run around like an excited bitch in a shoe store or something. Nah, you walk in smoothly, cool and shit. You act like you ain't buying shit and you let them beg you to buy something. When they see you looking like you look right now, they know they got them a dummy nigga willing to pay his ass for anything they throw his way . . . feel me," Fox lectured, his tone more stern than Sean had ever heard it.

Sean nodded his understanding and stepped away from the car he was admiring like it all of a sudden had poison on it.

"And a E-class is a bitch's car. As a man, you shouldn't be looking for shit less than an S or maybe that new G truck . . . nothing else. How am I going to retire if I can't trust you to make me proud out here?" Fox went on. Sean looked at him with wide eyes.

"What? You thought an old ex-NBA player with two bad knees and a bum hip would be hustling forever?" Fox asked, smiling. Sean couldn't answer because that's exactly what he thought. He had never even contemplated the fact that one day Fox might not be around to hold his hand through the game and help him navigate the streets.

"I just thought you had some more time," Sean said with a regretful tone.

"C'mon, man, this is what all of my work is all about. You . . . the next generation that will take the torch that me and your mother lit for you. Making sure you have a good grasp on the game before I sail away into the sunset is what it's about, baby boy. A nigga ain't never plan to stay this long, but I had to make sure Mook's kid was good. Remember the money you gave me in the bag the day your mother was killed? Well I'm about to show you what we gon' do with it. I told you it was yours," Fox said with genuineness. "Now let's go start this over again and let these white motherfuckers scramble for us out this bitch. Shit, I was looking forward to my glass of champagne from these cats. That's how I make them get down when I roll up in here," Fox joked.

Sean laughed, but he was seriously taking it all in. He was like a sponge learning everything Fox did and said. Sean felt like all of Fox's lessons would one day serve him in the streets, he just didn't know how soon it would be.

Chapter Four

After three hours at the dealership, three glasses of champagne each, and a lot of haggling, Fox handed Sean the keys to a brand new big-body, black-on-black Mercedes-Benz S500.

"This is how you do it. You are seventeen and your first car was a big-body Benz . . . Always remember how high I set the bar," Fox told him.

"Thanks, man. I don't know how I can ever repay you," Sean gushed, his foot itching on the gas pedal.

"You don't owe me or nobody else shit. I wanna see you at the crib tonight . . . you know a celebratory dinner and kind of like a retirement dinner for me. I got something I want to give you and talk to you about," Fox said.

"A'ight bet. I got that consignment paper for you, too," Sean told him.

"Just bring it tonight, wrap some in a gift box like you bringing something for my lovely wife. The rest, you go and buy some food items from a real nice restaurant or some wine and you box the money with it, you know like you're a polite guest not coming to dinner empty-handed. We gotta get smart out here now. Too many eyes in the sky on the streets. Never even speak on it like that out here. The Feds love to watch me. And if they love to watch me, it won't be long before they love to watch you," Fox told Sean.

"I got you," Sean agreed.

"Now go show off, but don't be late for dinner. Adina hates when m'fuckers show up late and so do I," Fox said. He smiled and stepped back from the driver's side window so he could admire his protégé in his new ride.

"Looking good, baby. Looking damn good," Fox beamed, nodding his head up and down with approval. With that, Sean pulled out of the dealership lot. He didn't care what Fox said, he was smiling from ear to ear like a boy getting his first taste of sex. That was exactly how he felt.

Sean drove straight to his grandmother's house with his new car. His adrenaline was pumping as he caught glimpses of dudes in the street stopping and trying to figure out who was driving the sleek, new Benz. Sean liked the attention, but he was heeding Fox's advice—*real niggas don't go seeking attention they command it without effort.*

Sean couldn't wait to show Sunny his new whip and take her for a ride. He was thinking, maybe he would ask Sunny to go to with him to Fox's retirement dinner tonight. Sunny was probably in the house pouting about her situation and Sean was always the one to cheer her up since they were younger.

When Sean pulled up to his house he squinted his eyes and pursed his lips when he noticed a black Suburban with shiny, chrome, spinning rims sitting out front. The SUV was kitted out with a custom grill, police-grade black tints, and a huge system in the back that was blasting reggae music.

"Who the fuck is this disrespecting my crib?" Sean growled under his breath. He could feel his insides heating up as he eyed the strange, intruding vehicle. The SUV was blocking the entire front of the house so Sean had to pull his Benz a few spaces back, which made him seethe inside.

"This m'fucker acting like he live here?" Sean said, his jaw rocking back and forth. He touched his gun that was stashed in the back of his waistband and moved it to the front to make it more readily accessible, just in case the occupant of the SUV was up to no good. Sean got out of his Benz and walked slowly toward the house, all the while eyeing the strange SUV with a scowl painting his face. The windows on the truck were tinted so dark, Sean couldn't see inside at all. He couldn't front though; the Suburban looked like money with its custom paint job, halogen lights and big wheels. It looked like a hustler mobile right off the back, a fact that caused Sean more unease. He gripped his gun under his shirt and moved forward slowly. Just as Sean made it to his grandmother's gate he heard the front door open creak open. Sean swiveled his head quickly, being careful not to turn his back on the strange SUV too long.

"Why you out here looking like you about to blow some shit up?" Sunny joked, smiling brightly. The passenger side window on the SUV went down as soon as she stepped out of the house and Sean could finally see inside.

"Aye, gal! I don't have all day to wait," the driver yelled out. Sean's eyebrows shot up on his face as the shock of the situation registered in his brain. He looked from the dude in the SUV to Sunny and back to the SUV.

"I'm coming, Faheem. I'm coming," Sunny called out, smiling and blushing like she was the happiest girl on the planet. Sean's heart started pounding so hard his head began swimming. He clenched his fists at this side and swayed a little on his feet.

"You know him?" Sean asked incredulously, his bottom lip turned in by itself—something that always happened when he was angry. Sunny giggled at him because she knew he was jealous.

"Boy, I told you I was seeing somebody. You never believe me when I talk or what? He's my new man. He's gonna be my ticket off this fucking block, too," Sunny said as she sauntered sexily down the porch steps.

Oh, so my offer from earlier was just bullshit? Another nigga gonna save you? Sean thought to himself.

Sean bit down into his jaw when he noticed that Sunny was wearing a very revealing, bright yellow sundress that hugged her body so snug he could even see the indent where her bellybutton was. The dress left nothing to the imagination and it outlined Sunny's smooth butt and legs and lifted her D-cup breasts into perfect mounds on her chest. She also wore a pair of high-heeled wedge espadrilles that made her look like a grown woman and nothing like a seventeen-year-old girl. Sunny had her hair pushed away from her face in a neat ponytail that hung down her back and for the first time she had on makeup. Sunny was so stunning Sean had to cough to keep from saying something. He could feel his mouth hanging slightly open because he had never seen Sunny dressed up like that. She had never gone to those lengths to be around him; whenever they hung out she was always in jeans, sneakers and sweatpants. "You want to meet him? His name is Faheem," Sunny asked, now standing right in front of Sean.

"Nah . . . no need," Sean replied with an attitude. "Just tell that nigga when he come around here, respect my grandmom's crib and don't be blasting that monkey music 'n' shit," Sean retorted while he squinted his eyes into evil dashes and stared at the man behind the wheel.

In a bold act of bravado, the dude Sunny had called Faheem jumped out of his kitted-out Suburban and walked around to the passenger side door all the while eyeing Sean like he had something to say to him.

Sean noticed the huge diamond cross sparkling on Faheem's chest and the iced-out big-faced watch glistening from his wrist. Faheem was a pretty boy, with perfect cocoa skin, a small, neatly trimmed goatee, and deep-set intriguing eyes. He was tall like a basketball player and dressed pristinely in a pair of dark Levi's, a crisp white T-shirt that fit his body close enough to show off his muscular chest and six pack abs, and a pair of gleaming white Nike Air Force Ones. A pang of jealousy flitted through Sean's chest causing him to instinctively touch his waistband and snarl at the man he now saw as an immediate nemesis.

Faheem noticed Sean's little gesture and he laughed as he kissed Sunny on the lips and opened the door to let her into his ride. He closed the door once she was inside and turned his sights back to Sean. Faheem smirked at Sean as if he saw Sean as a little punk or a joke. The two young men shared a heated, glaring, staring exchange; neither of them wanting to be the first to back down.

Faheem finally broke the heated exchange by touching his waistband the same way Sean had a few minutes earlier.

"The way I got the info, blood . . . she's like your sister or more so you're like her little brother, so chill the fuck out. You don't know me and I don't know you. She's gonna fuck with niggas. That's life. Find you a bitch and forget about mine," Faheem said snidely as he bopped toward his driver's side door.

"Fuck you, nigga. You don't know me and I don't care to know you. Fuck from in front of my house," Sean snarled, baring his teeth like a rabid dog. Sunny rolled her window down.

"Faheem, get in this car and stop. Y'all both need to stop," Sunny said like what was happening was a joke. Faheem laughed and made his way back to his driver's side door. Sean stood there brooding, his chest rising and falling rapidly.

"Don't wait up for me. If I decided to come in tonight, I'll call first," Sunny said waving at Sean cheerfully. Sean stood there seething inside, his fists curled so tightly at his sides his knuckles ached. He didn't know if he was more angry at Sunny for having a man or at her man for taunting him; whichever it was, Sean made a promise to himself that day that he would never let himself be chumped like that again.

Sean went into the house, his pride and his feelings crushed.

"Sean? Is that you?" his grandmother called out from the kitchen. Sean smiled and headed to see his Big Mama. She would definitely make him feel better; she always did.

"Hey, Big Mama. How you today?" Sean asked, grabbing her affectionately from behind. He loved hugging his grandmother's soft, ample body. She reminded him of a big teddy bear and she always smelled like peppermint.

"I'm fine, baby, but I want to talk to you about something," his grandmother said, her voice going low and her tone sounding grave. In the years since Sean had moved in with her, his grandmother hardly ever sounded like that. She was always upbeat and happy.

Sean released his grasp on her and stepped around to her left so he could look at her face. When he did, he noticed her red-rimmed eyes and a flush of red on the tip of her nose. Sean could tell his grandmother had been crying.

"Big Mama . . . what is it? Somebody did something to you?" Sean asked, swallowing hard as all sorts of crazy things ran through his mind.

His grandmother moved away from him and shuffled her swollen feet to one of the chairs that sat at her kitchen table. She flopped down into the chair and let out a

winded breath like she had walked for miles. Sean was
starting to see signs that his grandmother was getting old
and he didn't like the feeling or thought that she might
not be around forever.

"Big Mama, tell me what's going on," Sean said, sliding
into the chair across from her. His nerves were on edge
because his grandmother was the only family he had left;
he couldn't stand to think that something or someone
was disturbing her.

"Well, baby, I have a problem," his grandmother sighed.
"After all these years of working, struggling and buying
my own things, I ain't never asked the government for
nothing." His grandmother hung her head and shook it left
to right. Sean's eyebrows dipped on his head as he listened.

"Now, they want to tell me that they taking the house
from me, Sean. Them people want to tell me that I owe
them taxes on property that been mine since the sixties,"
his grandmother lamented, cradling her head in her
hands. Sean's shoulders slumped and he twisted his lips.

"I ain't got it, baby. We might be getting put out of
here," she broke down and cried, her soft double chin
jiggling with every sob. Sean drummed his fingers on the
table, his mind racing in a million directions. He knew
that he couldn't just go upstairs to his shoebox stash and
drop the cash on his grandmother because she would
have too many questions about where he'd gotten the
money from, but he also wasn't going to sit by and let his
grandmother lose her house.

"Give me the paperwork, Big Mama. I'll have Fox take
me downtown tomorrow to take a look and see what we
can work out. I'm the man of the house, Big Mama, and
I'm not going to let us get put out. I promise you I'm
not going to let us get put on the streets," Sean assured,
standing up and hugging his grandmother around her
neck. She smiled and used her cloth handkerchief to wipe
her tears.

"I want you to always live your life right, Sean. Always do what's right or else things you do will come back on you with a vengeance," his grandmother said. Sean stood hugging her for what seemed like an eternity; her words were planting seeds in his mind, but he wasn't ready to let them grow roots.

"I will, Big Mama. I promise . . . I will," he said, crossing his fingers because he knew that an orphan like him would never survive if he always did the right thing.

When Sean pulled up at Fox's house he immediately impressed with the huge, wrought-iron monogrammed gates that protected the property.

"This nigga Fox living how I'm gonna live one day. This that shit I'm talking about," Sean said to himself, smiling from ear to ear.

Sean pushed the button on the intercom outside of the gate and when he was asked to announce himself he yelled out his name. The regal gold and white gates opened slowly and Sean drove his Benz through them slowly. He inched his car along the circular driveway and almost hit one of Fox's parked cars because he was busy admiring the grounds. Fox had the most beautiful, plush green manicured lawn Sean had ever seen. There were custom-cut shrubs, trees and bushes adorning the front of the house. The shrubs directly in front of the steps leading up to the door had a huge F and A cut into them and there were dozens and dozens of different colored roses, daisies and hibiscus flowers surrounding the letters. There were two water fountains outside of the house—one shot water straight up into a beautiful stream with green and blue lights around it making the water look colored as it shot into the air and the other seemed to be on a timer as different sized plumes of water flew up into the air from it, reminding Sean of a brochure he'd seen for the Bellagio hotel in Las Vegas.

"Yo . . . this is some rich man shit for real. I gotta step up my game. Damn, Fox, I wanna be like you when I grow up," Sean mumbled to himself, his eyes wide with awe.

Sean parked his Benz, but he was so dumbfounded by the beauty of the mansion's grounds, he only grabbed the nicely wrapped gift box off the seat.

Fox was waiting in the doorway smiling and waving Sean inside.

"C'mon, man. You too young to be walking up them steps like a old man," Fox joked.

"Nah, I'm just still trying to catch my breath from this house," Sean called out as he climbed the twenty white and gold marble steps that led up to Fox's front door.

Sean's eyes must have told the story of what was running through his mind because Fox was rolling laughing by the time Sean made it to the door.

"Man, you act like you ain't never been nowhere nice before," Fox laughed, taking the gift box from Sean's hand and giving him a quick hug and pound.

"Yo, Fox . . . your new house is the shit. I thought the other house was big, but this one . . . this like some rapper shit. Nah, more like some mafia don shit," Sean gushed, his eyes still wide and roving.

The inside of the house wasn't a disappointment either. Just like the outside, it was regal inside. The floors were made of all shiny gold marble and a huge mosaic tile design spelled FOX in the center of the floor. Sean was even scared to walk on the floors with his Timbs on.

"These floors got specks of real solid gold in them," Fox bragged as he glided with his usual swagger.

"I believe it," Sean whispered breathlessly.

"Go ahead, man, look around for a minute. See what hard work gets you in this game," Fox said, patting Sean on his shoulder. "When you're finished, go in and say hi to Adina. You know how she gets if you don't speak. Then go into the dining room and give me a few. I'm going to freshen up, I'll be back in a shake," Fox said. Fox set the gift box Sean had given him down on a small glass top table as if he didn't know what was inside.

Sean walked farther into Fox's mansion and to his left he noticed a room that resembled a shrine to the game of basketball.

"Damn," Sean gasped. He walked slowly inside, his mouth opened like a kid who discovered a mountain of candy. Sean rushed to the left side of the room where there was at least fifty basketball trophies lined up. Some were on shelves and others were so big they sat on the floor. Sean squinted and bent down to read some of the little gold plates on the trophies—MVP 1990, MVP 1991, SLAM DUNK CHAMP 1993, COLLEGE ALL PRO MVP, were just some of the trophy tags Sean read. He knew Fox had told him he was in the NBA, but Sean had no idea Fox had been such a decorated and celebrated ball player. Sean thought about something he had heard Fox say to his mother when he was younger: *"Shit, I make more money in the dope game than I would've ever made in the league."*

Sean wondered if that was true and if it was, could he be as skilled as Fox in the game. Sean looked over at Fox's desk and his heart sank. Sean picked up the framed picture of his mother and a hard lump formed in his throat. He stared at his mother's beautiful smiling face with Fox standing right next to her, both of them decked out in white fox fur coats. Sean put the picture back down and picked up the one next to it—a picture of Liam.

"I miss both of y'all," Sean whispered. He placed Liam's picture back down too. Sean shook his head left to right trying to shake off the gloomy feeling starting to creep up on him.

Sean rushed out of Fox's study and walked across the expansive foyer to formal living room. There, he took in eyefuls of the rich, priceless paintings on the walls. Sean could tell that Fox had put down millions on everything in that house.

"Millionaire status. That's what I'm talking about," he told himself.

After about fifteen minutes Sean remembered that Fox had told him Adina would be pissed if he didn't come speak to her. Sean rushed into the kitchen, but was stopped dead in his tracks once he made it through the doorway. Sean's eyes popped open and he immediately felt blood rushing to his private area as he took in an eyeful of Adina's thick, round behind and her perfect, hairless vagina from the back. She was bending over into the stove with a short skirt on and no underwear. Sweat immediately broke out on Sean's forehead and his heartbeat sped up. He tried to avert his eyes away from Adina's bare ass, but he couldn't help but stare at the perfection in front of him. Sean swallowed hard and cleared his throat, finally alerting Adina that he was there, but she had already glanced back and smiled slyly at him. Adina knew he was watching her all along, which made Sean even more nervous, but excited him at the same time.

"Hi, baby," Adina cooed, smacking her full, glossy lips.

She slowly stood up and with the sexiest motion she shook her beautiful, fluffy head full of naturally auburn curls and turned around like a performer from a porn movie. It was the most erotic thing Sean had ever witnessed. It all seemed to be happening in slow motion, like he was watching his own personal porn movie. Sean put his hands in front of his zipper to hide the pulsing hard-on growing in his pants.

"Um . . . hey . . . um . . . hello, Miss Adina," Sean stammered, gulping the ball in his throat. *Damn she is fine as shit!* he said to himself.

"Come over here and give me some sugar," Adina said sexily; pointing her long, red-painted nail at her smooth, blemish-free cheek. Sean tried to bop over like Fox would, but he stumbled because he was so thrown by her beauty.

"Don't hurt yourself now." Adina winked and giggled. Sean gave her a quick tap kiss on the cheek and a little hug. His pulse quickened from the contact.

"I ain't gonna bite. Give me a real hug," Adina chimed, thrusting her double-D cups into Sean's chest. When he felt her firm, erect nipples against his chest, Sean thought he would just bust a nut on himself right on the spot.

"Mmm, you smell good," Adina complimented. "I love a young man who takes pride in himself, it's sexy," she said in a throaty sex kitten voice.

"Th . . . thanks," Sean huffed, wiping sweat from his head. Adina laughed heartily, her huge breasts jiggling and seemingly teasing Sean.

"I tend to do that to men," she joked. "Go ahead on inside to the dining room. Dinner is almost ready."

Sean started for the door, but before he left, he turned back and looked at her one more time. Adina was a straight beauty from head to toe. Time had been kind to her because her smooth butte-colored skin didn't show one sign of aging. Adina had unmistakable Hispanic features—her long, luscious, dark eyelashes; thick, pouty full lips; round, deep brown eyes and her distinctive hourglass shape told the story of her heritage right off the back.

"Go ahead now before you get caught staring." Adina smiled, shooing Sean into the dining room. Sean snapped out of his ogling daydream and rushed into Fox and Adina's large, grandiose dining room. Sean was even in awe of that room.

"This house is fucking amazing," he whispered, touching the top of the table like it was made of something precious. The dining room boasted a long, shiny, black lacquer table with at least twelve tall back, black and gold plush cushioned chairs. The table was set with beautiful gold chargers and shiny black fine China dishes. There were four grand centerpieces made of roses, hibiscus flowers and long stems of baby's breath. It looked like someone was getting married the way the décor was put together. Fox was a king and that was definite in Sean's mind now.

"Aye. Made yourself at home I see," Fox called out, interrupting Sean's thoughts. Sean stood up and pushed his chair back, clumsily bumping his legs on the table and rattling the dishes.

"Oops. Shit . . . I'm . . . I'm sorry," Sean stuttered, finally making it from behind the table so he could greet Fox properly again. Sean rushed over and extended his hand for a pound and hug again, although he had seen Fox earlier.

"Why you so nervous?" Fox laughed. "It's dinner at my house. Relax and act like you at home. You ain't new to this," Fox told him.

Sean couldn't look Fox in the face and tell him that he had been lusting after Adina, which had put his nerves on edge.

"Nah . . . I'm not nervous," Sean lied with a fake smile painting his face. "It's just that this is all so nice. I ain't never been to a nice dinner like this unless it was a restaurant."

"This should be how you strive to live. If you don't treat yourself like a king, trust me, kid, nobody else will. Start thinking of yourself as King Sean and everybody will fall in line . . . feel me?" Fox told him. "Now let's sit because if we don't that beauty in there ain't gonna feed us," Fox followed up, smiling and laughing as he took his seat at the head of the table. Fox had Sean sit at his right hand, a slight gesture that Sean noticed and was elated about.

Adina came out and began putting beautiful silver platters of scrumptious-looking food down on the grand table. Sean was having a hard time trying to keep his eyes on the table and the food and not on her. Fox was speaking to him about something, but Sean could barely listen to him. The sound of the doorbell had finally saved Sean.

"Ahh, my other guest has arrived. Sit tight while I go answer the door," Fox told Sean. Fox stood up and patted Sean on the shoulder. "Don't hurt yourself watching her. She's way too much for you," Fox whispered.

Sean's cheeks flamed over with embarrassment. Had he been that obvious? He shook his head in shame and hoped that Fox wasn't pissed with him.

After a few minutes, Fox returned with a tall, older white man who had the iciest blue eyes Sean had ever seen.

"Meyer, this is my boy Sean . . . Sean, this is Meyer," Fox introduced. Sean got up, met the man eye to eye and shook his hand. Sean got an ill feeling in his stomach from the man. It might've been the fake, halfhearted smile Meyer cracked or the fact that he couldn't really hold eye contact with Sean; whatever it was, Sean decided right away he didn't like him.

"Let's sit," Fox said, breaking the awkward exchange between Sean and Meyer.

"Sean here is like my son. He is about to go to college this year," Fox said proudly. Meyer nodded and cracked another fake smile.

"Yeah. Sean is a good kid. He works real hard. Isn't that right, Sean?" Fox said, his left eyebrow raised expectantly.

"Yeah. Yes. I'm about to go to college," Sean played along. He had no idea where Fox was going with the storyline, but Sean only had plans on going to the school of the streets, not a lame college.

"Are y'all gonna eat all of this food or what?" Adina snapped, shooting Meyer an evil look. She hadn't even greeted Fox's guest with so much as a hello. Sean took that to mean that Adina didn't care for Meyer either. Sean felt slightly better about his gut feeling on Meyer now.

"Calm down, baby girl. We are digging in right now," Fox tried to ease the tension in the room. "Everything was made Kosher, too, Meyer . . . you know . . . we respect the Jewish religion." Fox smiled awkwardly.

"I'm not that hungry to tell you the truth, Fox. I had to attend one of those big Bar Mitzvahs right before I came here. Another bite and I might bust," Meyer replied, rubbing his stomach, another fake smile curling his lips. Fox's facial expression changed like he had just been told he only had days to live.

"Well then I'll eat later," Fox said, throwing his material napkin atop his empty plate. "We will all eat later," Fox followed up, his voice stern. Adina went to open her mouth in protest, but Fox threw his hand up in a halting motion and shot her a look that would've silenced anyone.

"You go in the kitchen and put us up a plate. I'm going to take Meyer out back . . . have a cigar or something," Fox said seriously, glaring at Adina as if to say, *keep your mouth shut and do what I say.*

Sean was silent, but his stomach was churning with hunger. He wanted to eat all of that good-smelling food Adina had prepared, but he wouldn't dare go against anything Fox told him to do. Adina looked crushed, her eyes went low and her lips dipped at the sides like she was about to cry.

"C'mon, boy . . . let me and Meyer show you how real men talk business," Fox said, shooting Sean a telling glance. Sean nodded his agreement, pushed away from the table and stood up. He could feel Meyer staring at him and Sean wanted so badly to pull out his gun and ask the

Jew what he was looking at. Sean bit down into his jaw to keep his cool. His ill feelings toward the white man wasn't getting any better with the passing time.

Fox led Sean and Meyer poolside to a beautiful, marble top outdoor table with several plush lounge chairs surrounding it. On the table was a small, shiny, mahogany cigar box with exclusive Cuban cigars inside and a bottle of single harvest 1858 Cognac Croizet, Cuvée Léonie cognac.

"Fox, I'm surprised you know about this cognac. It costs over $150,000 a bottle. You surprise me again, eh," Meyer said, his eyebrows up in arches on his face. Sean sensed a hint of jealousy in the man's comment.

"Why are you surprised? C'mon, if anyone knows class and taste it's me, Meyer. You know that. We've been doing business long enough for you to figure it all out," Fox replied. Sean could hear a hint of defensiveness and annoyance in Fox's voice and knew that Fox had been offended by Meyer's doubt of his knowledge of the finer things.

Fox lit a cigar for himself and Meyer. He winked at Sean as if to say, *you're too young.* Fox did pour a swallow of the exclusive cognac into three snifters for each of them.

"It's not for sipping," Fox told Sean as he handed him the little glass. Meyer threw his back immediately, Fox followed and Sean did as he saw them do.

"Nothing finer," Meyer said, then he took a long drag of his Cuban and blew out a smoke ring.

"Listen, Fox, let me get to the point of this meeting. I don't really have good news for you tonight," Meyer started, his voice raspy like an elderly man's.

"What do you mean?" Fox asked incredulous. He put his cigar down in a crystal ashtray.

"The partners . . . they've found out that you are . . . you know . . . you are . . . black," Meyer stumbled over his words like it was paining him to say them. "I tried to keep it away from them but they've found out . . . unfortunately," Meyer lamented.

"What the fuck that mean?" Fox retorted, moving to the edge of his chair with his jaw going square. Sean could tell Fox was growing more and more annoyed with his houseguest.

"Just what I said. Although you bring in a lot of money to the business, I'm getting major heat for dealing with you. They think you blacks get into the business to buy sneakers, cars, big chains and play loud music from your cars . . . that's it. They think eventually you will bring heat. They could never picture a black man living like you . . . like a real wealthy person. They can't see pass their prejudices," Meyer went on.

"Well tell them it's happening—a black man can and will live like a king, and will for generations. See him, he is like my son, he will learn to live like this too. Ain't no hood rich shit going on over this way. You just tell them that," Fox said defensively.

"Hey . . . I'm just letting you know. Now that it's out you're going to have some enemies if we keep doing business. I can't afford to have these types of enemies. I mean, these are the types of guys you'll never see coming . . . more dangerous than those that act like big bad mafia types. These are sneaky bastards," Meyer replied, steepling his fingers in front of his face as if he was in deep thought.

"Do I look worried? You haven't made it until you have enemies," Fox said like he had no cares in the world.

"Well we should talk about next moves then," Meyer said; he shot a quick glance in Sean's direction. Fox took the signal.

"Aye, Sean. Go inside and see if Adina needs any help putting the stuff up. I know she's pissed with me. Let me rap with Meyer for a minute," Fox said, nodding his head toward the huge, sliding glass doors that led into the house.

"A'ight, I got you," Sean said, jumping up from his chair. He gave Meyer one last evil glare before he bopped away.

"Seems like a good kid," Meyer lied.

"Next generation of this shit. Trust me, he'll be king after me," Fox said. Neither of them knew Sean could still hear them.

Sean walked back through the glass doors and walked around into the kitchen. He didn't see Adina in the kitchen. Sean peeked around, but still didn't see her. He picked up a piece of the nicely carved roast she had prepared and quickly shoved it into his mouth.

"Damn," he whispered licking his fingers hungrily. The meat was so juicy and tender that it melted in his mouth. Sean walked out of the kitchen looking for Adina, but he had to piss. Sean walked passed the dining room and Fox's study and found the door to a small bathroom.

"Here we go," he huffed, already starting to unzip his pants.

Just as he was about to push the door to the bathroom open, Sean heard moaning coming from his right. He crumpled his eyebrows and slowly backed away from the bathroom door. The moans got a little louder, piquing Sean's curiosity so he followed the strange sounds. He thought maybe Adina was crying over the way Fox had treated her.

"Ms. Adina?" Sean whispered, inching forward toward another door that was slightly cracked. The moans grew louder the closer he got.

"Ms. Adina, you all right?" Sean called out in a low voice. He was finally standing in front of the door where the sound was coming from. He put his eye into the crack in the door and immediately his breath got caught in his throat.

"Oh shit!" Sean wolfed, his nostrils flaring open as he stared at the sight in front of him.

Adina was lying on her back with her legs up on the bed inside of the guest bedroom. She had her thick, muscular, dancer's legs spread open with her clean-shaven, deep pink, wet pussy fully exposed. When Adina saw Sean watching her, she giggled, then she drove two of her fingers into her dripping wet hot box and pulled them back out over and over again. The sound of the wetness and her moans were driving Sean wild. He wanted to run but he was frozen in place. Adina smiled at him, pulled her fingers out slowly, put them in her mouth and began making slurping noises. Sean swallowed hard and used his hands to cover his rock hard, swollen manhood. Adina repeated the same action at least five more times until finally, her eyes closed, her thick legs began quaking and she groaned so loudly Sean jumped.

"Yes! Yes!" she called out as she busted her own juices all over her fingers.

"You want to taste it?" she cooed at Sean, extending her wet fingers toward him. His eyes shot into big round circles and he stumbled backward a few steps. Guilt trampled over his mood like an angry army, but he couldn't stop watching her. Adina sat up and began cleaning herself up with a white towel from the nightstand.

"Don't tell him. He won't believe you," she whispered to Sean.

Sean shook his head from left to right, letting her know he had no intentions of telling Fox what he'd witnessed.

"Next time you join me," she said, her voice kind of sounding sad like she felt guilty too.

Sean didn't say a word; instead, he rushed away from the door and rushed into the bathroom, which had been his original destination. He pulled out his rock-hard rod, closed his eyes and jerked it until he released a load into the toilet.

Sean put his hand on the wall for stability and lowered his head. He had to get his thoughts together before he could face Fox again. He jumped when he heard a light knock on the door.

"We have time for a quickie," Adina said softly from the other side of the door. Then she laughed. Sean turned around toward the closed door, his chest heaving wildly up and down. *Is she crazy?* he thought.

"Umm . . . nah . . . I . . . I . . . I'm good," he stuttered. He hurriedly put his dick in his pants and flushed the toilet. He rushed over to the sink, washed his hands and splashed water on his face. Still a bit out of breath, Sean looked up into the mirror.

You can't fuck Fox's lady. Not after all he's done for you. That shit would be foul and you ain't living like that, Sean told himself. Loyalty was a lesson Fox had been drilling in his head since he was a little boy.

Sean swallowed hard, with his nerves on edge; he unlocked the door and turned the knob slowly. When he stepped out of the bathroom he didn't see Adina. Sean let out a long sigh of relief and headed toward the kitchen. He ran right into Fox and Meyer.

"Aye . . . you good?" Fox asked, a strange expression on his face.

"Yeah . . . um . . . I'm good. Listen, I'm about to get out of here. I told you about that thing with Big Mama and the house . . . I need to get her down there early tomorrow to take care of it," Sean rushed his lies out of his mouth trying to find any excuse to get out of there. He knew Fox was real good at reading him and he didn't want to take a chance on Fox figuring out what had just happened.

"A'ight. That's a real standup thing to do," Fox said, pulling Sean in for a pound and a quick tap hug. "Call me if you need anything. You know I always got your back," Fox said with sincerity.

"Yeah . . . will do," Sean replied, a ball of guilt sizzling in his gut. Fox walked him out with one last pat on the shoulder. Sean gave Fox a weak smile, guilt keeping him from showing a real one.

Sean rushed into his car and quickly sped down Fox's driveway to the gates. Sean couldn't stop thinking about the hot, pink center of Adina's pussy and what it would've been like to touch it, kiss it and stick his pole all the way into it. Sean licked his lips as the images of Adina's beautiful box played over and over in his head. He was driving with tunnel vision and as he pulled to the first light after Fox's street he almost didn't notice the four black Chevy Impalas in a row that passed him going in the opposite direction toward Fox's house.

"Hmph, cops love that car," Sean said to himself assuming the caravan of Impalas was the police. "Fucking pigs," he murmured dying for the light to change so he could get the hell away from the area.

As he tapped his hand on the steering wheel waiting for the light to change, he casually glanced over into this passenger seat and noticed the box sitting there.

"Aww shit!" he exclaimed, slamming his fists on the steering wheel. "I fucking forgot the rest of his paper! Damn! I never forget to give him his dough," Sean cursed himself.

He had put the other half of Fox's money into a boxed wine set just like Fox had instructed, but when Sean had arrived at the mansion, he had been so enamored with the house, he'd mistakenly only grabbed the gift box. Now, he was riding with the rest of Fox's money, which was real risky.

"Nah . . . I gotta go back. I can't have him thinking I tried to short him. I'm not living like that," Sean mumbled, shaking his head, disgusted with himself for being so careless. When the light turned, Sean busted a U-turn and headed back to Fox's house.

When Sean pulled up, he immediately crumpled his face in confusion.

"Why they got the gate open? That ain't like Fox," he mumbled to himself, an eerie feeling coming over him.

Sean drove slowly through the opened gates and just as he pulled around into the circular driveway, he noticed Meyer rushing out and climbing into a black Impala. A cold chill shot down Sean's spine as he watched the car peel out of the driveway.

"White bastard . . . don't fucking trust you," Sean grumbled as if Meyer would somehow hear what he was saying. Sean grabbed the boxed wine set containing the remainder of Fox's money. He took a deep breath and told himself he would not look at Adina if Fox was around. Sean promised to just hand Fox the box with the money in it, give Fox a pound and rush back out of the house. He knew saying anything to Adina would be too risky because he was still fantasizing about her in his mind's eye. He couldn't risk Fox figuring him out.

Sean walked up the front steps of the mansion and once he was at the top of the steps he immediately noticed that the door was cracked open.

"Nah . . . Fox wouldn't leave his shit open," Sean whispered, instinctively grabbing his gun from his waistband. He pushed the door slowly with sweat forming on his hairline. "Fox? Ms. Adina?" Sean called out as he moved slowly and cautiously into the house.

"Yo, Fox . . . it's me, Sean. I forgot to give you the wine," Sean called out, his voice rising and falling with nervousness. Suddenly that eerie feeling from earlier became more like an ominous foreboding that shrouded Sean like a black veil. His stomach began doing flips, which made him grip his gun even tighter. The silence of the scene took him back to the day he'd found his mother slaughtered.

"Yo, Fox, man! Answer me if you're here!" Sean yelled, more frantic this time.

Sean walked slowly through Fox's grand foyer until he came to the study. He could see someone sitting behind Fox's huge desk in the high-backed leather office chair. Sean's shoulders slumped with relief when he saw Fox sitting at his desk although Fox was slightly turned away from Sean's full vision.

"Aye, Fox, man, I came back because . . ." Sean was saying as he stepped closer to where Fox sat.

"Oh shit! No! No!" Sean barked throwing his hands up, sending the boxed wine set went crashing to the floor. "Nah! Nah, man!"

Sean pushed the office chair all the way around so he could get a full view of what he hoped was all a bad dream.

"Fox, man! Nah! You can't go! Fox!" Sean screamed, shaking the chair as he stared at the two perfect bullet holes in his mentor's head. Fox's eyes were opened like he'd seen the shots coming and like he'd taken them like a man.

"Fox! Fox!!" Sean screamed, falling to his knees. He sobbed for a few minutes, but then, as if a bolt of lightning hit him, Sean jerked around and scanned the room. It had suddenly struck him that he didn't see Adina or hear her screaming for Fox. Sean scrambled up off the floor, gun in hand; he ran out of the study and bolted toward the kitchen.

"Adina? Adina!" Sean shouted as he busted through the kitchen door.

"Oh shit! Adina!" he huffed as he found her slumped on the floor, her hand over her chest, blood covering and seeping through her fingers.

"Hel . . . hel . . . help mmm . . . me," Adina gasped, blood bubbling from her mouth, too.

"I'm going to help you! I won't let you die!" Sean called out as he grabbed her up into his arms. "I promise," Sean said with feeling as he rushed toward the front door with Adina in his arms.

Chapter Five

Sean sat vigil at the hospital while the doctors worked to save Adina's life. He had slept in a small chair in the waiting room until his legs and neck were cramped and painful. Each time he closed his eyes, Sean envisioned the gunshot wounds in Fox's head and the shocked look on his face. Sean surmised that whoever shot Fox had definitely caught him slipping with his guard down, but when Fox saw it coming he had taken death like a man. The first person to pop into Sean's mind was that white Jew Meyer. Sean promised himself he would make sure he found out where Meyer laid his head so he could pay him a visit. It was the least Sean could do to repay Fox for the years he'd taken care of him.

"What? What?" Sean huffed defensively jumping up and touching his gun when the doctor tapped him on the shoulder and snapped him out of his sleep. The doctor stepped back and put his hands up in surrender.

"I'm sorry if I startled you. I'm here to speak to you about your friend . . . um . . . the young lady you brought in," the doctor explained, his voice quivering a bit.

"Yeah, yeah. Sorry, you just caught me off guard," Sean said, easing the tension in his body while he stretched. He swiped his hands over his face in an attempt to settle his nerves.

"It looks like she's going to pull through. She took a pretty bad hit in the chest, but she was wearing a solid platinum pendant that kind of deflected the full impact of the bullet," the doctor told Sean. "She's out of it now, but we are going to take her off of the meds that had induced the coma so we could treat her at the time. When she wakes up, she'll be looking for someone to be here. You can go in now . . . just hold her hand and be there. We find it helps with the healing in these types of touch-and-go situations," the doctor went on.

When Sean walked into Adina's hospital room his legs went slack and he almost hit the floor. "Goddamn," he gasped, shaking his head. He had never seen so many tubes and machines attached to a person in his life. He walked slowly over to her bedside, his jaw tense and anger welling up inside of him for the people responsible. Sean did just what the doctor said, he reached out and grabbed Adina's hand, being careful not to move the intravenous line stuck in the top of it, and held it as tightly as he could.

"You gotta pull through, Adina. You're the only connection I have left to Fox. He was all I had out here. He was the only person who could show me how to survive. I need you. You have to pull through this," Sean said aloud hoping Adina could hear him. He put his head down on the side of the bed and kept a grasp on her hand. After a few minutes Sean felt Adina's hand move slightly.

"Adina?" He raised his head slowly, his eyes wide with excitement. His shoulders slumped when he saw that her eyes were closed and she was still out of it. He went to put his head back down but before he could, Adina squeezed his hand with much more force than the first time.

"Yes! I'm here, Adina! I'm here!" Sean exclaimed, excitement welling up inside of him. Although her eyes were still shut, Sean knew she was still with him. He promised that he would wait there as long as he needed to until she got better. He didn't know it yet, but he needed her as much as she needed him.

After two and a half weeks of being at the hospital twenty-four-seven, Sean began going home at night and returning to the hospital during the days to sit with Adina and help her.

"I'm going home today so just give me the release forms!" Adina shouted as Sean walked into her room from one of his trips home.

"But . . . but . . ." one of the doctors was saying. A group of doctors stood around dumbfounded by Adina's ranting and raving when not even three weeks ago she had barely been clinging to life.

"But shit! I'm out of here! I feel better and I'm not sticking around here for all these people to keep coming and asking me questions, poking at me and shit! I need to bury my man with a proper burial and that's it!" Adina screamed, disregarding the blood starting to seep into bandages that still dressed her healing wounds.

"C'mon, 'Dina, calm down, they are trying to help you," Sean stepped closer to the bed and tried to comfort her.

Adina shot him a blazing look. "Don't you start no shit, boy!" she gritted, a nerve at her temple twitching. Sean and the doctors were no match for Adina's fiery attitude. "Don't get like them and I won't have to serve your ass too!

"Look! Either y'all give me the fucking release papers or I walk out without them . . . Choose, but do it now because a bitch is ready to go!" Adina boomed, coughing afterward which was a clear sign that she wasn't really ready to go home.

One of the nurses finally relented and slid a stack of papers toward Adina. Adina snatched the stack and rolled her eyes. "About fucking time!"

Within seconds she was signing her discharge papers and signing herself out of the hospital. Sean just stood by, his hand shoved into his pockets, waiting to take Adina wherever she wanted to go.

"Did you bring the stuff I told you to bring?" Adina asked him.

"Yeah, a few days ago, but I didn't know this is what you wanted it for or else I wouldn't have," Sean said snidely. He walked over to the small hospital closet and pulled out a navy blue silk pants suit Adina had told him to get from her house, along with a short white mink jacket and a pair of beautiful black patent leather Giuseppe Zanotti pumps.

"What about my makeup bag and my curling iron?"

"Yep, right here," Sean replied shoving the Louis Vuitton makeup holder toward her.

"I'll be right out," Adina said, nodding her head toward the door. Sean looked at the door, then back at her.

"Oh . . . oh you want me to leave while you get dressed?" he said, his face turning red.

Adina smiled slyly. "What you think you my new man or something?" she said jokingly. "Of course I want you to leave so I can make myself look decent. I can't leave here looking like I look now."

Sean stepped out of the room shaking his head. Adina was a handful and then some.

When Adina walked out of the hospital room Sean's mouth dropped open. *Dayum this woman is bad!* Sean thought.

He had become so accustomed to seeing Adina a sickly mess in her hospital gown since the shooting that he couldn't believe his eyes at that moment. Adina was seemingly glowing, her skin looking angelic against the white mink. Although she had bandages on under her clothes, Adina glided in her silk suit and heels like a celebrity on the red carpet. She had pulled her thick hair into a neat, classy bun at the back of her head and applied her make up with the perfection of a professional. *Flawless. Bossy. Gorgeous,* were just a few of the words that popped into Sean's head as he watched her.

"Let's go, boy. We have an important stop to make before we make the funeral arrangements for Fox," Adina said, her tone all business.

"Anywhere you need to go," Sean acquiesced falling into step at her side. "It's not where I need to go . . . it's where *we* need to go. We both need to know that we can always eat, so business first," Adina said as she and Sean exited the hospital like they were a couple. Sean wasn't sure what she meant and where they were going, but without Fox to guide him now, Adina's lead was the only one he had to follow.

When Adina directed Sean to drive to the airport he finally broke his silence.

"I hate to ask a million questions, 'Dina . . . but what's up with the airport? We flying somewhere?" he finally questioned after driving for what seemed like forever to the airport farthest from their town.

"Yup, we are, baby boy. I didn't want you running your mouth or bragging to nobody so I arranged it all from my hospital bed. We going to meet a very important man to make some very import moves. It's time for you to take the helm, this is what Fox would've wanted," Adina replied like his mother, but touching Sean's knee like his lover. Sean seemed to contemplate what she was saying for a few minutes.

"So tell me what's up before we go. I mean, what is this meeting all about?" Sean inquired further, very aware of Adina's outwardly sexual pass at him.

"Listen, baby, you're going to meet God right now. Not in the literal sense, but almost. God was Fox's connect before Fox let the white Jew snakes sweeten a deal and steer him to them . . . a move I always told Fox would come back and bite him in the ass and it did," Adina explained, looking at Sean seriously.

"God? Who calls themselves God?" Sean asked, his eyebrows dipping low on his face.

"God . . . mmm, mmm, mmm, what can I say about that man. You'll have to see for yourself. He calls himself God and he lives up to the name every day. I used to be his sweetie, but me, I was too jealous for the way God lived. He had too many of us beauties and I'm the type of bitch that needed to be number one. I never told Fox how it was between me and God . . . didn't want to muddy the business waters . . . you know? Nah, never told Fox that I was so in love with God that I was crushed when I finally had to leave him. Fox believed it was me and him against the world, baby boy. Only lie I ever told Fox . . . yeah . . . told Fox God was my godfather when I introduced them. Didn't feel bad about it neither because Fox would've never got where he was without that little white lie. God was good about it, too . . . He played along. He is a businessman over everything else," Adina recalled dreamily. The lie she told Fox didn't sit right with Sean, but he hid his feelings about it right then.

"So, if Fox wasn't doing business with God anymore why we going to meet him?" Sean asked the next logical question. Adina shot him a look like he was asking the dumbest question on the planet.

"Look, Sean . . . in everything there is succession. With kings when they die their first born sons take the throne, with the mafia the one who proves himself worthy takes the title as boss, in the streets when the head gets cut down we replace it. Fox is gone, somebody has to take over. I know this is what he wanted for you and I'm not letting you get eaten up by the Jews like he did. You need somebody like God to get you on your feet, so just trust an old lady and follow my lead," Adina relayed, cracking a beautiful, comforting smile. Sean stared out of his front windshield thinking about and absorbing what she had said. *Me taking over? Walking in Fox's shoes? Hell yeah I can!* he told himself.

"So you ready to go meet God?" Adina asked, looking at her watch and letting out a long sigh afterward.

"As ready as I'm going to get," Sean replied. With that, they both exited the car and headed toward the terminal for their flight.

Adina and Sean landed in Toronto, Canada with no problems. They had ridden in first class and had been waited on hand and foot. As Sean understood it, Adina had simply placed a call to the man she called God and everything had been arranged within days.

As Adina and Sean exited the plane, she grabbed Sean aside and leaned in close to him.

"Follow my lead through customs. God's guys work on terminal ten so that's where we are going. We don't need any questions about our trip. Feel me?" Adina whispered, keeping a fake smile on her face like she was telling him a private joke.

"I got you," Sean acquiesced, chuckling like he had gotten the joke. Sean had become real good at catching signals and following along with her leads, but that didn't change the fact that her warnings had sent a flock of huge butterflies into his stomach and suddenly he felt like he would lose his lunch.

From the outside, no one could tell he was nervous though. Sean had become a master at keeping his cool and standing up like a man. He bopped through the airport like he was on vacation—smooth and calm as ever.

Just like Adina had said, they went through terminal ten at the Canadian customs like a breeze. The officer didn't ask for their birth certificates, passports, or anything. He acted as if they were married and had all of their paperwork.

I guess God pays well, Sean said to himself as the man stamped some documents and cleared them through.

Once they were officially allowed into Canada, Sean followed Adina through the airport to a man holding a sign with their names on it.

"That's us. Going to see God," Adina had said to the man. He just bowed slightly at the waist and waved Adina and Sean to follow him.

Outside, the man led them to a waiting all-black, heavily tinted Maybach. Sean's eyes widened as the man opened the back door for him and Adina to enter.

"Yo! This the shit right here!" Sean exclaimed excitedly as he climbed in behind Adina.

"I told you . . . God lives up to his name in every sense of the word. It's always nothing but the best if he trusts and respects you," she replied, settling into the cozy, reclining leather back seats.

Sean was suddenly excited about this meeting with God. He didn't get as relaxed as Adina did on the drive because he was too busy imagining what God was like and what the outcome of the meeting would be.

Sean watched his surroundings closely as the Maybach drove up quite a few tall hills and more than one narrow, winding road.

"Damn where we going in the mountains?" Sean joked, a hint of nerves apparent in his voice. He didn't like being in a strange place with no gun on his hip.

"That's exactly where we're going. God's house is at the top of a mountain . . . Don't you read your Bible?" Adina said, laughing afterward.

Adina wasn't lying; God's mansion sat regally atop one of the biggest mountain ranges in Canada. When the Maybach finally came to a stop in front of a huge pair of white gates with gold trimmings all Sean could do was picture what he'd heard heaven described as when he was a kid.

"Damn," Sean gasped.

"Shit, this ain't nothing, baby boy. Wait until you get a look inside this bitch. Why you think I went all out to dress for the occasion? I will never let God see me slipping," Adina said, quickly checking her makeup and hair in the rearview mirror.

Sean and Adina were let out of the vehicle and led up a huge set of gold, marble steps. There were so many steps Adina had to stop to catch her breath a few times because of her injury, but with Sean's assistance, she finally made it to the top. The expansive porch that led up to the door was also paved in gold. Sean was starting to see where Fox had gotten his ideas for his new house from.

"Right this way, Ms. Adina and Mr. Sean," a beautiful, tall, slender, woman dressed in a female tuxedo said, nodding and bending at the waist to welcome them inside. *A female butler? Now that's boss,* Sean said to himself eyeing the woman's long, statuesque legs as they followed her. That wasn't all though. As they entered farther into the mansion, Sean noticed several other drop-dead gorgeous, sexily clad, perfectly made up model type of women who all seemed to serve in different roles—one was dusting wearing a French maid's outfit with a tiny gun strapped to a garter belt on her leg; one was carrying a tray of food wearing a body-hugging dress that accentuated every curve on her body; another had a clipboard and seemed to be taking care of the business of the house her gun holstered on her waist like a cop; and, the one who'd let them in led them through the grand foyer. Sean stumbled a few times because he was so busy looking around. God's mansion had huge, twenty-foot gold ceilings that were decorated with paintings that resembled the Sistine Chapel in Italy. The gold foil paint and detailed art embedded on the ceiling had actually taken Sean's breath away so much that he couldn't keep his mouth closed.

"This shit is unreal," Sean ogled.

"This is not even the half of this place," Adina said like she'd been a regular at God's mansion. "You see that?" Adina pointed out a large area to their left between two big Roman-style columns. "Those are all solid gold busts of God at different times in his life," she told Sean. "He had them all hand made from solid gold. They gotta be worth almost a billion dollars together," Adina educated him.

Sean blinked a few times because he couldn't believe his eyes. He started toward the museum of God, but his steps her halted.

"God will you see now," the tall female butler said stepping into Sean's direct path. Sean put his hands up in front of him to let the woman know he had gotten the message she was sending.

Sean rushed back over to Adina's side and they both followed another long-legged beauty to finally meet God. *If this is what heaven is like count me in,* Sean told himself.

Stepping into God's office the familiar aroma of cigars made Sean immediately think of Fox, which immediately dampened his mood.

God's office was bigger than Sean's grandmother's entire house. There were floor-to-ceiling mahogany bookshelves with what appeared to be thousands of books. Even the carpet, with its embedded gold fibers, was more regal than anything Sean had ever walked on. There was a large bay of windows behind God's desk and the view of the mountains was breathtaking from where Sean and Adina stood.

"Your guests, sir," the female butler announced after they had all stepped into the room. Then she bowed and stepped aside like something out of a movie or television show. There was another girl dressed in an all black leotard and stiletto heels, with her hands folded, standing at the side of the desk where God sat as if she were waiting for her next command. Sean thought it was adorable that she had a gun strapped to her leg as well.

"Ahhh, Adina, my love. I haven't seen you in how long?" God said coolly as he spun his huge chair around to face Adina and Sean. "Still beautiful as ever," God smiled, blowing out a lung full of cigar smoke. "As beautiful as ever."

"God, baby . . . it's been way too long," Adina sang, extending her arms and rushing toward him with a huge smile on her face. Sean shifted on his legs because he was thinking about Fox and how he would feel if he knew Adina had once been God's woman.

Sean watched God and Adina's interaction, immediately wondering if Adina had forgotten about Fox already. Sean eyed God closely, trying to keep a poker face, but also trying to read the man's eyes to see what feeling he got from him.

God was a smooth-faced older man; not so old he would be considered an old man, but older than Fox for sure. God still had a full head of hair, but it was speckled with gray streaks that gave him a distinguished look. Although he was in his home, God wore a burgundy suede smoking jacket with black silk lapels accented by a gold silk ascot at his neck, a huge solitaire diamond pinky ring that had to be at least fourteen carats, and, one of the rare solid gold Presidential Rolexes with the full diamond face.

This nigga think he Hugh Hefner or some shit, Sean thought to himself as he watched God embrace Adina and slide his hands down over her ass. A pang of jealousy gnawed at Sean's psyche and his jaw instinctively began to rock.

"Who you got here?" God asked unhooking himself from Adina and training his eyes on Sean. God stuck out his hand that was holding the cigar and the gorgeous girl jumped into action. She rushed over, took the cigar from God's fingers and stubbed it out in the ashtray that sat only a few inches from God's hand.

"This here is Sean. He was one of Fox's number ones and he is good people, God. He got a good head on his shoulders," Adina introduced proudly like she was speaking about her own son. Sean shifted his weight from one foot to the other uncomfortably as he felt the heat of God's gaze on him.

"Awful young ain't he?" God asked without blinking or moving his eyes from Sean's face.

"Young, yes, but he ain't dumb like some of them. Fox was looking to make him number one. I think you'll like him. I mean, I know he can do great things if you give him a chance," Adina replied, smiling at Sean.

"So should I give him a chance only for him to turn around and shaft me like Fox did? I mean . . . that ended up being a waste of my time, Adina . . . you know that," God said dismissively, easing himself back down into his throne-style chair.

"Naw, baby, I already spoke to him about that. God, I'm telling you, he's ready. I wouldn't put my good name on the line again if I didn't know for sure. He's going to pledge his allegiance to God . . . ain't that right, Sean?" Adina said, shooting Sean a telling glance.

"Let's talk . . . you know, man to man," Sean replied, sticking his chest out like he was an animal about to fight for territory. He had remembered Fox always telling him to never let what a man has in material things intimidate him into thinking that man is more of a man than he is.

God laughed at Sean's show of bravado like he was being amused by some circus act.

"Have a seat, kid, and let me see if you're a man," God chuckled. "Adina, give us a minute." Adina was led out of the room by yet another exotic beauty.

"I'll be right out there if you need me. I got faith in both of you that this will work," Adina said, winking at God and Sean as she sauntered toward the door. She knew they were both watching her, too.

When she was finally gone, Sean turned back toward God with a stony look on his face. God returned the icy gaze as well. After a few seconds, Sean extended his hand toward God. At first, God looked at Sean's hand like it had something dirty in it, then he softened his facial expression and accepted Sean's hand for a shake.

"So start talking, kid . . . You said you wanted to talk man to man," God said. With that, the floor was Sean's. It was up to him to convince God to take a chance on signing on as his connect.

Chapter Six

Summer 2000

"Big Mama, keep your eyes closed. Don't peek," Sean chuckled holding on to his grandmother's chubby arm.

"Don't you let me fall now. I don't like walking where I can't see now," his grandmother complained as she held his arm in death grip.

"Now would I let anything happen to my favorite lady in the whole world? Just a few more steps and we almost there," Sean told her lovingly. His grandmother followed his lead, shuffling her feet slowly in an attempt to keep up. Sean's heart melted when he looked at the crown of silver hair covering her head now and her feet that were barely able to move anymore. Sean was becoming more and more aware that his grandmother wouldn't be around forever, so this day meant even more to him.

"All right, Big Mama, when I count to three I'ma take the blindfold off you," Sean said playfully, finally bringing their steps to a halt.

"Boy, I'm gonna get you if you don't stop playing around soon," his grandmother came back at him. "I do not like no surprises," she complained. Sean laughed, stepping behind her and slowly untying the black material blindfold he'd put on her when they'd left her house.

"Okay . . . here we go. Five, four, three, two, look up!" Sean cheered. His grandmother opened her eyes; blinking a few times to adjust them against the bright sunlight. Her eyebrows creased and her lips pursed with confusion.

"What is this, Sean?" she asked, simultaneously placing her hand over her chest as if she was clutching her pearls. "Whose house is this, boy?"

"It's yours, Big Mama. It's from me to you," Sean said proudly, smiling so wide even his back teeth were exposed. He opened the beautiful, brand new, gleaming white picket fence that surrounded the newly built 2,000–square foot house and ushered his grandmother through. Once she walked onto the freshly manicured lawn with its beautiful rose bushes and sunflower stalks, Sean grabbed his grandmother's hand and dropped the keys to the house into them.

"Oh, Sean! How did you? I can't . . . no . . . oh my goodness, boy!" his grandmother cried, her entire body shaking. Sean grabbed her into a big bear hug and squeezed her as tight as he could.

"You know I told you whenever I made it big, you would be the first person I took care of. Well I always keep my promises," Sean said getting emotional himself. He meant every word of it, too. Where Sean stood in the game at that moment, his grandmother would never have to worry about another thing in her life.

Sean's introduction to God had put him at the top of the heroin game. At just eighteen years old he had become one of the biggest names in the game. He'd masterminded a human pipeline from Canada to the United States that brought in twelve and a half pounds of heroin each week, which netted a half million dollars on the streets. All of the other street dealers had dubbed Sean, the King, and Sean had become the man to see about heroin because he sold his in its purest form at half the wholesale price of others and he was one of the only weight dealers fronting the drugs on consignment at a slight markup. With that business acumen, Sean had changed the heroin game in his city and all the street bosses were vying for a sit-down with him. He had literally become King Sean: the youngest kingpin in the history of his city and it hadn't even taken a full year.

"Big Mama, you make yourself at home. I have a few errands to run but I'll be back tonight to check on you. Everything you need is inside. You don't need nothing from the old house," Sean told his grandmother, giving her a big kiss on her cheek.

"Make sure if she needs me or anything, you hit me on my new cell number," Sean told the lady he'd hired to help his grandmother around the house. He slipped the lady three crisp one hundred dollar bills and walked away.

Sean climbed into his brand new shiny silver Range Rover and took one more look at the house he had bought his grandmother and smiled. "It's what you would've done, Mook. I know it," Sean murmured. He knew his mother and Fox would've been proud of him. Thinking about them always made Sean think of Sunny, too. Their friendship had fallen off since she had started dating Faheem, but Sean had tried to meet up with her at least twice a month. He looked at the date on his big-faced Rolex and realized it had been almost a month since he'd heard from Sunny or had a lunch date with her.

"That ain't like her," Sean mumbled under his breath as he headed to his meeting. He pulled out his throwaway cell phone and dialed the number to the cell phone he'd given Sunny the last time they'd had lunch. Sean listened as the phone just rang and rang.

"This is Sunny, if I ain't answer I don't want to or I can't. I'll holla back or not."

"Corny-ass message," Sean grumbled as he disconnected the call without leaving Sunny a message. "Probably up that nigga's ass," Sean spat, letting his imagination run wild. He had heard from the street reporters that Faheem was bad news. Sean was told that Faheem was a low-weight weed pusher, but he had a big-time heroin addiction. Sean had also heard Faheem liked to get chicks hooked and then turn them out. Sean knew it was useless trying to tell Sunny about Faheem because Sean knew his best friend was extremely stubborn.

Sean had been thinking about Sunny a lot lately since he couldn't seem to keep a steady relationship with any of the chicks he was sleeping with. Sean couldn't build a friendship with any female like the one he had with Sunny. The longer he thought about it, his new come up in the streets was nothing without being able to share the highs with her. Sunny had missed a lot of firsts in Sean's life; things he would've wanted to share with his best friend, like buying the Range Rover on his own; buying his newly furnished condo and moving out on his own and now, presenting his grandmother with a fully paid for brand new house. Sean hadn't realized how much he was missing Sunny. He picked up his cell and dialed her number again, but he got the same result—no answer.

"What the fuck is up with you, Sunny? You forgot a nigga . . . best friend?" Sean spoke out loud as if Sunny would somehow be able to hear him.

Sunny took another swig of the white Hennessy straight from the bottle and the warm liquor and loud reggae music soon took hold of her soul. She swayed her naked body in front of Faheem laughing like a silly schoolgirl. Sunny was flawless—her breasts sat up, perky and ripe on her chest; her stomach was flat as a board and her hips were smooth and round with not one hint of cellulite. Sunny's green cat eyes glinted in the dim light of the bedroom casting a glow over her face that made her look magazine-model perfect.

"Bring ya ass over here, gyal," Faheem said, rubbing his dick lustfully as he watched her. He had a lot of plans for Sunny. "Come here, gyal," Faheem whispered.

Sunny could not resist his fine cocoa-skinned face, his cut muscular chest and abs and that sexy Jamaican accent always drove her wild. Sunny reached down and touched her clitoris, putting pressure on it until it began to visibly swell.

"Feed me what I need, gyal," Faheem demanded as he stroked himself roughly. Sunny took another swig from the Hennessy bottle, giggled, and then stuck her pointer finger into her creamy middle. She crawled over to Faheem and put the same finger into his mouth. Faheem sucked her finger like it was the last thing on the planet to eat. Sunny let out a mouthful of hot breath and her chest began rising and falling with excitement. Faheem had Sunny completely open with his sex game. There was never anything off-limits with them and Sunny felt she had never found her perfect sexual fit until now.

"Beg for it," Faheem hissed, his accent thick.

"Mmm mmm," Sunny moaned, refusing his commands. She knew what would happen if she playfully refused. "I don't want it," she groaned out sexily.

"Oh so you wanna be a rude gyal. You don't wan' to beg for it, huh?" Faheem grumbled getting up onto his knees. Sunny chuckled drunkenly as he threw her down on the bed forcefully.

"You take me for a joke?" Faheem huffed, dick in hand. "Joke me a joke?" he gritted with that Jamaica patois Sunny loved. Then he rammed his dick into Sunny's dripping hotbox from behind with the force of a wrecking ball.

"Ow!" Sunny hollered out clutching handfuls of his Egyptian cotton sheets. Faheem plowed into her from the back with no mercy. The loud clap of their skin slapping together filled the room. Sunny could feel him so far into her that his balls here hitting up against her clit from the back. The slight touches from his hairy beanbags were driving her insane with lust.

"Yes! Fuck me! Fuck me harder!" Sunny yelled out. She loved it when he gave it to her rough sometimes. Faheem was so much fun to be around and his bedroom work had her head completely gone. Sunny wanted to be with him every minute of every day. She had left her mother's house without looking back and recently Faheem had cut her visits with Sean all together. Sunny felt like all she needed was Faheem to make her complete.

"Agggh!" Faheem screamed as he reached orgasm. Sunny followed with an intense cum of her own. They both collapsed onto the bed. Sunny rolled onto her side and drew her legs up to her chest. Faheem was so good in bed he often made her curl into a fetal position afterward. He looked over at her beautiful form and smiled to himself. He sat up on his side of the bed and pulled out a small glass mirror. He started chopping his heroin up to get it ready.

"Aye, gyal . . . you wanna try this?" Faheem asked Sunny for the fiftieth time since they had started dating. She didn't even have to look over to know what he was talking about. Sunny had watched Faheem snort heroin on numerous occasions.

"My answer is still the same . . . no, I don't wanna try it," Sunny slurred, closing her eyes as she listened to Faheem snort like a pig. She wasn't that drunk.

Once Faheem fell back onto the bed, she knew he was gone off the heroin. His eyes were closed and a satisfied smile curled on his lips. Sunny was curious, but she had still resisted the urge to try something as hardcore as heroin.

Sunny eased out of the bed on wobbly legs, grabbed her cell phone and went into the bathroom.

She sat on the toilet and while she relieved her full bladder, she scrolled through her missed calls—all from Sean. Sunny snapped her phone shut and rolled her eyes. She knew calling Sean now would just lead to a bunch of questions about where she's been staying and what she's been doing and why she don't call him and did she go back to school and what is she planning to do with her life . . . blah, blah, blah. She wasn't in the mood for his protective brother/father role right now. Sunny admitted to herself that she missed Sean, but she wasn't going to call him back and tell him that or let Faheem know.

"I'm grown. I don't have to explain nothing to nobody so you might as well stop fucking calling me. I'll call you when I'm ready," Sunny said out loud like Sean was standing right in front of her.

"Yo, King Sean, don't let them do me like this man. I . . . I . . . I'm gon' get your paper . . . I swear, man. Just don't let them do me like this," an overweight, dark-skinned dude name Boogie begged as he tried to use his hands to cover his naked body.

Sean sat calmly, eyeing the groveling mess of a man in front of him. He despised weak men and Boogie looked like a real female at that moment. Sean looked on serenely; he prided himself on being cool under pressure and never getting his hands dirty. Sean's number one henchman, Beans, stepped closer to Boogie with an evil glint shining in his eyes.

"Listen, nigga, King Sean is the only m'fucka on these streets frontin' niggas grams and for half the price of that bullshit y'all was buying that been stepped on a million times and you can't have the king's paper when you supposed to?" Beans growled, so close to Boogie's face the heat of Beans's breath threatened to singe the hairs in

Boogies nostrils. "You beggin' now but was you thinking about the king when you was stealing?" Beans spat. Then he drove his bare knuckles into Boogie's fat face, busting his nose, resulting in a stream of blood that seemingly would not stop.

"King Sean took a risk on you, just like he did with the whole city, yet you the only nigga that never pay the king on pay up day and rumor has it you back door dealing, too. So you tell me, as a king, how King Sean supposed to take that? The way we see it, it's like treason 'n' shit," Beans growled, looking around at his cronies for agreement.

Beans was young and fearless and although Sean was only two years older than Beans, Sean saw himself in Beans a lot of the times.

All of Sean's other crewmembers mumbled their agreement as well. Sean didn't say a word; instead, he inhaled the long toke he'd take from his cigar. He was not fazed by the pure, unadulterated violence taking place a few feet in front of him. Sean was into sending messages by any means necessary.

"You think you deserve another m'fuckin' chance to do the same thing again?" Beans asked through his teeth as he grabbed the fat dude's face roughly so he could look the dude in his eyes. "Kings behead traitors who commit treason, nigga, so I guess you know your fate," Beans gritted, releasing the slobbering dude with a shove. Beans had something to prove to Sean if he wanted to move even closer to his boss, so this was the perfect opportunity.

"Please, King Sean! Please! I'm sorry," the fat dude cried looking over at Sean as he cried for mercy. Sean didn't even flinch, blink, or say a word. He seemed bored with the crying and begging show the traitor was putting on.

"We heard you been making side deals with somebody else who is stepping on our territory. We also heard you gave them permission to step on that territory at that . . ." Beans hissed, while Freddie and Ak, two of Sean's other crew members, pulled Boogie's arms so far behind him his shoulders bulged and popped.

"Agghh . . . nah, man!" Boogie cried out. "I would do that, man! I wouldn't do that!

Beans let out a long breath, his face turned up as he circled like a hawk. He knew Boogie was lying and it was making the heat of anger rise into his chest. Beans signaled for Bo, one of Sean's younger flunkies to bring him a machine that was sitting in the corner. The young kid jumped into action and retrieved a handheld machine with a round sandpaper wheel on the front of it. Boogie's already bulging eyes grew even wider when he noticed that his tormentor had a car sandblaster that was used to take paint off of cars in his hand and heading straight for him.

"Please! Please!" Boogie screeched as urine splashed from his bladder and his knees began knocking together. It was too late for all of that; Beans snatched the tool from the young kid.

"Now you gon' tell the truth?" Beans snarled as he drove the sandblaster right into Boogie's chest immediately stripping away a few layers of his skin. "Agggghh!" Boogie screamed so hard and loud that eventually his mouth just hung open until he couldn't produce any more sound. His body jerked violently from the pain and shock starting to take over his senses.

"Now, we gon' ask you again. Who the fuck you working with on our blocks?" Beans asked, the bloodied machine out in front of him menacingly. The heavy scent of his victim's seared flesh and freshly drawn blood was fueling Beans's crazy psyche.

Sean had enlisted him as his closest associate because of Beans's penchant for violence and this was just a prime example of what the kid was capable of.

"'Cause you ain't smart enough to be doing it on your own nigga!"

Boogie hung his head and slobber dribbled from his mouth. Ty, another one of Sean's men, rushed over and roughly lifted Boogie's downturned head. Just for the hell of it, Ty drove his fist across Boogie's already broken and severely swollen face.

"Who is it, m'fucker? Who dares to fuck with King Sean? Huh? Huh?" Ty barked. He really just wanted in on the action. He was another loose cannon that Sean was happy to have on his team. Ty was older than Sean, but never dared to show anything but respect for his younger boss.

"B . . . B . . ." Boogie muttered through his battered lips, a long line of spit and blood dangling from his lips.

"Say the name, nigga?" Beans growled with a sinister snarl on his lips as he powered the sandblaster back on again.

"B . . . B . . . B . . . G . . . G . . . it's BG," the fat dude blurted barely above a whisper.

"Who? BG? What the fuck is you saying, nigga?" Beans asked.

"BG! It's BG! Just please," Boogie begged, more bloody slob bubbling from his mouth. "BG made the side deal," he said barely above a whisper.

"Who the fuck is BG?" Beans and Ty said at the same time. Sean didn't say a word, but his squinted eyes and squared jaw said enough.

Everyone in the room seemed to contemplate the question. Who would be bold enough to step on the toes of King Sean?

***

Sean didn't say a word during Boogie's torture, but when Sean finally heard that someone named BG was violating his spots in the streets, he was all ears. Calmly Sean stood up and got ready to exit the building. He looked at all of his men in one long eye scan around the room. His face remained stony.

"Find out who BG is. Then find out where he rest at and everything else about him. Take your time. Be smart, because obviously this nigga BG thinks he's smarter," Sean gritted, fighting to keep the anger welling up inside of him under wraps.

Two weeks after the name BG came up, Sean sat at the end of the beautiful lacquer conference table in the conference room above his new boxing gym, where he usually discreetly conducted his business. Sean sat calmly, smoking a cigar, a new habit he had picked up in homage to Fox. Sean was patiently waiting for his men to report back to him what they'd found out about BG.

"From what we peeped whoever this nigga BG is, he sends a bitch, who drives a white Benz CLS with license plates that say BG to his spots to pick up his paper," Beans spoke up.

"She's a bad bitch, too. Must be his lady. Sexy as hell though," Ty chimed in, his tone a little too excited and hype for Sean's liking. "She usually has a car full of dudes following her pretty ass. But they look like lame-ass wannabe thugs anyway. Whoever BG is, I could tell he a lame."

Sean took a long toke on his cigar and blew the smoke out slowly. Contemplating what he was being told, Sean finally looked down at his sparkly diamond pinky ring. He stared at the blindingly shiny diamonds as he always did when he was thinking hard. The information he was getting just wasn't sitting right with him. Any real hustler wasn't going to send his lady to risk herself picking up his paper unless he was locked up or in some other predicament where he didn't trust his street soldiers.

"Y'all sure y'all got the right info? How y'all know the bitch is picking up?" Sean asked, his voice slow and steady.

"You can see here yourself," Beans said like he already knew Sean would be skeptical. "She's like clockwork most of the time," Beans continued, sliding some pictures across the conference table. Sean looked down and squinted at the photographs. He was having a hard time keeping a poker face at that moment.

Damn! he said to himself while fighting to keep his visible reaction even and unfazed. Sean didn't lift the picture, but he could see her as clear as day. The woman in the pictures was beautiful to say the least. She was the color of a Hershey's chocolate bar; her eyes were covered in oversized shades but that didn't keep Sean from seeing that her eyebrows were perfectly arched. She had a slim nose, high cheekbones and thick full lips that were painted with a deep burgundy lipstick. She wore her hair long and silky with a perfectly cut bang covering one of her eyes. It was probably a high-priced weave, but it was perfectly styled nonetheless. From what Sean could see in the picture, the woman's clothes screamed designer and appeared expensive as she donned a short mink vest, a gleaming white shirt that hugged and pushed her breasts up at the same time, and a pair of close-fitting, destroyed jeans that accentuated her round, wide hips. The woman in the picture reminded Sean of a black actress or one of those reality show chicks. Flawless—was the word that came to mind as Sean surveyed the pictures one more time.

Yeah, she gotta be a hustler's wife, Sean told himself. He wanted to know more about her and this dude BG she was riding for. Sean took one last look at her and decided that woman in the picture seemed like an easy enough target.

"I guess to get to the man we will have to get his lady . . . grab her . . . I want to have a talk with her," Sean said coolly. His men knew exactly what that meant.

Chapter Seven

Sunny's speech was slurred, her eyes were rolling around uncontrollably and she kept laughing at nothing in particular. She was so drunk out of her mind after a night of heavy partying, that when Faheem introduced a girl named Lucky, Sunny smiled and made kissy faces at the beautiful, blue-eyed, statuesque white girl.

"Damn she look like a broke version of Angelina Jolie," Sunny hiccupped and laughed, her half-opened eyes moving up and down over Lucky.

"Lucky gettin' down with us tonight," Faheem announced like it was something normal for him to say. Sunny just smiled lazily and laughed some more.

"She gettin' down with who? You? Me?" Sunny slurred, her eyes rolling around like she couldn't control them. Sunny had never been as gone off liquor as she was that night, but she would've also never guessed that Faheem would slip anything into her drink either.

"I like men with dreads and big dicks . . . you know . . . like you," Sunny garbled, running her hands through Faheem's newly growing dreads. "I like dick . . . your dick," Sunny went on, sticking her tongue out sloppily. Faheem wasn't budging. His face was flat and stony, unmoved by Sunny's advances.

"Get up off ya ass and give me a show. Both of y'all, I wanna see y'all together," Faheem said, directing Sunny and Lucky with hand movements.

"Don't make me say it again," Faheem said bending his head down over the small mirror on his nightstand and inhaling a line of his poison of choice. Lucky sauntered over to where Faheem stood and followed his lead. She was a pro at sniffing H just like Faheem; in fact, that's how he'd met her: through their shared heroin connect.

Once the drugs hit Lucky's system her body seemed to relax, her mouth went slack and a sinister grin cropped up on lips. She threw her head back seductively and fell down to her knees. Lucky whipped her hair around and around, then got down on all fours and crawled toward Sunny like a hungry lion going to eat a smaller helpless prey.

"Open ya legs for her, gyal," Faheem demanded with dick in hand. He slapped Sunny on her right thigh. "Ya hear me? Open ya legs!" Faheem insisted again. Sunny laughed like a silly kid and stuck her tongue out tauntingly.

"I'm not no fucking lesbian," she slurred, her words barely understandable. "I don't fuck girls, you . . . ass . . . asshole." Sunny struggled to get her words out straight, her tongue clucking on the roof of her mouth with every syllable. She was twisted out of her mind, but still had enough sense to know that she wasn't trying to have lesbian sex with another woman.

"Open ya fuckin' legs now or get the fuck out of me house! You act like ya can't do nothing . . . laying around all day . . . and partying all night. I'm feeding you, clothing you, and dealing with ya bullshit. You think ya pussy alone can satisfy me? Eh? Nah . . . fuck that . . . I want some fun and you will give it or get the fuck out. Go back home and suck that old, fat nigga's dick like you did all ya life," Faheem boomed cruelly, his face drawn tightly into a monstrous grimace. Sunny threw her hands over her ears and fought the tears welling up behind her eyes. Even completely, sloppy drunk, she understood the cruelty of Faheem's words and they had landed like hard slaps to her face. Sunny had never heard him speak to her like that, but lately, she could tell that he had been getting frustrated with her resistance to some of his sexual requests and had become increasingly mean toward her.

Even completely inebriated, Sunny understood that if she didn't bend to his will and Faheem threw her out she'd be forced back home or worse, forced to call Sean to save her, which would also come with his "I told ya so" speech.

"Do it now, gyal, or get the fuck gone from me," Faheem spat, sniffing another line of heroin.

Sunny closed her eyes and reluctantly let her legs fall open. Just as she did; Lucky buried her face between them like a hungry dog. Lucky didn't care about putting on a show, so long as there was heroin as a reward at the end of it. At first, Sunny was tense, but once Lucky drove her warm, wet tongue deep into Sunny's middle, Sunny opened her legs wider, closed her eyes tighter and began grinding her hips toward the hungry girl's mouth.

"Ssss, yeah, that's what I'm talking about," Faheem hissed as he stroked his growing member. He dropped his pants down around his ankles and got behind Lucky, who was on her knees lapping away at Sunny's clit. Faheem let a glob of his spit fall from his mouth and land between the crack of Lucky's ample behind. He then took the head of his manhood and swiped it up and down her crack, making sure the area was wet enough for an easy entrance.

"I know what you white gyals like," Faheem said, his accent thick as he forced his pulsing rod deep into Lucky's semi-loose anal cavity. Lucky let out a whimper, but she knew at the end of that pain would be more heroin for her so she took Faheem's swollen inches like a champ. Faheem banged into her from behind like he was a dog in heat. The sound of skin slapping together filled the room and the musty, acrid smell of body fluids and hot, deviant sex wafted around.

Sunny was thrusting her hips harder and faster now as Lucky reached up and pinched Sunny's nipples between her fingers while simultaneously sucking and putting pressure on Sunny's pink, swollen clitoris.

"Ahh, ahhh," Sunny groaned, her body tingled everywhere. Even Faheem had never given her head so good.

"Stop . . . don't let her cum," Faheem instructed, grabbing Lucky's long blond hair and yanking her head from Sunny's hot box. Sunny's eyes popped open.

"Let her finish . . . please," Sunny slurred her body so hot with lust she felt like she'd explode.

"Nah . . . you want it you work for it," Faheem said cruelly, pulling his dick from Lucky's anus. Lucky laughed and watched hungrily as Faheem put a line of heroin on is rock hard shaft. Faheem tempted Lucky with the heroin.

"Ya see Lucky . . . she loving this dope dick. You . . . you're a scared little gyal Sunny. Ya call yaself a woman? Nah . . . a woman knows how to take the dope dick, see," Faheem teased Sunny, his words upper cutting her each time. A fiery ball of jealousy welled up inside of Sunny's chest as she watched Lucky sniff the line of heroin off of Faheem's dick.

"Mmmm, shit . . . yeah," Lucky moaned, falling down onto her back as the drugs took hold of her.

"I love a woman who takes it like that," Faheem said, moving between Lucky's legs and thrusting himself into her with no mercy. Faheem moved in and out of Lucky like a jackhammer, all the while keeping his eyes trained on Sunny. He could see the mixture of lust, pain, jealousy and wanting on Sunny's face. Faheem knew her so well, he figured it would just be a few more minutes before he'd have her exactly where he wanted her.

Faheem thrust hard and harder and the more Lucky moaned in ecstasy the angrier Sunny got. Her drunkenness was fading and she wanted that feeling back. She needed to feel high to escape her realities. Faheem knew it too.

"You want some of this dope dick? Huh? Or you gon' keep turning me down. The dope makes it better . . . harder . . . slower . . ." Faheem teased, bending down and plunging his tongue deep into Lucky's mouth as he continued to pump his hips into the girl's small pelvis vigorously. "C'mon . . . stop being scared," he urged, with Lucky's saliva wetting his lips as he eyed Sunny. "Sunny is a little gyal. Scared of a little heroin. Scared of a real man's dick," Faheem pressed as he grinded farther and farther into Lucky.

Sunny couldn't take it any longer. She got up onto her knees and forcefully pushed Faheem away from Lucky. Faheem busted out laughing as he toppled over.

"Give me some! Give me some now!" Sunny demanded. "I am not a little girl. I can handle it all. Stop playing with me before I fuck this bitch up!" Sunny screamed, her face turning deep red. Faheem laughed raucously as he was forced to pull himself out of Lucky's insides.

"That's what I'm talking about. Fight for this dick. Fight for the dope dick, baby," he taunted, stroking his prize. "You're finally growing up," he said. He grabbed his heroin from the nightstand and did the same thing again, making a neat line on his rock hard meat. Sunny shot Lucky an evil look and without hesitation Sunny leaned down and snorted the heroin just like she'd seen Faheem do so many times.

"Ahhh," Sunny winced throwing her hands up to her face.

"Pinch your nose. Pinch your nose," Faheem shouted. "The first time it burns . . . but after that . . . shit this is the best feeling in the world," he told Sunny.

As soon as the drugs hit her central nervous system, Sunny fell back onto the bed and her eyes snapped shut involuntarily. Her ears were ringing with some sort of music and she felt like she was floating on air. Every worry or care or painful experience Sunny had ever had seemed to float away. She saw the faces of her mother, stepfather, and Sean floating in her head. Sunny couldn't hear anything, but she felt damn good. Her eyes were closed tight, but not for long.

"Aye, gyal . . . aye, gyal," Faheem was yelling and slapping Sunny's face roughly. He had interrupted the floating feeling and suddenly Sunny could tell she was just lying on his bed. She finally forced her eyes to flutter open and looked up at him.

"Shit . . . I thought you had OD'd," he huffed, a glimmer of terror creasing his face. "Didn't I tell you that was some good shit," Faheem said, his winning smile now painting his gorgeous face. Sunny smiled at him with her pointer finger at her lips seductively.

"More . . . I want more," Sunny groaned, a lazy grin contorting her face as she reached toward the nightstand where the drugs lay.

It had been only been a month since Sunny snorted her first line of heroin and she couldn't get enough now. Sunny was dependant on the drugs to function on a daily basis.

Now she sat on the toilet seat in Faheem's bathroom with one end of a belt tied around her arm and the other end between her teeth while she slapped the center of her arm vigorously searching for a ripe vein.

Faheem had made the mistake of telling Sunny that if she shot the drugs directly into her arm it would get her high faster. The first time she tried it, Sunny had almost fainted when she hit the wrong area in her arm. She had missed the vein and caught muscle. The pain was like nothing she'd ever felt and Faheem had slapped Sunny across her face until her nose bled because she had wasted the drugs.

Sunny hated that her veins took so long to find. If she trusted that Faheem wouldn't take her hit away, she would've asked him for his help.

Bang! Bang! Bang! Sunny jumped, releasing the grip she had.

"What?!" she screamed in response to Faheem banging like a madman on the locked door. "I'm coming!"

"Fuck," Sunny whispered harshly. "Now I'll never find one."

Sunny sniffled back the snot threatening to leak from her nostrils. She was dope sick already and needed that hit more than anything.

"It's a party going on out here . . . our party so hurry the fuck up!" Faheem barked. Sunny could tell he was probably seconds from busting the door down. It was too late for her to sniff the heroin because she had already cooked it and got it ready for the needle. Sunny tied her arm again, this time her veins were a little more cooperative. She found one that plump and ready. She picked up the needle and with her hands shaking, she eased the drugs into her vein. Immediately her body relaxed against the toilet seat. The needle dropped from her slack hand and she slid down to the floor. Sunny felt at ease now, but she still couldn't recapture the feeling from her very first high.

"I'm not going to call you again!" Faheem screamed; this time he kicked the door in.

Faheem practically dragged Sunny into his living room where the mixed crowd of strange and familiar partygoers were mingling. Loud reggae music blared from two huge black speakers set up in either corner of Faheem's expansive living room. There was enough drugs and liquor spread out on side tables, the coffee table and even the mantle over the fireplace. Sunny was high, but she was aware of everything. There were men and women on couches, the floor, and the balcony all engaged in different sexual acts.

Faheem had moved from selling weed to throwing what he called dutty wine parties. In Sunny's assessment it was just another word for orgies. Sunny wasn't a fan of the parties, but Faheem's increasingly aggressive behavior toward her usually made her go along with it.

"I got three people that want to meet you," Faheem yelled over the music into Sunny's ear as he pulled her along by the arm. Sunny groaned something, but when she saw all of the drugs that were laid out on the tables she quickly swallowed her words of protest back down her throat.

"Dreads, mon . . . this is my gyal Sunny," Faheem announced to three dreads who were standing around in his kitchen. "I told yuh she was a hot piece," Faheem continued with his accent on thick as palmed a handful of Sunny's ass.

Sunny's stomach flipped in her gut and she had to clutch the side of the kitchen counter to keep from falling down. One of the dudes with dreads smiled lustfully at her. "She like to party?" he asked, rubbing his hands together.

"Hell yeah," Faheem said, nodding his head toward Sunny. Sunny couldn't move at first, she stood there seemingly rooted to the floor. She shot him a dirty look and folded her arms over her chest. Sunny had been doing a lot of things she wasn't proud of since she'd started getting high but this. . . .

"Don't fuckin' play around. I'll put you on the streets," Faheem whispered in her ear harshly. Then he pulled a packet out of his pocket and shook it in her face like he was dangling a carrot in front of horse to get it to move.

Sunny followed Faheem and the drugs to the back. The stilettos he'd purchased for Sunny the day before were clicking against the tiles on the floor. The party dress she wore hugged her curves and as beautiful as she looked, she felt ugly.

Sunny counted each step because each one got her closer and closer to another hit.

The three dreads were laughing and speaking excitedly as they approached the bedroom.

"Stay out here for a second, dreads. Let me get her ready," Faheem told them, halting their steps. All three men watched Sunny like she was the last meal that they were about to devour.

Faheem pushed Sunny into the bedroom. "It's no big deal, gyal. I love you and I won't let nothing happen that I don't approve of," he was saying as he immediately started preparing the heroin for Sunny.

"I don't want to sniff . . . I need to bang it," Sunny groaned, throwing herself down on the bed.

"Ya nah have no time for that. Sniff it," Faheem replied through his teeth.

"C'mon, Fah. It'll be better for me," Sunny pleaded, her legs swinging in and out anxiously. Faheem rushed over to her and pushed her forcefully back on the bed. He used one of his knees to force her legs apart, ripped the split on the side of the dress she was wearing and forced his rock hard dick into her dry vagina.

"Ahhh," Sunny cried out. "Please, Fah . . . I'm sorry. I'm sorry," she cried as he took her mercilessly. Faheem put his hand roughly over her mouth as he thrust into her with the force of a bulldozer.

"I told you . . . you do what I say or you will suffer," he growled in her ear. "Now, get up like a good girl. Sniff the line and fuck these dreads like you never fucked anyone. This is money," Faheem huffed, fire flashing in his eyes. He quickly jumped up, pulled himself out of her and shot his load all over her face and chest.

Sunny couldn't even feel emotions anymore. She was numb. She used a Kleenex from the nightstand to wipe Faheem's body fluid off of her. She got up, sniffed the line of heroin and fell back onto the bed. Sunny heard when the three dreads entered the room. She heard the excitement in their voices as they discussed who would put his dick in which opening on her body. She also heard her cell phone buzzing on the nightstand on the side of the bed she usually slept on. Suddenly Sean popped into her mind. He was the only person who would be calling her.

As if she was possessed by some kind of sex demon, Sunny jumped up, smiling and laughing like a mad-woman.

"Let me suck your dick. And you . . . put that shit in my ass while your friend gets the pussy," Sunny commanded like a pro. She pictured Sean's face again, which seemed to anger and propel her further into the indecent acts with the strange men. Sunny felt like Sean had betrayed her. Yes, he had tried to call her a few times, but he had never come looking for her. Sunny had heard that Sean was on the serious come up in the streets, yet he had abandoned her. She was in so much pain and agony, yet her best friend who she loved like no other person had never come looking for her.

"Bring in some girls, too," Sunny moaned as one of the men plunged himself deep into her anus. In between acts, Sunny would stop, sniff a line of heroin and get right back into it.

Within minutes Sunny and Faheem's bedroom was the site of an all-out orgy. Sunny had almost every place on her body filled with a piece of a man. Then she would switch places and bury her face between a woman's legs. Faheem was loving every minute of it. He had made a ton of money that night, with the secret promise that there would definitely be more parties with Sunny as the star.

Chapter Eight

Beans, Ty, Freddie, Bo and Ak sat outside of the spot they had watched the woman, who worked for a dude named BG, enter for the past month. They had it timed down to the minute and knew exactly where her security car was going to be and what it looked like, but so far, the spot and outside of it looked dead. They had been there over an hour and there had been no sign of the woman driving the Benz with license plates that read "BG."

"This bitch is late today," Ty complained, looking down at his watch for the tenth time.

"Word . . . all of these days and she ain't never been late," Freddie followed up.

"Well we wait," Beans said flatly. "We will not fuck this up under my watch. Sean is sick of waiting now so that's that."

"Can we at least spark a L? I mean waiting in this car to snatch a bitch off the street and blast on her lame-ass security got a nigga needing something to take the edge off . . . feel me?" Ty asked and proclaimed all in one breath. Beans looked up into the rearview mirror and shot Ty a dirty look.

"G'head, m'fucka, damn. You act like if you don't get high for two hours your ass gon' die. Weed fiend-ass nigga," Beans snapped, shaking his head in disgust. He had to admit it though; sitting there waiting was nerve-wracking. In the weeks they had been watching BG's woman, she wasn't usually ever late. Suddenly an ominous feeling came over Beans. He looked up into the rearview mirror again and just as he did, he saw a heavily tinted Yukon Denali slowly creeping up on his Escalade. A bolt of fear struck Beans like lightning.

"Yo, Bo . . . pull out! Pull out now!" Beans shouted to Bo who was driving. The nervous young boy threw the car into drive and pulled away from the curb as fast as his reflexes allowed. The tires squealed against the blacktop. Beans turned around in his seat and craned his neck to see if the Denali was still there.

"What's up, nigga? We ain't waiting for her?" Ty asked, his eyes wide, his blunt gripped tightly between his fingers. Before Beans could answer Ty's question.

Tat! Tat! Tat! Tat! The sound of rapid gunfire and shattering glass cut through the Escalade.

"Oh shit! Niggas firing on us!" Ty shouted, ducking down in his seat. Just then, more gunshots rang out.

"Niggas bangin' on us! Get y'all fuckin' ratchets out!" Beans commanded, pulling his .40-caliber Glock from his waistband.

"M'fuckas!!" he screamed, sticking his hand out of the passenger side front window and firing back at the Denali. The driver had been bold enough to pull right next to the Escalade now.

"Yo, swerve over! Now!" Beans screamed at Bo. More deafening shots rang out. Two shots hit the side of the Denali as Ty, Freddie and Ak squeezed off freely.

Bo was swerving the Escalade all over the road because his nerves were going haywire. Ak leaned up to scold the young boy, but right away he understood what was going on.

"Yo, he's hit! He's hit! He can't drive like that!" Ak yelled from the back seat. Beans couldn't look over; he was too busy keeping the driver of the Denali at bay by firing shots straight for the driver's side window.

"Somebody gotta grab the wheel!" Beans screamed. "Yo, Bo keep ya foot on the gas, man!"

Ak leapt over the seat and took hold of the Escalade's steering wheel. Bo was breathing hard but he was able to keep his foot on the gas.

"Yo, li'l nigga, just don't stop hitting that m'fuckin' gas or we are all dead," Ak said, while he struggled to steer the truck. Just as the words Ak's mouth, right next to them the Denali slammed into a lamppost on the street.

"Pull over! Pull over! Yo! Pull the fuck over!" Beans screamed at Ak. "This shit ain't over!"

"Yo, nigga we a nigga hit. Fuck what they talking about . . . we can snatch the bitch another time. We need to take this nigga 'cross town before he bleed too much," Ak screamed, noticing that Bo was slumped with blood seeping into the material of his shirt.

"Nah. These niggas know what it is . . . they soldiers. Shit happens. We take care of it now. We ain't gon' get this chance again," Beans said, gun in hand as he slowly opened the Escalade door.

"Fuck! This nigga here acting like he m'fuckin' Superman," Ty spat, grabbing the back door handle with one hand while keeping a tight grip on is Beretta with the other. "Stay here with Bo," Ty told Ak. Ty and Freddie followed Beans out of the Escalade, all three approaching the Denali with guns leading.

Beans would see that he had spilled the driver's brains and the dude was hunched over the steering wheel. There was a dude in the front passenger seat rocking back and forth with blood all over the front of his shirt. Beans couldn't see much of what was going on in the back because the vehicle was so heavily tinted. He hand signaled for Ty to walk around the other side and for Freddie to get low and go around the front. Ty to the other side of the Denali approaching from the back. Just as he made his way around the back bumper, he came eye to eye with the barrel of a cute little silver .22 revolver. Ty raised his gun to eye level as well.

"Yo! Beans! I found her," Ty called out, standing toe to toe with the beautiful woman they had been waiting to snatch. Ty and the woman were in a standoff, each pointing their guns in the other's face. The scene was like something out of an old Western movie. Beans rushed around and was quickly taken aback. The woman was even more drop-dead gorgeous up close. Her coral-colored pantsuit had splashes of blood on the left side.

"Tell him to drop that fuckin' gun or we both just gon' die," the beautiful woman spat, her eyes squinted into dashes. Beans thought there was something extra sexy about her bravado.

"Nah, ma . . . seems to me you the one that is outgunned right now," Beans said, nodding. The woman felt the kiss of Freddie's weapon on the back of her neck.

"We just wanna talk to you. We ain't about hurtin' no bitch . . . feel me?" Beans negotiated further. The woman didn't seem like she was budging.

"Why the fuck y'all been following me? Robbing me would be a mistake, take my word for it. Y'all don't know who I am," the woman snarled, moving her finger into the trigger guard on her gun.

"Nah, ma, we don't get down like that. If we wanted to rob you we woulda been did it weeks ago," Ty clarified, his arms burning from having them extended with the gun out so long.

"Our boss . . . King Sean . . . he wanna have a quick minute with you. That's all," Beans told her. "We look like we need to rob you, ma? It's bad enough your man sends you out here to do his job," Beans said mockingly.

The woman laughed, flashing a glimpse of her gleaming, perfectly straight white teeth.

"Fuck so funny," Freddie hissed at her back.

"My man? I work for myself. Y'all niggas got the story all wrong," the woman said, lowering her gun a little. "Where ya boss at?" she asked, clearly amused.

"Yo, this bitch mad disrespectful like she don't believe we will dust that ass right here," Ty growled. He already despised the beautiful creature standing in front of him. Ty hated to feel like people were making fun of him.

"Chill . . . she know what it is," Beans said, nodding at the woman knowingly.

She lowered her gun and looked at them expectantly. Beans lowered his, but Ty wasn't going for it.

"Nah, son, I don't trust no bitch this calm after all her peoples got dusted right in front of her fuckin' eyes," Ty snapped, keeping his eye on her.

She laughed at him. "I'm the only one that matters to me," she said calmly. "Security is replaceable. You should know . . . you're the security right?" the woman taunted Ty.

"Yo, Beans . . . tell this bitch something," Ty said through his teeth.

"Again . . . where's this so-called boss of yours?" she said, taking a few steps toward the Escalade.

Beans was alone with the woman when Sean arrived. Ty, Ak and Freddie had taken Bo to the in-house doctor they used in cases like this. No way they could take their people to the hospital with gunshot wounds because that would mean an automatic call to the police.

Sean bopped into the conference room above the boxing gym with a cool, even expression on his face. He had already heard about the woman's brazen standoff with his crewmembers and her mocking behavior. He was intrigued.

Beans stood up and rushed toward Sean, giving him their signature pound and tap hug.

"Well she here, but she ain't talkin' to me about BG. Beware she got a slick tongue that make a nigga wanna take her head off for real, son," Beans filled Sean in with a harsh whisper. Sean took his seat at the head of the table. The woman was sitting at the other end, also at the head of the table. Bold to say the least.

"I'ma get right to the point. I heard you work for somebody named BG . . . I don't know if he's your man or your boss, but I don't like his moves," Sean said, his voice even, calm.

The woman smirked, leaned back in the chair and crossed her long, slender legs. Sean was having a hard time keeping his eyes off of her cleavage. She had taken off her bloodied blazer and wore nothing but a close-fitting camisole now.

"Is that right?" she replied, seemingly uninterested. "You had me dragged here at gunpoint to get to my man or my boss . . . okay," she said sarcastically.

Sean bit down into his jaw. He quickly changed his lustful attitude toward the woman. He didn't like her tone and he surely didn't like to be tested.

"Look . . . you're a woman. I'm not tryin'a go back and forth with you. I just need to know who BG is . . . if he's your man . . . if he's your boss . . . don't really make me no difference. I have a talk with the nigga and I need to know from you where I can find him," Sean said sternly.

The woman smirked again. She stood up in a bold move. Beans immediately sprang to his feet and touched his gun.

"No need for all that, cowboy," the woman said smoothly, placing her well manicured hands up where Beans and Sean could see them. She shook her silky, long hair out of her face and started making her way toward Sean. When she was finally close enough, even with Beans breathing down her neck, she extended her hand toward Sean. Sean could smell the sweet scent of her perfume and he liked it . . . a lot.

"Hi . . . I'm BG, short for Black Girl, nice to meet you," she said smiling slyly, flashing her perfectly straight white teeth. Sean could feel his mouth drop open by itself, but he couldn't close it. For the first time in a long time, he was at a loss for words.

"What?" Beans shouted. "You? BG? Get the fuck outta here," Beans gasped in disbelief, twisting his lips for emphasis.

"In the flesh," the woman replied, her hand still dangling out in front of her.

Sean extended his hand and accepted hers for a firm handshake.

"A'ight, BG, I guess we got a lot to talk about then," Sean said flatly, although his mind was blown away.

Three weeks after his first encounter with BG, Sean sat across from God; both men deep in thought.

"I don't know, Sean. Seems to me this woman showed up out of nowhere and now she wants a partnership. Smells like setup or devious takeover to me," God said apprehensively. Sean let out a long sigh. He had been spending a lot of time with BG for the past couple of weeks and his gut was telling him that she was a stand-up person. Not to mention, she had the other side of the city on lock and was moving more than just heroin. BG was willing to open up a new methamphetamine market to Sean on a half-and-half partnership basis.

Sean could see his dollars growing by leaps and bounds partnering up with BG. Now he had to convince God of the same.

"Yo, God . . . I'm tellin' you. I seen her in action. She's smart . . . real smart. She about her business. Yo, she so good niggas in the streets thought she was a nigga when her name first started ringing bells out there. Nothing flashy, real demure, sexy as hell, too. If you see her you would never guess she's so powerful," Sean replied, trying to sell God on the idea of partnering with BG.

"She got certain areas on lock already without even tryin'a step on my toes. She started riding through my spots just to get my attention. I mean that shit is fucking commendable because she could've gotten her wig twisted but she stood her ground. All in the name of growing her business. There's niggas that ain't got the heart to do that shit. She ain't satisfied with the scraps niggas leaving behind and that's the type of people we need to align with . . . All these other so-called bosses let niggas come in, sell kilos a dollar cheaper and they automatically jump on the dollar cheaper team instead of standing their ground . . . not her," Sean went on.

God sat silently for a minute. He looked up and snapped his fingers. One of his beautiful servants rushed over with his signature cigar and a shot of Ace of Spades on a gold-plated serving tray. The statuesque model-like woman held the glass up to his lips and God sipped the liquor slowly. Then the beauty lit God's cigar and handed it to him.

"Sean, the years we've been in business have been sweet . . . I must say. You're a smart kid and I trust your judgment. If you vouch for her I'll take the chance . . . but only because it's you. You've made me a lot of money out there and I know you're loyal. You know how I feel about you, kid," God finally relented. Sean smiled and sprang to his feet excitedly.

"But . . ." God said, putting his free hand up in a halting motion. "Don't let me regret giving you and your new female partner this chance. Don't cross me for a bitch,"

God warned, his gaze hot on Sean's face. "It won't be a pretty picture if you do." Sean looked God in the eyes for a few seconds, the awkwardness of the situation almost palpable.

"Nah, never that, God," Sean said in earnest, finally breaking their heated eye lock on one another. "Never that," Sean repeated.

Chapter Nine

Club Azure was packed inside with wall-to-wall people. The DJ had everyone moving their bodies in unison to the extreme bass that was pounding through the clubs and making the walls shake. It was New Year's Eve and the crowd was ready to bring 2003 in with a bang. It was also Sean's twenty-first birthday and he planned on doing it big.

Sean and BG navigated slowly through the tightly packed swarm of people, taking in eyefuls of scantily clad women—young and old—who had probably saved up for months to buy the gaudy, ill-fitting outfits they wore and huddles of dudes rocking their obligatory diamond Jesus pieces—some fake and some real.

"You pack this shit out didn't you?" BG screamed into Sean's ear as their bodies were forced close together, flanked by Beans and Ak in the front and Ty and Freddie behind them.

"Everybody love a King Sean party. What did you think niggas was gon' do when they heard I bought out the bar tonight?"

"Bring they asses to the club," BG and Sean said in unison. Then they busted out laughing.

"Shit, you better know it," Sean joked, yelling over the music. BG laughed again, but it had registered with her how serious his statement was. Sean was the man in the city and it was widely known that he was sitting on major cake.

Sean's partnership with BG had grown by leaps and bounds over the course of the year since they'd had their first rocky encounter. Sean respected her business mind and she respected his status in the streets—a perfect combination that served their takeover well. Sean and BG had taken their collective businesses and merged them into millionaire status. It had taken them a little time to work on the friendship part of their partnership, but it was getting there.

Sean had shared with BG how much she reminded him of his mother, especially her smooth, dark skin and no-nonsense attitude. BG had opened up to him that she'd had a rough upbringing in the poorest part of Panama. She told him she had actually gotten her nickname—Black Girl—from being teased and called the name as a kid, because in Panama there was a lot of prejudice against darker-skinned people; therefore, she started referring to herself as BG, which was really a derogatory term. She thought embracing it showed how strong she was. Sean agreed.

Just as Sean and BG made it to the VIP section at the back of his club, a small commotion in the far left corner of the club caught Sean's attention.

Sean stopped for a few seconds, his abrupt pause causing BG and all of his crewmembers to look at him strangely.

"Everything good?" BG asked, looking at Sean with widened eyes.

"Yeah . . . yeah," Sean replied with his head turned in the direction of the distraction. His eyes were trained in on something and he would not turn away.

"Yo, y'all go ahead inside VIP," Sean told his crew, waving them on. He grabbed Beans's arm and stopped him from walking behind the velvet ropes that separated VIP from the rest of the club. "Yo . . . follow me over there,"

Sean told Beans, nodding his head toward the gathering crowd in the corner.

"A'ight, what's up?" Beans asked, more interested in getting to VIP with all of the beautiful women than he was in following his boss.

Sean didn't answer; instead, he forged ahead as if the club was empty.

"Damn I guess it's just . . . let's go," Beans said rushing behind Sean, hot on his heels.

Sean was pushing and shoving people out of his way as he steamed forward like he was on a mission. His chest was heaving up and down and his nostrils flared in anticipation that what the thought he was seeing might be true. The closer Sean got to his target, the clearer he could see that his initial suspicion had been correct.

"Fuckin' Sunny. I knew that was you," Sean grumbled under his breath, the vein at the side of his temple pulsing hard against the side of his skull.

Although he hadn't seen or heard from her in almost a year, Sean could still spot his best friend anywhere. Sean could see Sunny clearly now and he didn't like what he was seeing. She was surrounded by at least eight dudes, who were all touching the intimate parts of her body at will. Sunny was the center of attention as usual. She was laughing and giggling like it was fine with her that these men were basically violating her.

"Get the fuck out my way," Sean barked, pushing a few females and dudes aside. Once the crowd realized who he was, they began to part like the Red Sea giving Sean a clear path to Sunny.

"Yo! Sunny!" Sean called out. "Sunny!" But it was impossible for her to hear him over the ear-shattering music that was blasting. The men surrounding Sunny shot dirty looks in Sean's direction, but Sunny was too gone to even hear him or notice him right up on her.

"Sunny! Get the fuck up!" Sean growled, grabbing Sunny by her arm up off the lap of one of the dudes and pulling her out of the clutches of the other hungry dudes that had been taking advantage of her. Sean hadn't noticed until he was up on her that she was wearing nothing but a tiny piece of material that barely covered her butt cheeks and as a top, a thin sheath of cutoff spandex that barely made it over her ample breasts.

"Get off me," Sunny slurred, squinting to see who was grabbing on her. "Don't touch me." Her words came out so garbled Sean knew right away she was more than just drunk.

"Sunny! It's me Sean!" he shouted, grabbing her face trying to force her droopy, half-closed eyes to focus on his face.

"Ohhh, Daaaviid," Sunny sang drunkenly. "My best friend . . . where you been at, nigga?" Sunny slurred and laughed. "Why you tryin'a break up my fun?" she garbled, finally focusing her dilated pupils on Sean's face.

"Whatchu doin' in here dressed like a trick, letting niggas put they hands all over you?" Sean snarled in her face. "You ain't stayin' in here! Let's go!"

"I'm . . . I'm grown. Now get the fuck off me! You don't know nothing about what I do . . . *King Sean*," Sunny yelled putting a nasty emphasis on Sean's street name as she pushed him in his chest with all of her might.

"Sunny, this shit ain't up for discussion. You're drunk or some shit and you ain't stayin' over here like this," Sean declared.

"You think you know me?" Sunny spat, viciously yanking her other arm away from him and pushing him again. Sean was shocked to find her like that; he was at a loss for words.

"Yo, Beans grab her and bring her on," Sean demanded. Beans stepped closer to Sunny. Just then, Faheem stepped up behind Sunny. He smiled evilly at Sean.

"We got a problem, potna?" Faheem asked, trying to sound more American than Jamaican. He pushed Sunny behind him and shielded her with his body.

"Yeah, nigga, we do and what?" Sean growled, touching his waistband. "You supposed to be her man right? You got m'fuckas feelin' all up on her?" Sean gritted, the butt of his gun showing.

"When you gonna get it, nigga? She with me and she don't want you. It's been years now, li'l soldier . . . she don't want you. She don't want to be your friend . . . nothing like that," Faheem said viciously, stepping a few steps too close to Sean.

"Fuck you, m'fucka!" Sean barked, pushing Faheem in the chest so hard he stumbled backward into Sunny and they both fell. Beans was all over it. He slid his gun out of his waistband and put it to Faheem's head. Beans's eyes were flashing with fire and his bottom lips was drawn in between his teeth.

"I will spill this dread nigga's brains right here with a million witnesses, King . . . on my word I ain't got no problem. Just give me the word," Beans said through clenched teeth.

"Don't do it, Sean! Don't do it!" Sunny screamed and cried. She was sobering up real fast now. "For me! Just leave us alone! Don't do it! I don't want to go with you! I hate you! I'm happy with him! I'm happy with him!" Sunny cried out. Even she didn't believe her words, but she couldn't bring herself to give into Sean. She was too angry at him for that. Ever since they had been kids, Sunny would never surrender to Sean, but she had perfected the art of getting him to surrender to her.

"Leave me alone, Sean! I don't want to be your friend! I don't want to be with you! I want him! I want only him!" Sunny screeched through a waterfall of tears with the lies burning on her tongue.

Sean saw her tears, listened to her words and was immediately drawn back to their childhood. Sean tapped Beans on the arm calling him off.

"Nah, son, it is what it is. She wanna be with a nigga that's gon' let m'fuckas violate her . . . so be it," Sean spat coolly, pulling Beans back. "We came to enjoy our new year and it's my day. This wannabe bad boy fake-ass Jamaican nigga ain't gon' fuck that up," Sean proclaimed hawking a wad of spit down on Faheem.

Beans released Faheem with a hard shove and then kicked him in the stomach. Faheem doubled over and Sunny fell on top of him. The entire left side of the club was watching the spectacle now, but no one jumped back because everyone knew about King Sean and his crew.

"Fuckin' lucky . . . bitch-ass nigga," Beans snarled at Faheem. "You ain't gon' always be this lucky though. We gon' see ya m'fuckin' ass again."

Sean didn't even bother to take another look at Sunny, but he could hear her screaming at his back.

"You don't know shit about me and what I do! You don't give a fuck about me! You don't care shit about me, Sean! So what! You a millionaire! The same people you shit on going up you have to see on your way down, Sean! Remember I said that!" Sunny was screaming at the top of her lungs. Her words were breaking Sean's heart, but his face remained stony and unfazed.

"You ain't no better than me! We the same, Sean! We come from the same place! You just like me!" That was the last statement Sean heard Sunny say before he'd gotten so far away that the music had drowned her out.

"Fuck you, Sunny, and fuck me for ever loving you," Sean mumbled under his breath.

When Sean returned to the VIP section, BG was sitting on one of the huge leather wraparound benches. The table in front of her was decorated with hundreds of expensive bottles of champagne, exclusive cognacs and a variety of flavored vodkas.

"You good?" BG asked as soon as Sean slid onto the seat next to her.

"Yeah. Ain't nothin'," Sean replied, his tone flat and uninterested. He immediately poured himself a snifter of Ace of Spades and threw it back.

"Who's the girl?" BG pried further. "Your ex?"

"That's nobody. We here to bring this New Year and my bornday in like kings," Sean brushed BG's question off. He raised his glass and called his crew over. Just then Beans, Ty, Ak and Freddie moved aside and a gorgeous Korean model dressed in a fire engine red leotard walked over holding a beautiful, custom-made cake that was shaped like a throne.

"Happy Birthday, King Sean," the exotic Asian girl sang. "Happy Birthday, dear King Sean," she went on.

"Didn't I tell y'all niggas birthday cakes was for lame-ass niggas?" Sean joked. His mind was already starting to put Sunny aside.

"You ain't gotta blow out the candles, nigga . . . we got some bitches that's gon' blow you instead," Ak yelled out. Everyone erupted in laughter.

"Money is all we need, niggas! Fuck all the rest!" Sean cheered, raising his glass out in front of him. His entire crew screamed their agreement. "To money!" "Money over bitches!" "Money!" they all yelled out. Sean stood up and blew out the candles on his gold crown cake, but one candle was left.

"You blow it out," Sean said to BG. "It's the candle for good luck and shit," he told her. BG came to his side and blew out the candle.

"That's what's up! To us!" Sean started laughing, but BG wasn't buying it. She had seen the hurt etched on his face when he had returned from the dustup with

Sunny. BG found Sean's concern for Sunny attractive.
BG couldn't help the deep feelings that were starting
creeping up on her.

Chapter Ten

Spring 2003

Sean and BG sat at the long, shiny, wood table inside the small conference room in a beautiful, picturesque $10,000-a-night penthouse suite at the Mandalay Bay in Las Vegas. It was a few hours before the Oscar De La Hoya and Luis Campas fight, which Sean had purchased premium ringside seats to for the both of them.

"Yo, we ain't come to Vegas to discuss business," Sean said exasperated after listening to BG go on and on about a new connect she had in mind. Most of the time Sean appreciated her work ethic, but when he was trying to have downtime, BG never stopped thinking about business and business moves.

"I'm telling you, King, God is marking shit up too much now. After all the money you made him, he wanna go up now all of a sudden? Niggas recognizing that his shit is more like eighty percent rather than that one hundred he was supplying when you first got with him," BG told Sean, her tone serious. Sean reared back in his chair, stretched his arms over his head and shook his head left to right at her. He hadn't met another woman so driven since his mother. Sean couldn't front, there was something he found sexy about BG's constant tabs on the business side of things; however, he sometimes wished she had a chill button he could push.

"Nah, we good money with God. C'mon, B . . . God don't bother us, we don't bother him and shit is good," Sean replied with finality. He swiveled his chair around. "Look around. We living like royalty and that's off of God. I can't fault that man in no way," Sean said, opening his arms wide to bring his point home. He wasn't going to get into particulars with BG about his early promises to God and Adina, so he wanted to drop the subject.

"Side deals ain't my style," Sean said.

"Look." BG stood up and walked over to where Sean sat. She laid down a typewritten sheet of paper and slapped her hand on top of it so he would look at it. "This is just something for you to think about . . . something I worked up just in case you gave me pushback on this move," she said, pointing to the information contained on the paper. "This is a comparison of suppliers with no names written here. God and his prices and his quality on the left . . . a new prospective supplier out of Miami and his prices and his quality on the right . . . You think about it and you do the math," BG said pushing the paper toward Sean some more. She didn't wait for his answer or to hear what he had to say once he reviewed the sheet; instead, BG sauntered toward the suite door.

"I'll meet you in the lobby and we'll walk over to the main event together tonight. If that's all right with you . . . partner," she said flatly. Sean chuckled at her tone. BG was a hard ass and she wasn't always easy to deal with, but she was starting to grow on him.

"And if you're betting tonight and in business . . . I hope you're betting on the right dude," she said figuratively, letting the door slam behind her.

When BG finally showed up in the Mandalay Bay lobby, she was glowing . . . literally. Her gleaming ebony skin played up against the shocking white, close fitting, Nicole Miller wrap dress she wore. The dress looked as if it had been painted onto BG's body because it clung to her so closely and accentuated her slim, yet curvy frame. BG seemed to glide across the expansive hotel lobby; her white feathered Manolo Blahnik pumps giving her slender legs the right amount of lift to bring out her thick muscular calf. The diamond chandelier earrings that dangled from her ears were blinding as she walked toward Sean with the grace of a goddess. He couldn't keep his eyes off of his sexy business partner. In fact, he had to shake his head a few times to shake away lustful thoughts about her.

"Damn. I don't even wanna walk next to you, super star," Sean joked when BG was close enough. Sean was joking because he looked just as dapper as BG in his custom-tailored Armani suit, monogrammed Gucci belt and Gucci loafers.

"You don't look so shabby yourself." She smiled, putting her arm through his playfully. BG thought Sean was gorgeous with his smooth caramel skin and dark intriguing eyes. Even the small gap between his pearly white teeth was sexy to her and she was simply infatuated with the new neatly trimmed goatee and slim mustache he had been rocking lately. They walked through the casino together and definitely turned a lot of heads as onlookers tried to figure out what celebrity couple Sean and BG was.

"Stop right there and make a bet," BG said, halting Sean's step while pointing to the roulette table. "I'm feeling lucky." She winked.

"Nah, ma, I don't play roulette. I gamble on sure bets only," Sean protested half joking, but mostly serious. BG pulled Sean by the arm over to the side of the roulette table that she had been pointing to. She unclasped the latch on her small white Christian Dior clutch and took out a handful of chips.

"Here, pick a number and bet. If you lose we go with my connect. If you win, we stay with God," BG said, dropping the $10,000 worth of coins into Sean's right hand. Sean looked at her strangely and shook his head.

"You just not gon' let this go," Sean said, reluctantly stepping up to the table. "You about to lose and then I don't want to hear no more talk about it," Sean said sternly.

"A'ight. No more about it if I lose, but if I win . . . give me your word." BG stopped him and looked him straight in the eye.

"A'ight, you got my word and my word is bond," Sean said with sincerity. He was sure he wouldn't lose. Sean counted himself as lucky in life thus far, after all, he had scarcely missed the murder of his mother and his mentor, and both times he'd crossed paths with their killers right before he found them dead.

With that, Sean chunked all of the chips down on the red 16 in the middle of the roulette table. It was his grandmother's birthday number. Sean caught a few sideway glances from other betters at the table who shot him looks as if to say he must be crazy to bet all on one number with such a slim probability of winning.

"Feeling lucky," he said with a smile, although his heart was jack hammering in his chest.

"No more bets!" the table matron called out, waving her hand over the table as if she was about to show everybody a magic trick. BG and Sean both watched the small white ball jump around the round number plate. BG had her ass cheeks clenched together tightly and Sean secretly had his toes balled up in his shoes as the ring finally started to slow and the ball fell, popping around to find its place in a number slot.

"Eight! Lucky number eight!" the table matron shouted.

"Yes!" BG blurted out, almost jumping out of her expensive pumps. Now, the other betters shifted their gazes from Sean to her; eyeing her strangely, as if to say why would she be happy her friend lost all of his money.

"Your word right?" BG clarified, a big smile flashing across her face.

"My word," Sean said somberly, his hands shoved into his suit pockets and his jaw flexing feverishly.

"In the future . . . always bet on black," BG said snidely, winking at him.

Sean kept his word and agreed to meet BG's new connect—a dude she called Reemo out of Miami. Sean didn't expect to cut a deal with Reemo because Sean didn't think anyone could do better than God's prices. No matter how many times BG had told Sean that Reemo was willing to front the heroin and premium lab made meth at half of God's price, Sean thought that was impossible. "How the fuck he gon' make his profit?" Sean had asked her sharply the third time she told him.

At the airport in Miami, Sean bent his lanky body into the passenger seat of a gorgeous, silver drop-top Bentley Continental. BG slid behind the steering wheel and looked over at him. She had felt him staring at her.

"What?" she asked, her left eyebrow raised.

"It's sexy as hell to have a woman driving me around in a whip that many niggas ain't even up on yet in 2003," Sean said, flashing a huge grin. BG relaxed a little bit and chuckled too.

"It's boss as hell for me to drive a king around in my 2003 Bentley, so I feel the same way," BG quipped right back, winking at him.

"Nah . . . say word. This shit ain't yours. This a rental, stop frontin'. Tell the truth," Sean teased, knowing just how to annoy her.

"Nigga, you crazy as hell you think I would be caught dead driving a rental. I have a whip in every state I frequent . . . believe that," BG clarified, a hint of defensiveness underlying her words.

"I hear that hot shit." Sean shook his head in admiration. "Remind me to get like you when I grow up," he said sarcastically. BG cut her eye at him, then busted out laughing. She knew he was trying hard to get under her skin like an annoying younger brother.

"Nah, nigga . . . we both about to grow up after this deal changes the game for us," she replied.

As they drove down Collins Avenue with the thick, hot Miami air blowing on their faces, BG schooled Sean on the hot spots that celebrities frequented, the best places to shop and most importantly, the best places to party.

"We gon' celebrate tonight. Trust, my nigga, there will be a lot to celebrate for sure," BG said as she whipped the Bentley past the glitzy part of the strip and into a mini mall parking lot toward the end of the strip. The mini mall had a few stores but BG pulled up in front of a nondescript, pale brick building with blacked-out glass windows in the front and no sign describing what type of establishment it was.

Sean craned his neck so he could get a good look at the building. It looked abandoned to him.

"What's up?" he asked BG, his crumpled facial expression telling the story of what was going on in his mind.

"Be easy. This is Reemo's hot spot . . . you know . . . strip club," BG said jokingly as she grabbed for her door handle. Sean grabbed her arm halting her motion for a minute.

"Look. I don't know this nigga so don't get in there and act brand new," Sean warned in a serious tone. "I don't have my people with me, but I can handle mines."

"C'mon. You're my partner. This is business and that's it. You'll see," BG assured.

With that, Sean exited the Bentley and straightened his jeans out, swiped his hands down the front of his Lacoste polo shirt and adjusted his Rolex on his wrist. He didn't take too kindly to having a business meeting in jeans, but given that the meeting was being held at a storefront strip club, Sean relaxed a little bit. He followed BG to the front door of the weird looking club.

"I'm warning you ahead of time, Reemo is interesting . . . to say the least," BG said. "But that don't mean nothing when it comes to his prices and quality."

Sean would quickly find out what BG meant. Inside the club, Sean looked around with wide eyes. The strip club's drab outside was nothing like chic inside which boasted shiny black and purple lacquer floors, sparkly silver walls and expansive, beveled glass mirrors throughout. There were four stages with shiny silver poles at the centers and a glitter covered DJ's stand at the back. The bar was beautifully decorated with colorful glass shelves behind it and nothing but premium liquors stacked up. Sean and BG walked slowly, he was taking it all in, imagining what kind of money an establishment like that could bring in.

"BG! What's up, girl?" a tall, slender girl wearing a lavender wig, clear plastic five-inch heels and a purple bathrobe shouted when she saw them. Sean gazed at the beautiful woman up and down.

"Dream! Hey, chica!" BG hollered in response, rushing toward the girl. They hugged and rocked back and forth like long-lost sisters being reunited.

"Girl, you look damn good! Leaving all this has served you damned good," Dream sang, stepping back to take in an eyeful of BG's luxurious jewels, her oversized Chanel tote and her spiked Louboutin pumps. BG seemed a little uncomfortable, but she smiled through it. But, she could feel the heat of Sean's gaze on her face. BG could only wonder if Sean had caught on to what Dream had said.

"Um . . . Dream, this is King Sean . . . King, this is my girl Dream," BG introduced. "We go way back and she's the sweetest female you'll ever meet."

"Damn ain't he a tall drank of chocolate milk," Dream licked her lips and said sexily. Sean's cheeks flamed over, but he kept his face stoic.

"He's off-limits!" BG snapped playfully. "C'mon before she rings the feed bell and you get surrounded by a roomful of hungry stripper bitches," BG told Sean, pulling him along toward the back of the club.

"How you know I ain't wanna be surrounded by a roomful of hungry stripper bitches?" Sean whispered to BG. She shot him a look and punched him in the arm.

"Because we are here on business that's how," she replied, a red flush of jealousy cropping up on her cheeks.

At the back of the club, BG pushed aside a bunch of silver and crystal hanging beads that were covering a doorway. She held the beads aside and let Sean pass through the doorway.

"Now that's some old school shit right there," Sean laughed. "I ain't seen beads since the eighties."

"Yeah, the girls been trying to get Reemo to take them shits down for years."

Once BG and Sean passed through the beaded doorway, BG made a sharp left into a long, dimly lit hallway. Sean followed her, looking around a bit leery.

"Sure is a lot of m'fuckin' doors in this bitch," he grumped. Sean hated closed doors.

"What's strip club without champagne rooms?" BG answered, as if to say "duh." Just then, Sean passed one of the doors and it was slightly opened. He peeked through the crack as he passed, only to see a beautiful Latina with her lips sealed around a dick.

"Ah . . . champagne rooms. Forgot about them," Sean said amused.

Finally Sean and BG arrived at a black doorway in the back of the club. Sean could already smell the cigarette smoke coming from under the door. BG tapped on the door a few times and placed her ear close to listen.

"Who it is?" a man's voice with a distinct Southern drawl screamed from the other side.

"Black Girl!" BG yelled back. Within a few seconds Sean could hear the locks clicking on the door. There had to be at least twenty locks that clicked before the door finally opened a crack.

"Jumbo, move out the way. It's me BG," she demanded, pushing the door open wider causing a short, portly man to stumble back a few steps. Sean followed her inside. Immediately the smoke and odor in the room assailed his nose and he coughed. It was taking everything inside of him to not throw his arm or hand up over his nose.

"Black Gal! Goddamn, gal! Where the hell you been at? You told me you was coming weeks ago," Reemo huffed, his fast Southern drawl reminding Sean of a cast member from an old slave movie. Sean did a double take at the man thinking his eyes were deceiving him.

"What's good, Reemo? I told you I would get here when I got here," BG sassed walking closer to where Reemo sat on a black leather couch.

"Who you got there?" Reemo asked, tilting his head in Sean's direction. Sean stepped closer and he couldn't take his eyes off of the man in front of him.

Reemo had to be at least 400 pounds of pure fat. His body spilled from side to side and although he was sitting on a full-length couch, it still seemed too small for him.

Reemo's legs looked like the trunks of one-hundred-year-old trees and his arms where so short they seemed almost nonexistent. Reemo was dark as night and had at least three chins. He had a thick afro of hair that looked like it hadn't been washed, cut or combed in years. This couldn't be the man BG had described as a multimillion-aire looking like this, Sean was thinking.

"Reemo, this is King Sean. Remember, we talked about my partner up North?" BG introduced, moving aside so Reemo could get a better look at Sean through the haze of smoke in the dimly lit room. Sean reluctantly stepped closer as the Jabba the Hutt lookalike in front of him extended his fat, greasy, sausage hand toward him for a shake.

"What up?" Sean said, balling his fist and bumping it lightly into Reemo's hand. There was no way Sean was going to touch Reemo's filthy hands for a handshake. Sean was already regretting that he'd agreed to make a deal with the sloppy pig in front of him. Reemo was a far cry from God in terms of appearance and even place of business. Sean had to wonder if everything else about the overweight man was going to be as sloppy; including his deals.

"All right. All right," Reemo said, sounding a bit out of breath as he spoke.

"So I told King Sean about your offer and he's willing to at least listen to you. He is finding it hard to believe that you can beat the prices of his connect," BG told Reemo. She could feel Sean shooting daggers at her with his eyes.

"Mmmm hmm, mmm hmmm," Reemo drawled like a true Southerner. "I'm tellin' ya. I gets that premium boy straight off the banana boat. Right'chere in Miami they brings it right from they country. Ewww weee, it's so pure it would kill a elephant if it ain't cut at least a little bit. Them coconuts lets me gets the best deal, that's why I can offer it to ya half of what you payin'. My shit so sweet and so pure you can step on it one time and them fiends won't knows the difference," Reemo explained, his fat jiggling as he got excited about the details.

Suddenly his girth and odor didn't seem that horrible to Sean any longer because Reemo was talking Sean's language . . . money.

"How you gettin' it to me? Right now, I have a human pipeline riding from Canada to my city and it's been working for years. I ain't one to fuck up a good thing . . . feel me? You talkin' half price but who takin' care of the transport?" Sean replied seriously. He was in straight business mode now.

"I'll take care of the transport," BG interjected. "That's what I had told Reemo I would do. I have my people here and my ways. Getting it is not going to be a problem," she assured.

Sean raised his eyebrow at her. He thought they talked about all their business moves and didn't keep any secrets. She was coming out of left field with this.

"A'ight," Sean acquiesced; although, in his mind the discussion with BG was far from over.

"Good. Good. So e'erythang half cheaper than you pays now. Deal?" Reemo wheezed, a crooked smile on his lips. His accent was laughable to say the least, especially because Northerners like Sean always pictured country dudes to look greasy just like Reemo did.

"Deal," BG said excitedly, smiling.

"A'ight," Sean said dryly. He wasn't about to shake Reemo's hand to seal their deal.

"Y'all come back t'night and enjoy the club. On me . . . your new partner," Reemo told them.

"Thanks, Reemo. I'm telling you this is going to be the best deal you ever made," BG said confidently. Something between BG and Reemo was gnawing at Sean's psyche but he couldn't place it just yet. He was going to keep his eye out though. If Fox had taught him anything, he had taught Sean never to trust another human being 100 percent . . . ever.

Chapter Eleven

"Yo, Miami is a'ight. I might have to buy a piece of property out here," Sean yelled in BG's ear over the music pulsing through Mynt Ultra Lounge.

"Yeah, it's a sexy-ass city. This is definitely my home away from home," BG mused as she looked out into the exclusive lounge; the liquor starting to take hold of her senses. BG was a regular at Mynt whenever she ventured back to Miami. Mynt was one of the few invitation only spots on Collins that was frequented by only the finest in South Beach glitterati. Sean and BG didn't disappoint either. He wore a white Cuban shirt like the old school Miami gangsters, a pair of sleek, white linen pants accented by a pair of crisp white Hermès boat shoes. BG played up her curves in a deep purple one piece, spandex, flare leg jumpsuit with a gold Chanel, double C chain belt and a pair of snake skin Christian Dior strappy stilettos.

"I fuckin' love this place. I wish my dudes was here to celebrate with us tonight," Sean said, getting close to BG so he could speak directly in her ear. The heat of his breath made the hairs on the back of her neck stand up and something thumped between her legs. Sean put his arm around her as he looked out and took in an eyeful of the place. There was something real sexy about the lounge and BG. The atmosphere lent itself to a sexy vibe that was unmistakable.

The front room of Mynt Ultra lounge, where Sean and BG sat, was draped in egg white and mint green colors;

but right outside of their exclusive section was what they called the a Grand Lounge with a walkway nestled between an encirclement of plush couches and the bar; and another part referred to as the Ultra Lounge that was decorated with chic hanging mirrors and marble floors.

"Well it's just me and you tonight," BG replied, raising her tenth glass of Cristal. Sean raised his glass as well, only he had lost count. Their glasses clinked together, a sound and a sign that they were real partners.

BG was definitely showing him a good time and with the liquor easing into his system, Sean began to relax— something he very rarely did when he wasn't in his own city, surrounded by his own crew. And even then, it took a lot to get Sean to fully let his guard down.

"Owww this is my song," BG jumped up, her legs feeling a little wobbly. Sean laughed as she stumbled a little bit while she did a two-step.

"Your ass can't dance," he teased.

"Nigga, please. If you only knew," BG snapped back, turning around swiftly so he could get a bird's eye view of her assets. She licked her lips seductively as she winded her waist in front of him. With the beat of the music thumping in her chest, BG swung her body sexily and twisted her hips like only a pro could. Sean played it cool, but he could feel heat rising in his loins as he watched her without blinking.

"You ain't never have a grind unless you had one from a Panamanian woman," BG said, lowering her backside down onto Sean's lap. Sean threw his drink back and smiled slyly.

"Nah . . . guess not," he whispered as BG grinded into him like a paid professional. Sean eased his head back and let her work her hips into a frenzy. He could feel his manhood throbbing against the thin material of his linen pants.

"Hold on to me," BG yelled at him, grabbing Sean's hands and putting them on her waist.

"Yeah, like that," she said, grinding him even harder and bouncing a few times for good measure.

"Damn, ma. I didn't know you had it in you," Sean panted, grabbing her and spinning her around so she would face him. They shared a quick, yet deep gaze, then Sean grabbed the back of her head, pulled her face toward his and seductively thrust his tongue into her mouth. BG relaxed against his muscular chest and extended her tongue too. It was the first time they had crossed a very thin line between business and pleasure but neither of them could control it or stop themselves.

That night when Sean and BG arrived at her condo door they couldn't keep their hands off of each other. Both of them were intoxicated, but aware.

"Wait. Let me get the keycard out," BG huffed as Sean kissed and licked the back of her neck, trailing his tongue down the center of her exposed back.

"Hurry the fuck up," he huffed, starting to pull her bodysuit off of her shoulders.

"Ah," BG let out a gasp. She was dripping wet down below and could hardly steady her breathing.

Finally the door clicked open and as if it were some sort of signal, Sean pulled her away from the door, picked her up and pushed backward into her condo. BG crushed her mouth over his and straddled her legs around his waist. Sean stumbled backward, holding on to her, their tongues doing a wicked dance with one another.

"I need you," BG panted out, gently biting Sean's bottom lip. He swung around and carefully eased her down onto her white leather couch. He fell to his knees in front of her, pulled her jumpsuit down over her ample breasts and ravenously buried his face in her chest. Sean extended his long tongue and ran them over BG's erect nipples.

"Oh God!" she gasped, squeezing his muscular shoulders as he lapped at her. She was grinding her hips dying to feel him fill her up.

BG lifted her waist slightly and began easing her jumpsuit all the way down.

"Let me do that," Sean corrected her, his sweat dripping onto her stomach. When he was done with her breasts and sure she was soaking wet and waiting for him; Sean finally eased her jumpsuit all the way off.

"Damn you are fuckin' sexy," he breathed out heavily. He trailed his hands over her lace La Perla panties, then he placed his mouth over her mound and blew out a lung full of hot air.

"Ahhh!" BG yelled out, the heat causing her clitoris to swell so much she felt like she would bust before he even really touched her. Sean chuckled.

"I love to hear your satisfaction," he said. He eased her delicate panties over her hips. Then he stood up and stopped for a minute. BG popped her eyes open.

"What's the matter?" she said, slight panic in her voice.

"I just wanted to look at your pretty ass," Sean replied as he loosened his belt and took off his pants. When he released his snake, BG's eyes grew wide and she licked her lips.

Sean touched himself and looked at her as if to say "you better be ready." He lowered himself in front of her, gently moved her pelvis in front of his and slowly entered her dripping wet middle.

"Oh Go . . . ddd!" BG called out as she took all of him inside of her. Sean fell down on top of her and began with a gentle stroke. The more BG screamed out the harder his strokes became.

"Argg! Argg!" Sean growled as he pounded into her. While he was still inside of her, he grabbed hold of her, pulled her in closer and stood up. BG locked her legs behind Sean's back as he used his powerful leg muscles and arms to air fuck her.

"Yes! Yes!" BG groaned, biting down into his neck. Still aware, Sean flexed his head so that she wouldn't give him a hickey. BG noticed his small rejection, but his sex was so good she didn't complain. Holding BG tightly, Sean carried her into her bedroom. Once inside, he tossed her onto the bed, quickly flipped her over and took her roughly from behind.

"I never been fucked like this," BG cried out. "Never!" she screamed as she clutched her fluffy white down comforter. Sean kept thrusting until he felt the walls of her vagina close down around his manhood. He knew what that meant so he picked up the pace of his thrusts.

"Aggggggghhh!!" BG screamed as she had the most explosive orgasm of her life. Sean was next. He pulled himself out of her tight hole, propped his throbbing member up on her perfect, round ass and released his load all over it.

BG collapsed onto the bed, breathing like she had just run a marathon. Sean fell over onto his side, his chest also rising and falling rapidly. Neither of them said a word, but they were both thinking the same thing—*we crossed that line, but business and pleasure don't mix.*

Chapter Twelve

When Sean returned from Miami, he went straight to his office. He knew his crew wasn't expecting him and that was exactly what he wanted—to surprise them. Sean was big on seeing how his crew behaved when out of his sight.

Sean pulled back the two huge, wooden conference room doors and stepped inside. He was immediately taken aback by what he saw.

Beans, Ty, Ak, Freddie and Bo all had their backs turned huddled around a laptop watching something with loud music blaring from it. They were so engrossed in the screen and the music was so loud that none of them even heard Sean step into the room.

"Yo! This shit is ill for real. Look at that ass," Ty said excitedly, tugging at his crotch. "That shit got me on swoll and I ain't even there! I heard she got that good good for real, nigga."

"I would run up in that shit like a maniac nigga who just got outta jail," Freddie followed up laughing. "Straight raw dawgin' that pussy like a m'fucka!"

"I don't know if I would touch that shit with a ten-foot pole niggas. She a fuckin' straight fiend that would suck the skin off a dick for a nick," Ak declared with disgust in his tone.

"That's what I'm sayin' too," Beans followed up. "No fiend pussy for me."

"Ahem!" Sean cleared his throat loudly causing his crew to jump and turn swiftly in his direction. "I coulda blown all y'all niggas away and y'all wouldn't even know what the fuck hit y'all," Sean said, walking over to where they all stood with their mouths now hanging open. All of this crew members had turned toward him and meshed their bodies together in an attempt to hide what they were watching.

"Why the fuck y'all look like kids that just got busted doin' some ill shit?" Sean asked, his face crumpled. "Shit, put me on, niggas."

Beans started shaking his head in disgust. "I told y'all niggas to dead that shit from the gate," Beans said in a low tone. "Y'all hardheaded-ass niggas don't listen. Never fuckin' listen."

Ty slammed the laptop cover down. Freddie and Bo looked away, unable to hold eye contact with Sean. Beans just shook his head like he was giving up.

"Yo, boss, how was ya trip?" Ak asked, rushing over and giving Sean a quick pound and chest bump.

"Nah, nigga, don't try to change shit up. Y'all niggas was all into something, so put me on, niggas," Sean said, half joking, but really serious. His crew knew when he wasn't playing.

Freddie folded his bottom lip in between his teeth and let out a long sigh. "Might as well show him," Freddie-conceded, shoving his hands deep into the pocket of his low-slung jeans. Ak let out a long sigh, anticipating Sean's reaction. Bo lowered his head and just shook it slowly side to side.

They all moved apart to allow Sean to stand in front of the laptop. Beans reluctantly opened the cover and Ak pulled up the screen they had been watching.

Ak pressed play on the video icon and immediately loud reggae music blared from the computer. Sean squinted at the grainy images on the screen for a few minutes, then looked around at his crew with his eyebrows dipping low on his face.

"Fuck is this?" Sean asked, scowling.

"That's one of them dutty wine basement clubs and that . . . that's . . . " Beans didn't have the heart to finish his sentence. Before he could say anything more a clear image and direct face shot showed up on the screen.

"M'fuckin' Sunny," Sean finished the sentence for Beans. The vein at Sean's temple began throbbing fiercely. Sean's legs suddenly felt too weak to stand as the heat of anger engulfed his entire body. He flopped down in one of the conference chairs, but he wouldn't take his eyes off the screen and Sunny's image. He bit down hard into his bottom lip as he watched four men take turns putting their dicks in different parts of Sunny's body, including her mouth. Sean's fists clenched involuntarily and his chest started heaving.

"Yo . . . is that a m'fuckin' black eye?" Sean grumbled. He got a few nods of agreement from his crew. "That gotta be that dread nigga puttin' his hands on her! Nah! Fuck that!" Sean jumped up so fast and hard he sent the conference chair flying into the wall behind it.

"Word on the block is he been pimpin' her out, keeping her high off that boy and beating her ass when she don't wanna get down," Ty relayed, instigating now that he saw his boss was steaming mad.

"Yeah, niggas is saying they be lining up at the dutty wine joint just to run up in them guts. Niggas is actually paying to fuck her . . . some of them sliding her a little dime of H to get down," Freddie finished up like he knew firsthand. Sean's insides were churning and he felt like someone had pulled a veil of red over his eyes.

"Let's go!" he barked. "Make sure all y'all holding, too."

Just as his crew began scrambling to follow him out, BG walking in halted them.

"Where we going?" she asked playfully with a beautiful smile and the look of a woman in love glistening in her eyes.

"You ain't goin' nowhere," Sean barked at her as he pushed past her. BG spun around, stunned and thrown off by his reaction.

All of Sean's crew members were hot on his heels, but Beans stopped and turned toward BG. Out of respect he didn't want to leave her hanging like that.

"It's his girl Sunny again. She's into some real fucked-up shit. He's going to get her. I think it's for good this time," Beans told BG. Her mouth turned down at the corners and her hands fell at her sides with disappointment. "If you ain't know before, that nigga King love Sunny. I mean real love since they was kids and shit. He don't like to admit it, but that's always gon' be his first love from the gate," Beans said to BG and with that he was gone.

BG stood in the empty conference room astonished. She felt like someone had just gut punched her or slapped her across the face. Her mind quickly replayed what had happened between her and Sean in Miami, something she wished she could erase at that moment. It had seemed so sincere and so real when they shared their moment, but now reality was setting in on her. BG could feel a sharp pain in her chest and knew it was heartbreak she was experiencing. She slowly eased herself down in the chair at the head of the table where Sean usually sat.

"And that's why you don't fuck your business partner and catch feelings because in the end you look like the asshole," she mumbled, scolding herself.

The tension in the Range Rover was so thick it would need to be sliced with an ax to break it up. The pin drop silence had everybody's nerves and tempers on edge. None of Sean's crew members dared to speak and there was none of the usual rap music blaring for fear that any little thing would set Sean off. They all knew how unpredictable their boss's temper could be when he wasn't happy and especially when it came to the topic of Sunny.

Sean barely waited for the Range Rover to stop before he was opening the door and hopping out. Bo had to literally slam on the brakes in front of their destination to keep Sean from falling out of the vehicle. Sean had his feet planted on the pavement before any of his crew could react fast enough. His jaw rocked as he moved forward like some unknown force was pushing him forward.

"Yo! Let's go!" Beans shouted, scrambling to get out of the Range Rover and keep up with his boss. "This nigga on a mission like a m'fucka right now," Beans huffed, practically running behind Sean.

Sean had his gun in his hand when he hastily descended the cracked cement steps that led to the basement of the raggedy building. He could hear the reggae music pounding through the shabby wood door before he made it all the way there. Sean wasn't there to be politically correct, so instead of knocking, he lifted his foot and kicked the weak door with the power of a wrecking ball. After the second forceful kick, the door splintered open sending the weak lock and doorknob flying off. Women and men inside were startled and began moving aside when they saw Sean and his goons storming through the damaged door. Waves of gasps and screams filtered through the basement as Sean and his crew moved deeper inside. Most of the partygoers thought it was a stick up so they were clearing a path.

"Yow! Wha happ'nin', star? Wha de fuck yuh?" a huge dread with a barrel chest and big beer gut barked in Sean's face with a thick Jamaican accent.

"Fuck out my face, nigga!" Sean snarled, raising his gun to the dread's head. Scowling Sean pressed the barrel of his .40-caliber Glock hard against the man's forehead and moved his finger into the trigger guard. The dread immediately threw his hands up in surrender, but not before about six others came rushing toward Sean and his crew speaking hard with their Jamaican patois. Guns were raised and pointed in their faces before the basement makeshift security team could even get their bearings.

"E'erybody back the fuck up! Back up! We came here for one reason, so don't get ya m'fuckin' dreads twisted for no fuckin' reason!" Beans screamed, raising the chopper in the air so the dreads would know they were immediately outgunned. All of the dreads threw their hands up and stood their brooding but helpless.

"Yuh nah know a who yuh a fuck wit', star?" the first dread grumbled. Sean raised his Glock and brought it down on the man's head, sending the dread to the floor like a deflated balloon.

"Nah, nigga . . . you don't know who you fuckin' wit?" Sean spat. The crowd of partygoers who had been wining and grinding up on one another began flooding out of the makeshift club like roaches when the lights go on. They wanted no parts of the drama unfolding in front of them.

Sean forged ahead, interrupting a few intense grind and sex parties that were going on in random corners of the basement. He was in search of Sunny and wasn't leaving until he found her.

"Where Faheem at?" Sean asked one dude as Ak and Ty pulled the dude up off of a girl. "Back!" the dude spilled the beans right away, his dick dangling in the open. Sean tossed him down and steamed toward the back of the club like a madman.

There was a closed door next to the bathrooms. Sean bulldozed into the door with his shoulder and it crashed open sending the doorknob into the wall inside.

"What the fu . . ." Faheem started, jumping to his feet with eyes as wide as dinner plates. Sunny remained sitting, but her one good eye went round as well. Between her teeth she held a belt that was tightly wrapped around her arm and she grasped a needle full of heroin, ready to jam it into her vein. She saw Sean, but the urge to get high prevented her from letting go of the belt and calling out to him.

"You m'fucka! I warned you right?" Sean snarled, grabbing a handful of Faheem's long dreads. "I told you to make sure you treated her right!"

"Agh!" Faheem winced, swinging his arms futilely as Sean winded his hand tightly in the dreads.

"You not only pimpin' her out but you putting ya m'fuckin' hands on her, too? You ain't no fuckin' man," Sean hissed in Faheem's face.

"Sean!" Sunny finally screamed, dropping her needle on the floor. Before she could rush over to Sean her movement was halted.

Bang! Bang!

Faheem's eyes popped open and his body went limp immediately. Sean had put two in his dome right on the button at the temple.

"No!!! No!!!" Sunny screeched, her body folding over at the waist. "Why! Why!" she cried out.

"Get her and let's go!" Sean commanded. Ak rushed over and hoisted Sunny onto his shoulder caveman style. "No! Don't touch me! No!" She was kicking, screaming, spitting and scratching.

"You killed him! Why? Why?" she was hollering. "Get off me! I need to help him! Fah? Fah?" Sunny screeched so loudly she began coughing and wheezing. She stretched her arms out toward Faheem's stiff form, but she was no match for Ak.

"Let's get the fuck out of here!" Beans barked. They all rushed toward the exit.

"Sean!! I hate you! I hate you!" Sunny howled as she continued to flail her legs. "Fah!! Fah!!" she continued screaming for her dead man. With each scream Sean's insides churned harder and harder. If he didn't love Sunny so much he would've put one in her dome to shut her up too.

"You can hate me all you want. I'm saving your life right now," Sean grumbled as they all loaded into the Range Rover.

Pain shot like daggers through Sunny's head as she struggled to open her eyes. "Mmm," she moaned, moving her head side to side slowly.

Sean stirred in the chair he'd been sleeping in across from the bed where Sunny lay.

"Where am I?" Sunny croaked out, finally able to open her eyes slightly. Her mouth and throat were desert dry and her lips were cracked and painful.

"Big Mama's new house," Sean said, sitting up in the chair. He flexed his severely cramped neck and tried to work the kinks out of his back. He took a good look at Sunny and couldn't believe it. Sunny's once-flawless face was now marred with old and new bruises. Her left eye was healing, but it still had blue, green and purple rings around it. One of her front teeth was missing and her usually long, silky hair was matted and missing in a few places. Sean could still see remnants of her old beauty under all of the scars and he couldn't wait until she was well enough for him to take her for a full makeover.

"I need to go, Sean. I am going to be sick if I stay here," Sunny said, sitting up in the bed too quickly. She suddenly felt faint and collapsed onto the floor. Sean jumped up and rushed to her side. He grabbed her and pulled her back up onto the bed.

"C'mon, Sunny, just relax. You been through a lot. You don't need to go nowhere. I got my man to get you some methadone to wean you down and you gon' stay right here and detox off that shit. Big Mama knows what's up and she wants to see you get better, Sunny," Sean told her as he helped her lie back down.

Sunny began sobbing and rocking back and forth. She wanted a hit real bad and she couldn't stop thinking about Faheem.

"Why? Why you keep trying to help me?" she cried, rubbing her arms like they hurt really badly. "Maybe I don't want to be helped," she sniffled back a nose full of snot.

"Whatchu mean why? C'mon we been best friends since we were little. Why wouldn't I wanna see you doing better, Sunny? Being in clubs fuckin' niggas for drugs ain't you," Sean replied, stroking her hair. "You just don't know that you want to be helped . . . but you do. You want shit to be like old times. Remember when you used to be scared and stressed and would come over to my house and stay?" Sean said as he lay down next to her and held her like he would when they were kids.

"It's the same old us, Sunny. We are the same old us," he said softly, holding her tightly.

"I'm embarrassed. Look at me," Sunny said, extending her arm so Sean could see all of the deep, purple track marks on her once-flawless skin.

"You ain't never got to be embarrassed in front of me. I was the first nigga to smell you take a shit remember?" Sean said jokingly. Sunny elbowed him playfully and let out a halfhearted chuckle.

"Well I was the first chick to smell your deadly-ass farts," she joked back. They both busted out laughing.

Sean hugged Sunny into him and kissed the top of her head.

"You gon' be a'ight. I'ma make sure you get clean and live like the queen that you are," he said, his heart filling with love. More tears dropped from Sunny's eyes and soaked the pillow. Once again, Sean had showed her the most love she had ever received in her entire life. They lay there for a few minutes in silence. Both of them wondering what life had in store for them.

A soft knock on the bedroom door interrupted their moment.

"Come in," Sean called out in response to the knocks. He unlatched himself from Sunny and sat up on the side of the bed. The door slowly crept open and within seconds Sean's grandmother was standing there with her usual warm, inviting smile spread on her face.

"Good morning, babies. I had Lacy make y'all some breakfast so come on downstairs. I hope you're feeling a little better, Sunny girl," his grandmother said sweetly. Sunny turned over and smiled at her; tears welling up in her eyes.

"You still call me that after all these years, Big Mama," Sunny said, her voice cracking.

"You gon' always be Sunny girl to me," Sean's grandmother replied.

"See, this is gonna be the perfect place for you to stay to get back on your feet. Big Mama's lovin' will have you better in no time," Sean said, smiling from ear to ear. He couldn't be more happy to have both of his true loves together in one house.

Chapter Thirteen

Sean stood in the warehouse with BG on the opposite side of a long, wooden folding table. He looked down at the flawless, neatly wrapped bricks of heroin that were laid out perfectly on the table.

"Ain't this bitch pretty?" BG asked, waving her hand over the shipment like a game show host showing a winning prize. "You can't beat getting this shit as easy as we did."

"You ain't never lie," Sean replied, excitement apparent in his eyes, but his face showing that he was cool about it. He was still kind of stunned that BG had pulled off the transport without even consulting him on a shipping method.

"Like Reemo promised, this is straight off that banana boat. Not one bit stepped on at all. Purest shit you gon' ever get in the U.S.," BG told him, sticking her chest out proudly. She had something to prove to Sean and this shipment was just what she needed to make the point.

Sean looked over at her and he felt funny inside . . . a tingle that he didn't get from many women. BG was as beautiful as the first day he'd laid eyes on her, but today, after what she'd accomplished, BG looked even more gorgeous to him. Sean loved to see her in white, so the white blazer she wore with her perfect cleavage peeking out was doing something to him. He remembered the hot night they shared in Miami and wondered if BG ever thought about it like he did. Neither of them had ever mentioned it again and BG knew that for the past two months, Sunny had been living with Sean's grandmother and receiving frequent visits from Sean. BG also surmised that Sean and Sunny had taken things to the next level, so BG stepped back from the situation to protect her own heart.

"Why you staring at me like that? I got something on my face?" BG asked, snapping Sean out of his daydream.

"Nah. Nah. Nothing like that. So you, we need to get this out to the streets and see how it goes," Sean told her quickly changing the subject back to strictly business. He picked up a brick of the pure heroin and held it for a few seconds. "This is good . . . real good."

"So God is a dead issue now right?" BG asked for clarification. It had been bothering her that Sean hadn't kept her updated about the situation with God.

"I'll handle God. You handle distribution," Sean came back quickly. Sean had already been dodging calls from God for the past two months while he waited to see if Reemo would make good on his deal. Sean finally got tired of God's incessant calls and changed his phone number. Sean told himself he'd get in contact with God in due time. His plan was to make God whole for the last supply and then let God down easily with the hopes they could just part peacefully. It was a lofty goal and hope and Sean knew it.

Adina awoke to a loud crashing noise in her apartment. Not too many people knew about her new living arrangements, so she was immediately struck with panic. Her mind was still a little fuzzy with sleep, but Adina had enough clarity to grab for the small .22-caliber pistol she kept in her nightstand drawer. The noise came again, this time Adina was on her feet with her gun out in front of her. Her heart raced so fast she could barely breathe, but she was not going to lie down and let herself be an easy victim again.

Adina slowly turned the doorknob on her bedroom door and just as she went to step through the doorway she felt something pulling her forward.

"Ahh!" Her scream was short-lived as someone snatched her by her hair and dragged her down to the floor. Adina tried to get her finger into the trigger of her gun, but a brute force punch to the face dizzied her so badly her completely lost grip on her weapon.

"Help," she croaked out, but another slam to the face caused the words to tumble right back down her throat. Adina could feel herself moving now but not of her own will.

"Sit her in front of me," a male voice that she recognized demanded. Adina was weak, but her attackers slammed her into one of her own chairs, pulled her head up so she met their boss eye to eye.

"G . . . G . . . God," Adina stammered, her lips beginning to swell. She knew his voice and his scent anywhere.

"I told you that if this little boy you brought me turned on me like Fox did, you would be the one to suffer for it this time. You know I never go back on my word, 'Dina," God spoke calmly as if Adina wasn't in front of him bleeding from her mouth and nose.

"What? I . . . I don't know what you're talking about," she groaned, her legs swinging in and out nervously. As far as Adina knew, things between God and Sean had worked out perfectly for years now.

"I guess Sean really thinks he is a king huh?" God asked. "I hear that's what he calls himself these days . . . King Sean."

Adina shook her head from side to side. She hadn't heard from Sean in months. Once she was paid her cut for introducing him to God, Sean's visits became less and less frequent.

"So you didn't know he has been going around to clubs killing people at will?" God asked Adina. She shook her head again.

"I swear. I haven't seen him," she mumbled as blood dribbled down her slips.

"Oh yes. There was a big incident at a Jamaican club. I hear King Sean really showed his power by blowing a man's brains out in front of one hundred witnesses," God said sarcastically. "This young boy has brought heat with his antics and now I hear he has crossed me . . . gone with a new supplier and didn't even have the courtesy to sit down with me man to man like he always like to say it," God said with an eerily calm tone to his words.

"Please. Let me call him . . . He . . . he . . . can tell you that I don't know nothing," Adina pleaded barely able to speak through her swollen lips.

"No need to call him. I will send him a message," God said, nodding at the goons he was with. "Starting with you."

"No! No! Please, God! No!" Adina screamed, bucking her body in the chair she was being restrained in. It didn't take long for them to silence her.

It had been almost four months that Sunny had been clean from heroin. She had had a few slipups in the process, but Sean was always there to put her back on the right track. Sunny was feeling pretty good, but getting a little antsy about being in the house all of the time. It was wintertime so that made it easier to accept; however, Sunny didn't know if she would be able to stay stuck inside when the weather broke.

Sunny and Sean's grandmother sat in the kitchen laughing and talking about one of the television court shows when the doorbell rang and interrupted their laughter. Sunny crinkled her brow and looked at Sean's grandmother strangely.

"You expecting somebody, Big Mama?" Sunny asked, standing up slowly from the kitchen table with a pang of fear flitting through her stomach. They both knew that Sean would just use his keys to get in.

"No, baby. Since you been here I told Lacy to just stay on home. You been all the help I need. I don't know who would be ringing my bell this time of day," his grandmother said, a little concern registering in her voice. Sunny moved away from the table tentatively. The hairs were standing on the back of her neck and she was involuntarily holding her breath. The bell rang again and her heart throttled up in her chest.

"Let me see who this is then, because whoever it is they ain't going away," Sunny told Sean's grandmother, padding through the kitchen and into the living room. Sunny peeked out of the side windows in an attempt to see who it was before she opened the door. She had been super paranoid since Faheem's death that someone from his camp would be coming to find her for revenge.

As she peeked from the windows suspiciously, Sunny noticed a white FTD florist van out front and the tightness in her chest quickly eased as a sense of relief washed over her.

"Who?" she called out with her hand on the doorknob just to make sure.

"Flower delivery," a male voice called back. Sunny smiled and let out a long, relieved breath. If it was flowers she definitely knew who was sending them. Sean had been so good to her since she had gotten clean and been staying with his grandmother that Sunny didn't know how she would ever repay him.

"Sean . . ." Sunny whispered with a smile as she twisted the locks on the door. Before she could fully get a sentence out of her mouth the door banged open and three men with dreadlocks rushed into her with the force of a hurricane. Sunny stumbled backward and fell hard on her butt. Terror registered all over her face like she had put on a mask.

"Aggh!" Sunny screamed, but not for long. One of the men's hands closed around her throat immediately cutting off her air supply. Sunny instinctively threw her arms up over her head, but she was no match for the men that rushed her. After a few minutes of being choked, Sunny was yanked up off the floor by her hair. Pain shot through her scalp like stabs from a butcher's knife.

"Agghh!" she yelled, grabbing her attacker's hand, trying to free her hair from his grip. Sunny got a good look at him and immediately noticed his dreadlocks. The one holding her grabbed her roughly into a headlock while one of the other dreads drove his fist into her gut. Sunny wheezed and coughed because his blow had literally knocked the wind out of her. She actually felt like one of her ribs had cracked from the force of the next blow.

"Yuh man can't protect yuh nuh," one of the dreaded goons growled, his Jamaican accent unmistakable. Sunny knew he must've been referring to Sean.

"Please," she croaked, blood leaking from her busted lip. Sunny immediately assumed these were Faheem's people coming back to avenge his death.

"Where he deh? Where yuh man deh?" another goon barked getting so close to Sunny's face she could smell the weed odor on his breath.

"Where yuh man deh?" the dread growled, backhanding her. This time Sunny's nose busted and blood sprayed from it. Sunny refused to answer him.

"Fuck you," she whispered defiantly. She didn't care what they did to her; she would never give Sean up.

"Yuh wan' play hard?" the same dread gritted, punching Sunny across her face so hard more blood and a tooth shot from her lips. Sunny was taking the hits like a pro. Each time they hit her, she forced herself to raise her head to meet them face to face. Her attackers didn't know that Sunny had been being beaten all of her life and it took much more to get her to fold.

Sunny was fighting, flailing her arms and trying to kick her captors. She was fighting so hard, she didn't hear Sean's grandmother calling out to her.

"Hit she again. Make her shit on she self," one of the goon's growled evilly. When his partner moved in to hit Sunny, she extended her left arm and swiped at him, catching the end of one of his dreads. Sunny yanked wildly on the lock of hair she had and was shocked when the dreads came off of the man's head. Sunny couldn't believe that the dreads were a wig, but she didn't have time to think hard about the fact that all of Faheem's people were *real* dreads.

"This bitch!" the disguised dread barked. He was so angry that he'd been exposed that he punched Sunny in her chest like she was a man. He hit her so hard her back teeth clicked together. Sunny made a squealing noise and her body folded as pain shot through her chest so fast and furious she just knew her heart had exploded. Sunny's oxygen was being cut off, but before her world went black she finally heard Sean's grandmother calling her name frantically.

Be quiet, Big Mama! Run, Big Mama! Run! Sunny was screaming inside of her clouded head, but she could not get the words out with the amount of pain wracking her body. Another hard blow made Sunny's eyes snap shut by themselves and piss leaked from her bladder involuntarily.

"Somebody else here . . . go!" the goon holding Sunny barked at the other two. "Take care of it!"

"No!" Sunny rasped out, immediately thinking about Sean's helpless and innocent grandmother. "Big Mama . . ." Sunny gasped, her words barely audible, but it was too late. Both dreads were already heading toward the kitchen and toward Sean's grandmother.

"Shut up, bitch!" the one holding Sunny barked and with his last blow to her head her world finally went completely black.

BG and Sean sat across from one another at Ruth's Chris Steak House. The awkward silence between them caused both of them to squirm in their seats a bit. It had been awhile since BG and Sean had had any time alone and there were several long bouts of painful silence that had made BG uncomfortable. She had been killing herself trying not to think about Sean in a sexual or romantic way, but whenever she laid eyes on him it was extremely difficult.

"That profit is almost triple what we were making." BG cut the silence with business talk as she sliced her food properly using her knife and fork. "I told you that deal was going to be the sweetest thing for us," BG said with forced excitement in her voice. She was trying to make their time light, but it wasn't easy. Sean nodded like he wasn't really interested in talking about it, but BG wasn't ready to give up just yet.

"So did how did God react when you told him we found a new connect?" BG asked, taking in a forkful of asparagus. Sean reared back in his chair and shot her a look.

"Let me handle God and his reaction. Keep your mind on the new business and the distribution. Period," Sean snapped curtly. BG dropped her fork on her plate loudly and glared at him evilly. A few patrons in the restaurant looked over at her after hearing the fork clink loudly on her plate.

"Look, you been acting real different since your *girl* been back," BG gritted leaning into the table using a harsh whisper and doing air quotes with her fingers when she said the word "girl." "Don't tell me to keep my mind on the business because God's reaction is my business too. I can turn around and tell you to keep your mind on the business and not on the drug addict, but I don't." BG could feel the blood rushing to her face and her heart pounding so wildly it moved the silk material of her shirt.

Sean looked at her strangely, his jaw rocking feverishly. "Nah . . . God is my business and only my business. And you sound jealous," he snapped cruelly. Sean wasn't stupid; he knew how BG felt about him and sometimes he toyed with her. BG laughed like he'd told a real funny joke.

"Me, jealous of a fucking broke-ass, run down, sucking dick for money, heroin addict? I don't think so. You got me fucked up. Yeah, we fucked and your dick was decent, but it's all business with me and you. It was purely physical. You needed to get off that night just as much as I did . . . *King*," BG retorted, fighting real hard not to jump up and slap Sean. BG was jealous of Sunny because BG felt she had much more to offer Sean than Sunny did. BG had become very sensitive when it came to the topic and tonight was no different.

"You be talkin' real breezy. Don't mention her and I won't have to say shit like that to you. Don't worry about the heroin addict. It's business with us . . . simple and plain," Sean gritted with a stiff jaw.

"Matter of fact," he grumbled as he dug into his pocket and took out four crisp one hundred dollar bills and threw them on the table.

"I'll see you tomorrow for the shipment," he said standing up. "No need for dinners and small talk and shit. Let's just keep shit strictly business between us."

BG was looking at him like he was crazy. She couldn't believe he was walking out on her.

"From now on all business," he spat before he stormed out of the restaurant.

BG sat back in her chair and stared at Sean's half-eaten steak and the empty seat in front of her. This was the second time he'd left her hanging by herself over something that had to do with Sunny. There wouldn't be a third time. BG's insides were boiling and her mind turned with ways to get Sean back for this one. Since Sunny had come back into Sean's life things were slowly but surely changing . . . and not necessarily for the better.

Sean drove in silence after his failed dinner with BG. He felt bad about what he'd done at the restaurant, but he felt he had to let BG know that he was still in charge and not her. Sean let the silence in his car and the serenity of the drive ease his mind. It was one of the rare times he had driven himself around without his crew and he was cherishing the mind-clearing time. Sean was thinking . . . thinking long and hard. Sunny had come back into his life struggling with getting clean, he had cut off all interaction with God without facing God like a man, and, now he was beefing with BG. Sean had the weight of the world on his shoulders and was feeling overwhelmed to say the least. He knew the one person who would make him feel better though. Sean made U-turn and headed toward his grandmother's house.

"Big Mama, I really need a hug from you right now," Sean mumbled as he dialed his grandmother's phone number. Sean pursed his lips and crumpled his eyebrows when he didn't get an answer.

"Sunny, why you ain't answering the phone if Big Mama can't get it?" Sean grumbled out loud. He disconnected the line and called again. Still no answer. The first thing that Sean thought was Sunny had probably relapsed again and gone out to get high and left his grandmother alone. That thought alone made him bite down into his jaw and grip the steering wheel so hard the veins in his hand popped up under his skin.

Sean stepped down on the gas and sped his Range Rover through the streets. A cold chill came over his body because it wasn't like his grandmother and Sunny to ignore his calls.

Sean finally pulled up to his grandmother's house and nothing looked immediately different from the outside. He pulled into the driveway, threw his Range in park and hopped out. As Sean climbed the front porch steps he immediately noticed the front door to the house was slightly ajar.

"What the fuck? No way Big Mama gonna have her door open and it's this cold outside," Sean whispered, grabbing his gun from his waistband. He pushed the door in and slowly stepped inside. "Big Mama . . ." Sean started to call out, but his words were clipped short by what was in front of him.

"Nah! Nah! Big Mama!!" Sean hollered as he looked up at his grandmother's naked, gutted body hanging from the large, overlook center banister. Her intestines were dangling from the center of her body and her tongue protruded grotesquely from her mouth. But, her eyes being open is what had hurt Sean the most. "Big Mama!" he screamed again. The smell of rotting meat and death choked Sean and threatened to make him throw up. He was immediately thrust back to his childhood when he'd found his mother nearly decapitated. Even the sharp metallic scent of his grandmother's blood reminded him of that day.

"Agggh!" Sean screamed, falling to his knees; his gun skittering across the floor. It wasn't until he hit the floor that he noticed Sunny's battered body lying behind the couch.

"Sunny! Oh God! Not you too!" Sean rushed over to Sunny's side; his insides were boiling. He lifted her swollen and bruised head into his hands. "Sunny! Sunny! Not you too!" Sean whispered holding her head carefully.

"Sssss," Sunny made a low hissing sound, blood and spit bubbling from her battered mouth. Sean lowered his ear to listen for more breath sounds. Sunny made the hissing sound again, this time louder.

"Sunny?" Sean shouted, realizing that she was still alive. He couldn't even stand to look at the mess that used to be Sunny's beautiful face. Both of her eyes were completely swollen shut. She had at least six huge knots on her head and the bridge of her nose was caved in. Blood leaked from her nostrils, mouth and ears and she had purple rings around her neck. Her chin was gashed open and her cheek had been slashed down to the white meat.

"Sunny, who did this to you? Hold on! Hold on!" Sean cried out as he tried to get his phone from his pocket. He went to put her head down so he could call 911. Sunny squeezed his arm and made more hissing noises.

"What? What do you want to tell me?" Sean asked her, putting his head close to hers. Sunny mumbled something but he couldn't make it out. "What? Who?" Sean urged her.

"Dr . . . ea . . . ds" Sunny managed through her severely swollen lips.

"Dread? Dreads came in and did this to you and Big Mama?" Sean asked for clarification. Sunny moved her head slightly and after that she was immediately unconscious again.

Sean's chest heaved up and down. "Arrrggggh!" He belted out a loud frustrated growl, which signaled that he was waging war against the dreads that he thought were responsible for the tragedy in front of him.

Sean cut his grandmother down before the police, ambulance and coroner arrived at the house. He lay her down and tried to make her look as presentable as possible by placing a blanket over her naked and severely disfigured body. Sean was covered in Sunny and his grandmother's blood by the time the police came flooding into the house with their guns drawn. At first they took him as suspect, until they realized he'd been the one that found Sunny and his grandmother in that condition.

It didn't take long before the entire block was crawling with emergency vehicles.

Sean's crew was waiting outside as the ambulance brought Sunny out on the stretcher with Sean right behind them.

"Yo, son . . . what the fuck is going on?" Beans rushed over to Sean. "I figured when BG told me you wasn't with her that you was here. But when we couldn't get you on the phone we all came. What's up?" Beans rambled.

"War, nigga. We at war," Sean said cryptically as he watched the EMTs load Sunny into the ambulance. Sean waited for the black bag that carried his grandmother's body to be carried to the coroner's van, then he calmly climbed into his Range Rover and headed to his office. Beans had already rallied up Sean's crew for the war they were about to engage in with the dreads.

Chapter Fourteen

"Four of them m'fuckas is dead tonight. All them m'fuckin' clubs being shut down as we speak. Niggas ain't leaving nobody breathing," Beans reported to Sean as they stood together in the hospital waiting room. "We shuttin' down all dreads in this m'fuckin' city and that's a promise, bruh," Beans assured with sincerity. Sean nodded and gave Beans a pound and a hug. When he turned around to head back to Sunny's room he ran into BG, who had just arrived at the hospital. Sean and BG both paused for a minute, unsure of what to say to one another next.

"I'm really sorry about what happened," BG started off sincerely. Sean softened his facial expression letting their differences fade away for the moment.

"Thanks," he said flatly. "I gotta go back in and see about her. It's real touch and go right now, but I appreciate you showing your support though," he said with halfhearted sincerity. BG shook her head up and down signaling that she understood. She stepped aside and as Sean passed her she grabbed his arm.

"I know shit has been sketchy between us . . . but I'm always here for you. Outside of the business, I do care about you, Sean," BG told him, love and admiration glinting in her eyes. Sean didn't change his facial expression and he didn't have time to deal with BG's emotions right now.

"Appreciate it," Sean replied coolly, then he walked away toward Sunny's intensive care unit room. Once again BG was left alone with her feelings. No matter what she did, BG could not take that number one spot in Sean's heart. It was clear that Sunny had that spot now and seemingly forever.

Sean buried his grandmother in a small, private, dignified service with tons of security around. He'd been able to take his mind off of losing her sitting vigil at the hospital through Sunny's recovery. It was almost two months before Sunny was finally able to come home from the hospital. The physical therapy had taken longer than anything else with her recovery process. Sean had been by her side the entire time. He'd even brought in his twenty-second birthday and the New Year at Sunny's bedside. Sean and Sunny had toasted and promised that 2004 was going to be a better year for the both of them.

"This is it," Sean said cheerfully as he pushed open the door to his waterfront penthouse condo. Sunny smiled brightly and stepped inside with a look of awe on her face.

"This is it? Please . . . this is crazy! Sean, you have moved up in the world, boy!" Sunny gushed in amazement. "I can't believe how many windows you have," she exclaimed rushing over to the huge bank of windows that extended the whole length of the place. "And this view is breathtaking." Sunny stood in front of the window staring out in awe. She couldn't believe her friend Sean had come so far. When Sunny was strung out on heroin, she had heard about Sean making it big in the streets, but she could've never imagined that he was really living like a king.

"Now it's ours . . . not just mine," Sean said moving close to her. Without warning Sunny spun around and threw her arms around his neck, just like she used to when they were kids. A bit taken aback, Sean took a few steps back. "Whoa, whoa, what's this for?" he asked chuckling, but hesitantly returning Sunny's embrace.

"For years of being the best friend a girl can have," Sunny said, her voice going low.

"Don't start no sentimental shit," Sean griped playfully.

"Shut up," Sunny mumbled into the skin of his neck. "Let me have a moment."

Sean and Sunny held on to each other for a few minutes, both realizing how much they'd missed one another. Then Sunny moved her face in front of his in an unexpected show of affection. They locked eyes for a long minute and without even saying a word, they both moved closer and began kissing. Sunny melted into Sean's embrace and he held on to her like he never wanted to let her go. The heat between them was enough to start a forest fire as their hands moved like snakes, curling over every inch of each other's body.

"What are we doing?" Sunny whispered through labored breaths as Sean trailed his tongue down her neck.

"What we've been wanting to do all of our lives," he panted, undoing the buttons on her shirt. Sean pulled Sunny's shirt down over her shoulders and touched the raised scars on her collarbone. Sunny flinched, lowering her eyes, embarrassed at her marked body.

"I love every one of them. Each one shows how strong you are and why I admire you so much. Don't be afraid to show them," he said softly, kissing her war marks. Sunny closed her eyes as Sean lifted her off her feet and carried her toward his bedroom.

"You haven't even given me a tour yet," she giggled playfully.

"You gon' get a tour all right," he joked back.

Once inside his bedroom, Sean placed Sunny in the center of his California king-sized bed. Her healthy skin and striking green eyes glowed against his dark gray silk comforter. Sean took off his pants and slowly climbed onto the bed. Sunny removed her pants and as Sean took in her beauty his manhood rose to the occasion.

"You are still the sexiest m'fucka I know," Sean wolfed, crushing his mouth over hers again. They kissed like two teenaged kids in heat, darting their tongues in and out of each other's mouths. Sean let his hands roam down to Sunny's hot box, where he used his fingers to gently massage her swelling clitoris.

"Ah," Sunny let out a breath, letting her legs fall apart.

"That hurts?" Sean asked, quickly moving his hands.

"No. Don't stop," she whispered, guiding his hands back to the right spot. Sean smiled up at her.

"Yeah, you like that," he panted, biting down on his bottom lip eagerly. Then he moved up onto his knees so he could get better leverage. He started at Sunny's mouth, moved to her neck, licked down her chest, making sure he gently sucked her nipples before he finally trailed his tongue past her navel to her throbbing clit.

"Oh, God!" Sunny called out as Sean sucked lightly on her little man in the boat. She could feel herself creaming from the inside out.

"I want to feel you," she told him, trying to move his head. Sean jerked away from her grasp and continued to eat her cake. He took his long, strong tongue and darted in and out of her hole. Sunny couldn't take that and her thighs started trembling. She began thrusting her hips toward Sean's tongue.

"Yeah, yeah," he growled, loving that he had her so hot.

"Please . . . give it to me," Sunny whined. It had been so long since she'd been touched with such gentleness and caring. So long since she'd had sex because she wanted to and not because she was being forced to do it.

"You ready?" Sean asked. Sunny had her eyes closed, but she moved her head up and down in the affirmative. Sean raised up and slowly parted her legs with his knees to make room. Kneeling in front of Sunny, Sean slowly entered her as he balanced his weight on one arm.

"Ahhh," Sunny sighed as she felt him fill her up.

"You all right?" Sean asked her, taking his time.

"Fuck me please," Sunny whined as she wrapped her legs around his waist and used the strength in her thighs to pull him farther into her. Sean took her overt aggression as a sign. He started picking up the pace and the tighter her walls closed down around his throbbing pole, the harder he thrust.

"Yes! Yes!" Sunny shouted, grabbing handfuls of the skin on Sean's back.

"Ah," he panted, her nails digging into him hurt so good.

"Let me ride it," Sunny whispered. Sean quickly complied, but he never took himself out of her. Instead, he grabbed her tightly and flipped onto his back. Sunny giggled playfully as she looked down into the handsome face of the man she was always meant to be with. With love in their eyes, they stared at one another as Sunny moved up and down slowly on Sean's rock-hard love stick. Sunny grinded her waist, then went up and down and grinded her waist again. Sean's eyes rolled in ecstasy as he felt himself ready to bust. Before he could nut, Sunny began bucking wildly.

"I'm coming!" she called out.

"Yeah . . . give me that nut," Sean growled. Within seconds he was shooting his load too. Sunny fell down on top of him, both of them breathing like they'd just run a race.

Sean began stroking her hair as she played with the hairs on his chest.

"I love you, Sean," Sunny said softly.

"And you already know what it is, Sun," Sean replied. Ever since his mother died, Sean had been unable to say the words "I love you" to anyone, but he knew at that moment that he'd always loved Sunny.

"Let's go, sleepyhead," Sean said, pushing Sunny's shoulder playfully.

"Mmmm," she groaned, putting the pillow next to her over her head.

"Nah . . . we got a lot to do, so c'mon. I took the whole day . . . told those niggas don't call me or come by, all for you. We going shopping and spending the day out," Sean announced, pulling the pillow off of Sunny's face. She was smiling from ear to ear and when the sunlight streaming in from the big windows danced across her face and Sean immediately saw the first flashes of his old friend shining on her face.

"You're still a major pain in the ass. You know that?" Sunny grumbled jokingly as she stood up and stretched. Sean couldn't resist her beautiful legs and round hips, so he rushed over, scooped her up off her feet and whirled her around.

"Agh! Sean, put me down, silly!" Sunny laughed so hard her face went flush.

"Yup, I'ma put you down . . . right on this dick," Sean joked, putting his mouth over hers and kissing her deeply. He didn't even care about her stale morning breath. Before either of them knew it, they were back on the bed in another heated lovemaking session.

Sweaty and out of breath, Sunny looked over at Sean and out of nowhere she slapped him as hard as she could on the shoulder.

"Tag, nigga, you're it!" she yelled, then she jumped up and raced to the bathroom. "I get the shower first, slowpoke!"

Sean wasn't fast enough to beat her to the bathroom because he was laughing so hard. Sunny slammed the bathroom door and turned on the water. Sean flopped back on his bed and stared up at the ceiling. His Sunny was finally back and he was loving every minute of it.

Sean and Sunny laughed and talked about the past all the way to the high-end mall Sean finally pulled into. When Sunny saw the store names—Gucci, Cartier, Louis Vuitton and Saks Fifth Avenue—she looked over at Sean with an expression that read confusion and surprise.

"What? You thought I was taking you shopping at that bird-ass Macy's?" Sean said with one eyebrow raised. "Don't insult me. I ain't shop at Macy's and them little stores in years."

"I hear that," Sunny said, turning her head so she could continue scoping out the stores.

Once they parked Sean grabbed Sunny's hand and led her around to all of the stores. Their first stop was his favorite . . . Gucci. There was something about the Italian designer that Sean found timeless and classy.

"Pick out shoes, sneakers, clothes, bags . . . whatever you want," Sean instructed. At first, Sunny was apprehensive. She was still a little shell-shocked from an experience with Faheem when he'd tried to use a stolen credit card at a high-end store and he and Sunny had to run for their lives as the store clerk tried to secretly call the police.

"What? You mean to tell me that nigga ain't never buy you nothing nice?" Sean asked. Sunny rolled her eyes and let out a long sigh.

"Can we not talk about him," she snapped.

"A'ight. My bad. But, go shopping and stop playing. This is every girl's dream 'n' shit," Sean told her.

It was a slow start, but when Sunny finally got her bearings in the store she damn near burned it down running around. The usually snobby personal shoppers in the store didn't show one bit of cold shoulder; they all knew Sean very well. They also knew he bought thousands in merchandise every visit and paid in cash, which meant lovely commissions for them.

"Your total is $11,210.90," the smiling store clerk told Sean. Then she shot a quick glance over at Sunny.

"She lucky right?" Sean said, winking at the girl behind the counter.

"Very," the girl answered quickly. Sunny raised her brow at the girl and looked at Sean.

"No, she lucky I don't poke her damn eyes out for looking at you," Sunny whispered, but loud enough for the girl to hear. Sean laughed out loud.

"Take your bags and let's go to the next store," he told Sunny. "I ain't tryin'a bail you out of jail for no girl fight."

Sean and Sunny burned through every high-end store in the mall. They even went into La Perla and spent $4,000 on lingerie for her to model for him. They were both exhausted by the time they made it back to the car, but that didn't stop Sunny from leaning over from the front passenger seat and reaching down freeing Sean's jewel from his pants.

"Whatchu doin'?" Sean asked her.

"I'm thanking you," Sunny said, getting ready to lower her head into his lap.

Sean put his hand under her chin, halting her and pushing her head up. Sunny raised her head and looked at him strangely.

"What?" she asked incredulously. "You don't like head?"

"You don't have to thank me like that. Gimme head because you can't resist my shit . . . not because I bought you some clothes. You don't live like that no more," Sean told her in the softest tone he could muster. The tears burst from Sunny's eyes like a faucet that was just turned on.

"Don't cry," Sean comforted. "This new life is going to take some getting used to, but it's gonna be worth it." Sunny just turned her head, too embarrassed to look at him. She wondered if she'd ever get used to this new life or if she was even worth living it.

Chapter Fifteen

Summer 2006

Locked in the bathroom, Sunny sat on the toilet seat
with her legs nervously shaking as she gnawed on her
bottom lip. She looked over at the little white stick again,
but the results still hadn't showed up.

"C'mon . . . mmm . . . c'mon," Sunny groaned, lowering
her head into her hands. She looked at her watch. It had
been two minutes. Sunny held her breath and picked up
the pregnancy test. She squinted down at it. Then she dug
the box out of the garbage and held the test against the
back of the box.

"Two lines pregnant . . . one line not pregnant," she
whispered. Sunny jumped up from the toilet seat and
covered her mouth with her hand.

"Oh my God," she gasped, her heart speeding up in her
chest. Sunny started pacing around the bathroom, biting
her bottom lip.

"What if he gets mad? What if he's not happy about
this? What if he acts stupid? Where will I go?" Sunny
asked herself a million questions.

A loud knock on the door made her almost jump out of
her shoes.

"Sunny? You a'ight?" Sean called from the other side
of the door. Sunny rushed over to the garbage can and
stuffed a bunch of tissues on top of the pregnancy test
box.

"Um . . . yeah . . . um . . . I'm . . . I'm coming," Sunny stuttered.

"Yo, whatchu doin' in there?" Sean asked. Sunny could hear the concern in his voice. He was always worried about her relapsing so if she was behind a closed door too long he immediately came knocking.

"I'm using the bathroom, Sean. I'm coming," she said a little annoyed that he was always jumping to conclusions. Sunny knew she had to tell him what was going on . . . but how?

She slowly opened the door, a look of panic and worry creasing her face. Sean hadn't moved either. "What's up?" he asked her as she breezed passed him.

Sunny flopped down on their brand new leather sectional and lowered her head. Sean's heart immediately started thumping. He was hoping Sunny didn't tell him she'd gotten high.

"I might as well just come right out and tell you the truth," Sunny said, avoiding eye contact with him.

Sean swiped his hands over his face and started shaking his head. He was expecting the worst. He squared his jaw and lowered his eyes at her.

"Matter of fact . . . you can just see for yourself," Sunny said, standing up and walking over to him slowly. Sean was squinting at her evilly, waiting for her to show him her arms with the track marks.

"Here," Sunny said, extending her arm forward. Sean was scowling until he looked down and saw the little white stick in her hand. His eyebrows went into arches on his face and he tilted his head to the side.

"What? What is . . . I mean . . . you?" Sean stumbled over his words.

"I know you might not be ready. I know it's fast and everything, but I swear to you that I didn't mean for it to happen. I will do whatever you want me to do about it . . ."

Sunny started rambling nervously, rubbing her hands over her arms.

"What the fuck is you talkin' about, Sunny? You having my seed? You carrying my baby!" Sean said excitedly, grabbing her into his arms. "Yo! You just made me the happiest m'fucker living! My seed?" Sean shouted like he'd just hit the lottery. Sunny was relieved and her heart rate finally started to slow down.

"You . . . you a'ight? You feeling sick? I mean . . . you need something. We need to go shopping for all healthy foods. No more eating bullshit from this day forward. You got a doctor in mind? I mean you have to make sure you a'ight right?" Sean started rambling himself. Sunny laughed at him.

"Um . . . it's real early so just calm down," Sunny told him.

"Nah! I can't calm down. I'ma be a father!" Sean said, grabbing Sunny's face and kissing her deeply. "That's the greatest fuckin' gift I have ever received in my life, Sunny. Word up. I'll do anything for you, ma. Anything." Sean proclaimed. He didn't know then how prophetic his words would turn out to be.

"I heard BG is the one who convinced him to get a new connect out in Miami named Fat Reemo," Ty said, sitting across from God. God nodded at Ty as he took in the information. Although it had been almost two years since Sean had betrayed him, God wasn't over it. It had taken awhile, but God was finally able to send one of his beauties into Sean's camp to infiltrate and turn one of Sean's closest soldiers against him. Ty had fallen for the beautiful woman and God's irresistible proposition hook, line and sinker.

"I'm trying to make a way for myself . . . feel me? Even though niggas is saying Fat Reemo got that good shit, I heard you was the man to see up here in the mountains for better prices." Ty got right to the point.

"I want to speak more about Sean. Or excuse me . . . *King* Sean," God interjected. Ty let out a long sigh. He wasn't really comfortable being the snitch, but he was also tired of watching Sean rise higher and higher while the rest of the crew had to put in much more work to make money.

"A'ight . . . we can speak about him real quick, but then we need to get back to the point of all this," Ty said. "Me making my own come up out there."

"I want to know all about where Sean lives, where he distributes, where he parties . . . everything," God demanded. "No detail is too small. If Sean takes a shit I want to know about it."

"And what's in it for me?" Ty asked, growing annoyed with the old man sitting across from him.

"I let you live another day," God said calmly as he blew a ring of cigar smoke in the direction of Ty's face. Just then one of God's deadly beauties stepped closer to Ty and rested her gun on his shoulder.

Sunny was four months pregnant and she was finally able to see a small pouch growing under her belly button. She loved the glow that had settled on her cheeks and couldn't wait to get a little bigger so even strangers would notice that she was going to be a mother. Sunny had never been so excited about anything in her entire life and it showed. Sean had been waiting on her hand and foot and not letting her do anything for herself, sometimes to the point of annoyance. Sunny couldn't cook, wash clothes, or even take a shower without Sean right there making sure she was all right. She could tell he was also over the moon excited about their expected bundle of joy. With all of the tragedy that they'd both suffered, the baby was going to be a welcome miracle and blessing for them both.

"Let me help you." Sean rushed over to help Sunny climb up into his brand new, gleaming silver Range Rover.

"Would you stop. I'm barely showing." Sunny waved him off with a fake attitude. "I am pregnant, not handicapped." He laughed at her.

"You don't have to be showing for me to know my seed is growing in there. I'm going to bug the shit out of you until the end," Sean said, bending his head down and kissing her belly through her flowing sundress.

"I have to stop by the office and pick something up from BG and then I promise we will go get whatever you want to eat, plus I think it's time for some hot new maternity clothes for my hot woman," Sean told her. Sunny rolled her eyes. "Ugh, BG?" Sunny mumbled. She didn't like BG and Sunny knew BG didn't care for her either.

"Can't you stop later? You know my mood swings . . . I don't know if I want to see that chick," Sunny griped.

"Just for a minute. A quick business decision and then I'm all yours. I swear . . . ten minutes flat," he replied, leaning over and kissing her on the nose. Sunny smiled and then pouted like a baby. They both laughed.

Sean pulled up to the boxing gym where his office was located and left the car running.

"You wanna go inside with me or wait here real quick?" he asked Sunny. "It's up to you." Sunny thought about it for a few seconds. She really hated the way BG always glared at her like she knew something about Sunny that she was keeping a secret.

"I can do without seeing your crispy face girlfriend, so I'll wait here," Sunny said, twisting her lips.

"Yo, be nice, grumpy," Sean joked. Sunny watched him go inside, but she had no desire to see BG. Sunny had tried several times to convince Sean to find a new business partner. There was just something about BG that didn't rub Sunny the right way. Sunny wasn't sure if it was the fact that BG was gorgeous and didn't have a past drug problem, in which case, she had one up on Sunny, or if it was the fact that Sunny could sense that there was some sexual tension between BG and Sean. Whatever the reason, Sunny had already made up her mind that she was never going to like BG.

After a few minutes of waiting, Sunny looked at her watch and sighed.

"Mmmm, hmmm, I know his few minutes," she mumbled, reaching down to turn up the music. Sunny turned the music up so loud, she didn't hear the sound of the motorcycle approaching. Sunny had her eyes closed singing along with the music when suddenly . . . Clang! Clang! Clang! Clang! The sound of rapid fire gunshots rang out and the Range Rover shook like a earthquake had hit.

"Ahhh!" Sunny screamed, instinctively throwing herself down in the seat as bullets slammed into the metal doors of the car. Glass from the windshield rained down on Sunny's head as she squeezed herself between the dashboard and the seat.

More shots rang out as Sean and his crew raced outside and returned fire with the masked gunman on the motorcycle. It was too late; the motorcycle disappeared down the street.

"Sunny!" Sean screamed, yanking the car door open. "Sunny!"

Sunny was shaking fiercely and the tops of her hands were bleeding from the window glass that had shattered on her a few minutes earlier.

"Sunny? Baby? You all right?" Sean huffed, helping her unfold her body up off the floor. Sunny was shaking her head no. She was sobbing uncontrollably because she had felt the blow she'd taken to the abdomen as she'd thrown herself down to prevent herself from getting shot.

"No!" Sunny cried over and over again. Then she lowered her head and looked down because she had already felt the warm blood leaking down her legs.

"C'mon! We have to get her to the hospital!" Sean barked at Beans. Beans rushed down the block and got his Benz. He reversed back to Sean's Range Rover like a madman.

Sunny just kept shaking her head and saying no. Sean eased her into the back seat of Beans's car, but there was so much blood, they all knew what had happened.

It was two hours before the doctors came back to the waiting room to get Sean. The black female obstetrician walked over to Sean with a glum look on her face.

"Hi, I'm Dr. Whitaker," she spoke softly. "Are you the father?"

Sean stood up and nodded. His stomach churned and he swallowed hard waiting for her to make it official.

"It was way too early to save the fetus. Your wife took a very hard blow to the abdomen and caused a placental abruption. A fetus can't survive once that happens, even if the baby was fully developed without the placenta it would've suffocated in utero anyway," the doctor lamented. "I'm really sorry for your loss. You can go see your wife now and please let us know if we can help you in any way."

Sean bit down into his jaw to fight back the tears that were filling up behind his eyes. He felt sharp pains stabbing him in the heart.

"I'ma let you have a moment alone," Beans told Sean, giving him a brotherly hug and pound. "I'm real fuckin' sorry, bruh."

Sean walked slowly down the hospital hallway as if he were being led to the gas chamber. He actually felt like something inside of him had died that day. He swiped his hands over his face before he entered Sunny's hospital room. Once he felt strong enough, he walked in.

Sunny was sitting up in the bed, holding the small, wrapped bundle with only a tiny face exposed. She was rocking back and forth, sobbing. Sean walked over slowly and sat next to her on the bed. She looked at Sean pitifully through swollen and red-rimmed eyes.

"This is your son. I named him King . . . his middle name is Sean," Sunny said through tears. "King Sean," Sunny broke down. Sean looked down into the tiny face of his dead baby son. Although the baby wasn't fully developed, Sean could tell the baby was going to look like a good mixture of him and Sunny.

"Why? Why did they take my son away from me!" Sunny cried out. "Everything I love is gone. Why does God keep punishing me?!" she asked choking on her words. Sunny wasn't speaking about Sean's connect God, but she had no idea how on point her words were when she said them. God, Sean's scorned connect, was hell bent on punishing her to get back at Sean.

Chapter Sixteen

Sunny was released from the hospital after the miscarriage and given a prescription for pain medication. Sean was in too much of a grief-filled haze with everything that had happened to make sure that the doctors didn't give Sunny any pain meds that contained opiates. Sean knew full well that if Sunny had gotten one taste of anything with opiates in it, her yearning for heroin would be awoken again like a hibernating beast. The death of his son had caused Sean to drop the ball this time.

Once Sunny was settled in at home she wanted to be left alone for the most part. She didn't speak much and she cried more than anything during the weeks that followed the loss of her baby.

Sean assigned one of his young dope boys Freddie to sit security at his house while Sean worked to find out who had put the hit out on his life, but had gotten his unborn son instead.

Sunny began taking the pain meds two at a time in an attempt to try and wash away the physical and emotional pain she felt. Sean didn't even notice that Sunny had stopped eating, barely went out and had completely stopped caring for her hair, nails, and skin. Sunny was slipping and no one noticed.

Within a month after the miscarriage, Sunny was fully addicted to the pills and yearning for something stronger. The urges had become so strong, Sunny contemplated leaving to go find drugs, but she knew that would just cause Sean's little goon to call him and send a search party out looking for her. Sunny couldn't chance it. She had to be smart about things this time.

One afternoon, Sunny was home alone with Freddie sitting guard in her living room. She reached over onto her nightstand and picked up the little tan bottle that held her pain meds.

"Shit! Fuck!" she cursed as she turned over the empty medicine bottle and nothing came out into her hand. Sunny was out of pain pills and feeling terrible. Sunny need something for the pain and she needed it right away. There was no way she could just leave to go out on the street to find pills or better yet drugs for herself. Aside from Sean going crazy looking for her, Sunny didn't even know where to look in the new, posh neighborhood Sean had her living in anyway.

"Shit!" she huffed, thinking and pacing. She could feel the pain and sickness already starting to creep up on her. Sunny knew how bad sickness could get from any opiate addiction and she wasn't trying to deal with that pain, on top of the heartbreak pain.

As usual Sean wasn't home when Sunny needed him. In Sunny's assessment, since the miscarriage, Sean had become obsessed with the street life and he didn't give a damn about her and her feelings anymore. Sunny had started to convince herself that Sean probably blamed her for what had happened to their baby and that he was purposely punishing her by staying out. Sunny never took into account that Sean might've been working hard to stash for their future or that he might've been trying to find out who had shot at her. Sunny was making Sean out to be her enemy in her twisted mind. It was her usual; whenever she started using, Sunny became extremely paranoid, and this time was no different.

Sunny closed her eyes and started thinking like the old, dopefiend Sunny would think. *How can I get something? Who can I game? Even if I have to go back to my old ways behind his back . . .* Sunny's mind raced with all sorts of sinister thoughts. Nothing was coming to mind right away and she was feeling trapped in the house.

"Swoosh on that ass, nigga! Y'all can't fuck with LeBron!" Freddie yelled out at the basketball video game he was playing in the other room. It was like a sign from heaven. Sunny stopped pacing and turned toward the door, a flash of excitement filling her chest. It quickly dawned on her that Freddie was in her living room doing what he did best: playing video games. Like a light bulb had gone off in her head, suddenly Sunny's eyebrows went up and her bottom lip folded in. She had been struck with an idea . . . a way to satisfy her thirst to get high.

"This little nigga won't be no match for me," Sunny mumbled under her breath as she straightened out her hair and went about making herself as sexy as she could, given the fact that she felt sick. Sunny was going to have to work her magic on Freddie, that was the only way she would be able to get what she needed. Sunny was confident that the young boy would have no wins once she started throwing down her manipulation game. Sunny checked herself one last time in the mirror. She wasn't 100 percent, but she thought she looked good enough to accomplish what she needed, especially from a young, horny boy. She had seen how all of Sean's crew members looked at her whenever she was around them. Sunny knew they all lusted after her.

"What's up, Freddie?" Sunny said sexily as she sauntered into the living room in just a wife beater and a pair of thin lace panties. "You good?" she asked, licking her lips seductively at the young boy.

Sunny's erect nipples were clearly visible through the thin material of the shirt and more of her ample ass was exposed than covered by her sexy panties. Freddie jumped up from the couch and looked at her with wide eyes. He thought he must've been seeing things wrong because there could be no way his boss's lady was standing in front of him, practically naked, smiling and licking her lips at him invitingly. Freddie bit his bottom lip just to make sure he wasn't dreaming. He had always had a major crush on Sunny.

"Oh ... um ... Ms. Sunny, you need something?" Freddie stammered, his heart going crazy in his chest and his cheeks turning beet red. He gripped the game controller so tight the buttons made an imprint in the center of his hand, but he could not stop staring at her.

"Relax." Sunny smiled at him. "You seem nervous. All I came to ask you for is one huge favor . . . between me and you," Sunny said, batting her long lashes at him. If it was one thing Sunny knew how to do, it was get what she wanted from a man. She had learned that very early in life.

"Sure," Freddie blurted out. "You need me to go to the store or something? Or I can call King and tell him you need something."

"Naw, none of that. Let me tell you in your ear what I need," Sunny said in a deep throaty sex kitten voice. When Freddie moved closer to her, Sunny breathed into his ear and grabbed a handful of his crotch. Freddie jumped and tried to push her hand away. He was holding his breath, but he couldn't stop his nature from rising as Sunny whispered her request into his ear.

"Don't be scared. I don't bite unless you want me to," Sunny cooed in a deep throaty voice that was driving the young boy wild.

"Um . . . nah. I . . . I . . . shouldn't. If King Sean finds out I did something like that he would kill me," Freddie said right away, his voice quivering just thinking about his boss. Sunny whispered something else in his ear, but this time she fell to her knees in front of the bulge in his pants and began taking his zipper down.

"You still want to tell me no?" she said, looking up into the young boy's eager face. Freddie's legs were shaking and he didn't want her to stop. He would've done anything for her at that point.

"O . . . okay, I can do what you asked. And . . . and . . . I won't tell King Sean if you don't," Freddie gasped and as Sunny closed her mouth down around his flesh, sweat danced down the sides of his face and total ecstasy engulfed his body.

When Sunny was sure she had him under her control, she let him go. Within minutes Freddie was gone and back with what Sunny had asked him for. She grabbed the small bundle of heroin from his hand and raced into the bathroom without saying a word to him. Once she was alone, Sunny unwrapped the bundle and her mouth began to water. Her hands and legs shook with anticipation of what was to come. She stared at the little ball of drugs for at least ten minutes. All sorts of thoughts ran through her mind, but not once did she contemplate throwing the drugs into the toilet and flushing them.

Sunny wanted so badly to shoot the drugs directly into her veins, but she figured she'd have to snort it, because Sean might notice if track marks showed up on her arms. Sunny crushed the drugs to prepare it for snorting, but it was taking long and her conscience was starting to toy with her.

Think about Sean. Think about how upset he will be if he finds out what you're doing. Think, Sunny. Think. He's the only person that loves you. You can't betray him. Her mind was going crazy. *Fuck that! You're a grown woman.* Her thoughts suddenly turned on her.

Sunny leaned down to sniff the first line and immediately felt another horrible flash of guilt fill her mind. This time she did think of Sean and how good he'd been to her since she had been clean. Sunny could see his smiling face all of the mornings they had awoken in bed together. She could hear his laughter now, since they had been the happiest they'd been in years together. Sunny thought of how good her life was right now and how devastated Sean would be if he found out she was doing this. Sunny stood up abruptly and looked at herself in the mirror that hung over the his-and-hers marble-top sink. Her heart was telling her to flush the heroin down the toilet, but her mind and body was telling her she needed the drugs.

"Nobody loves you. You don't even love yourself. You ain't even worthy of being loved so if somebody says they love you they don't mean it," Sunny said out loud, repeating words her mother had said to her over and over as a child. Sunny believed that she was unlovable and although she wanted to believe that Sean loved her, she felt like she didn't deserve to be loved.

With those self-defeating thoughts trampling through her brain, Sunny hurriedly leaned back down and snorted the first and second lines of heroin. The drugs stung the inside of her nostrils and her head jerked back involuntarily. As the heroin took hold, Sunny collapsed onto the floor, pulling her entire vanity tray down with a loud crash.

"Ms. Sunny! Ms. Sunny, you a'ight?" Freddie called from the other side of the door in a panic, jiggling the doorknob to try and get in. When he finally forcefully busted into the bathroom, he found Sunny lying on the floor with her head moving slowly from side to side. Her eyes were glazed over and she wore a lazy grin on her lips.

"Thank you," Sunny slurred, reaching out for his hand. Freddie gave her his hand, not fully understanding what he'd done.

Sunny was humming and mumbling. She felt like she was flying over the entire world like an eagle. Sunny had finally recaptured that first-high feeling that she had experienced the very first time she did heroin with Faheem. Sunny didn't realize she would spend the rest of her life chasing that same elusive high and never get it back again. She also didn't realize how much damage the chase would cause.

That night when Sean came home, he was exhausted; so when he found Sunny knocked out in their bed, he didn't bother to wake her. Sean slid close to her in the bed and hugged her from behind. Sunny opened her eyes and stared into the darkness as she listened to him fall off to sleep. Tears drained from the sides of Sunny's eyes and wet her pillow. She had betrayed Sean's trust in the worst way, but the addict inside of her wouldn't let her stop and she knew it. The old Sunny was back and probably worse than she ever was before.

Two weeks later, BG paced up and down as she waited for Sean to arrive at their new shipment spot. The information BG had for Sean was burning a hole in her brain. She couldn't keep her nerves at bay because she knew how sensitive Sean could be when it came to Sunny.

The shipment of premium heroin worth millions in street value that was laid out in front of BG didn't mean anything compared to what she needed to tell Sean about his woman.

"What up, BG? Sorry I'm late. I been pounding that pavement trying to get some info on that hit," Sean huffed as he rushed into the warehouse with Beans, Ak and Ty flanking him. BG turned to face him and her heart immediately dropped when she saw his gorgeous face. Sean always looked so good to her and the full beard he was rocking these days was sexy as hell.

"It's all good," BG said softly, cracking a weak smile. "Everything is here just like I promised," she said softly. Her heart was already galloping in her chest because what she had to do wasn't going to be easy.

"Damn, that nigga Reemo comes through every time," Sean said looking at the largest heroin shipment they had ever received. Sean and BG had had a good run in the streets with Reemo's product. They both had made a boatload of money and their names were at the top of the list out in the streets. Sean was starting to contemplate having his hands in two more big shipments, taking his stash, taking his woman and getting out of the game. He remembered Fox telling him that you always needed an end game when it came to the streets; Sean was seriously thinking about his end game. Sean wanted to surprise Sunny by moving her far away from all of the pain and suffering that their city held for her.

"You don't look all that excited," Sean said to BG, noticing the pained look on her face. She lowered her head and shook it from side to side.

"What's up with you?" he asked her, his face crumpled in confusion.

"King . . . I gotta tell you something and it ain't the easiest shit to say," BG replied, looking at him square in the eyes. She let out a long breath, willing herself to go forward with the information she was holding.

"A'ight . . . I'm a man. I can take it. What is it?" Sean came back.

"Maybe we should speak about this in private," BG said, nodding toward the rest of Sean's crew.

"Nah, whatever you can say to me you can say in front of them," Sean told her with annoyance in his voice. BG let out a long exasperated sigh.

"Yo, you ain't never been at a loss for words before, BG, don't start now," Sean said sternly. He was growing wary of the guessing game she was playing. "Is it about Reemo? The shipments? What?" Sean probed, his eyes trained on BG's face so hard she could feel heat from his gaze.

"I'm just going to come out straight no chaser. It's about your girl Sunny," BG said, followed by a disgusted sigh.

Sean immediately twisted his lips. "Here we go. Look, I know you don't like her but . . ." Sean started. BG threw her hand up and stopped him from speaking.

"This ain't got nothing to do with how I feel about her or how you *think* I feel about her. I don't have to make shit up about her because the proof is all over the streets," BG said, pulling out her cell phone. "You the only one that don't seem to know."

"Fuck is you talkin' about?" Beans growled at BG. He was real sensitive about people talking breezy to his boss. Ak and Ty mumbled their disapprovals too. They all shot eye daggers in BG's direction. Her new security guards stepped closer to her side.

"One of the little flunkies at the downtown trap been forwarding this shit all around town," BG said, extending her cell phone toward Sean. "Word on the street is your own boy Freddie sent it out first and now mad niggas got it," she said solemnly. "They laughing at you, King. As a friend, I thought you should know," BG followed up. A sick sense of "I told you so" satisfaction came over her like a comforting blanket.

Sean stared at the cell phone pictures through hooded eyes. He could feel the heat of anger rising into his chest and his nostrils began flaring. Beans and Ak stepped closer so they could see what had their boss at a loss for words.

"Yoooo!" Beans exclaimed taking a good long look at the picture. Ak just shook his head from left to right and lowered his eyes. Neither of them wanted to stare too long at the disturbing image of Sunny on her knees giving somebody a blow job while he held a dime packet of heroin over her head. Sean grabbed BG's phone and smashed it into the cement floor.

"Yo, whatchu doin'?" one of BG's security guards grumbled stepping forward.

"It's okay. He's upset and by all rights," BG said, calling off her guard. "I can get a new phone, that's nothing."

"I'm sure you're fuckin' happy to see that kind of shit since you always hated her," Sean growled at BG before he turned swiftly and stormed toward the door.

"This ain't got nothing to do with me not liking her! I'm trying to protect you! I'm always the one looking out for you, Sean! Remember that shit! None of these niggas out here care about you like I do!" BG screamed at his back. "You're the only one who can't see that Sunny is going to ruin you," BG whispered as she turned back toward the table and began bagging the heroin for distribution. "That bitch is your Achilles heel."

Sean busted into his condo door with the force of a tsunami. His little worker Freddie jumped up from the couch where he had been posted up while Sunny was locked in the bathroom.

"Ki . . . Ki . . . King," Freddie started with widened eyes. He never got to finish his sentence. Beans was on him within seconds with his hands clamped down around Freddie's skinny neck.

"You little nasty m'fucker! You wanna be out here fuckin' niggas wives . . . you little dirty dick bitch," Beans gritted, then he slammed his one of his fists into Freddie's face so hard everyone in the room heard the bone in the center of Freddie's nose crack. Freddie's nose began leaking like a faucet, but Beans didn't care, he hit the frail body boy again. This time Freddie's jaw cracked and his body folded. Freddie couldn't fight back, scream, kick or anything. He was in too much pain.

"You crossed the king, m'fucker! Huh! Huh!" Beans barked, his hands clamped tightly around Freddie's scrawny neck again. Sean stood there looking on, his chest pumping up and down unnaturally.

"Lift his ass up," Ak growled, cracking his knuckles. Beans loosened his grip on Freddie's neck, but right after, Beans drove his knee into Freddie's balls. Freddie was coughing and gagging uncontrollably as he tried to get his lungs to fill back up with air.

"Lift him up I said! Let me get a piece of this little bitch nigga," Ak growled again. Beans pulled Freddie's weakened body up off the couch and brought him to face Sean. Sean's eyes glinted with rage and his jaw rocked. Sean pulled his Glock from his pants and raised it.

"Please . . . please! No! It wasn't my idea. She begged me to do it. She begged me," Freddie gurgled and cried with his hands up in front of him. Freddie's word hit Sean like someone had landed an open-handed slap to his face. *She begged me to do it,* kept playing over and over in Sean's head. *Sunny begged him to fuck her for drugs.* The truth was too hard for Sean to accept.

"What, nigga? Whatchu say?" Sean growled bringing the butt of his gun down on Freddie's forehead.

"Aggh!" Freddie screamed as his skin split and instantly a wide gash opened up on his head. Beans let go of him and Freddie crumpled to the floor, but Sean wasn't finished with him. Sean brought his gun up and down on Freddie's head and face at least fifteen more times, until there was so much blood the boy's entire face was completely covered. Freddie could barely keep his head up and two of his teeth lay next to him on the floor. Sean was completely out of control now.

"Yo, King . . . you gon' kill this nigga," Ak said, trying to call Sean off. Sean looked up and saw that Sunny had closed and locked their bedroom door. He knew then that Sunny was fully aware that he knew what she'd done with Freddie.

"Take this m'fucker out of my house before I spill his brains all over my expensive furniture," Sean wolfed, out of breath from beating Freddie so badly.

"You gon' be a'ight here . . . you know . . . ?" Beans asked, nodding toward the bedroom where they all imagined that Sunny was probably cowering.

"I'm good. I'll catch up to y'all niggas later," Sean said as he tried in vain to straighten out his clothes and clean himself off. "I'll take care of her alone."

"A'ight. Holla if you need anything. I'll take care of this little dirty nigga right here," Beans said, lifting his foot and kicking Freddie in the stomach for extra emphasis. "Get this bitch nigga out of here," Beans demanded.

Sean's crew scraped Freddie up off the floor and dragged him from Sean's condo. Once they were all gone, Sean flopped down on his couch with his gun next to him. He needed a minute to collect his thoughts before he dealt with Sunny. He didn't even know what he would say to her at that point. Sean felt angry enough to kill her, but he also felt devastated inside. For the first time in his life since his mother's death, Sean felt a deep sense of grief, because he knew that whatever he had tried to build with Sunny was now dead.

Sean felt stupid for trusting her. He had offered Sunny everything. He had saved her from her abuser and given himself to her even after he knew half the city had already had her. Sean loved Sunny from a place deep within, but he was starting to believe that she never loved him and never would. The more he thought about her betrayal, the more his anger crept back up on him. Sean got up from the couch, stormed toward his bedroom door, leveled his gun at the doorknob and fired. The lock flew off and the door jumped open.

"Aghhh!" Sunny screamed, dropping her needle and ducking down on the side of their bed. "Please don't kill me, Sean . . . I'm . . . I'm . . . sorry," Sunny cried out as she balled her body up on the floor, using her hands to protect her head. Sean stood over her brooding with his gun in hand. He could've blown her brains out right there, but he couldn't bring himself to do it.

Sunny was sobbing uncontrollably and Sean was dying inside. He could literally feel his heart breaking apart in his chest.

"Why, Sunny? Why?" Sean asked her through his teeth. "You wanted to go back to being a ho for drugs? You never wanted what I had to offer you? I gave you everything, but you ain't want the good life," Sean said, his voice unsteady with pain evident behind his words. "I guess once a fiend-ass ho always a fiend-ass ho," Sean said cruelly. He wanted to hurt Sunny as much as she'd hurt him.

Sunny uncurled her body and although she was trembling like she was sitting on a block of ice, she looked at him with tears streaming from her eyes.

"Sean, I never meant to hurt you. I didn't ask to be like this . . . it's just the way I am now. Somebody like you will never understand," she cried. "I'm a drug addict, Sean. Once an addict always an addict. Once you start . . . you can't stop. You have to believe that I love you. I always have, but you can't save me. Nobody can save me from this shit. It calls out to me every morning and every night. Even if it goes away for a little while . . . it always comes right back. Once you use that first time you're gone forever. I'm gone forever," Sunny said through wracking sobs. "I'm gone forever."

"That's bullshit! You can stop if you want to, Sunny! You're fuckin' weak! You don't want to stop! You wanna be out here fuckin' other niggas and selling your pussy for drugs! You're fuckin' weak!" Sean boomed wanting so badly to choke Sunny until the lights went out in her eyes. He was fighting back his own tears now. Sunny let out a long whelp of sobs as Sean's words cut her like a knife.

"You wanna see how fuckin' weak you are? Huh? Huh?" Sean gritted. He bent down and picked up the needle full of heroin she had dropped.

"You're the only one who can't fuckin' stop," Sean said as he extended his own arm.

"No, Sean! No! Don't do it!" Sunny screamed trying to scramble up off the floor to stop him. "Don't do it!"

"I'ma prove it to you that these drugs ain't more fuckin' powerful than me or you!" Sean growled and in a flash, before Sunny could stop him, he plunged the needle into his vein and slammed down on the back until the drugs blasted into his arm. Blood squirted everywhere because Sean had hit the vein wrong. Sean's eyes popped open wide as the drugs and the pain hit him at the same time. He didn't feel the pain for long though.

"Sean! No!" Sunny belted out. She was too late. Sean's knees went weak and his body folded to the floor with a hard thud. His eyes were closed, but he could feel all of his problems seemingly fading away. His mother, Fox, and

Big Mama showed up in his head right then. They were all smiling and laughing and telling him they loved him. Sean suddenly saw himself lying on a bed covered in one hundred dollar bills and music was playing all around him. He felt damn good for the first time in a long time.

"Sean! Sean!" Sunny screamed, slapping his face and splashing water on him. Sean's eyes fluttered open and he realized he was back in his condo. That first high euphoria was gone just as fast as it had come.

"Sean, why did you do it? There's no going back now. There's no going back," Sunny cried hysterically, laying her head on his chest. She knew that Sean had just made the worst mistake of his entire life.

Chapter Seventeen

Fall 2008

"Hurry up and hit me off, Sunny. I got a meeting with BG and I'm already late," Sean growled, flexing his fist in and out trying to get his veins to pop up to the surface of his skin.

"You need to start a new line, Sean. This vein is dead," Sunny replied, pressing down on his arm looking for a new place to shoot.

"You keep saying that. This like the tenth new line you started on me. I can't be all tracked up or niggas gon' notice shit like that. I can't be seen like that," Sean griped. Finally Sunny found a ripe vein without having to find a new place in his arm to inject the heroin.

"Hold still," she complained as he fidgeted. With the precision of a registered nurse, Sunny punctured Sean's skin with the tip of the needle. When she got a tiny drop of blood to back up into the needle Sunny knew she was in the right place. She pushed down on the plunger slowly and loosened the rubber tie on his arm so the drugs could get through faster. Within seconds Sean's head fell forward and his mouth hung open, proof that he was flying high at that moment.

"You be bringing that good shit home, boy. You in another world right now," Sunny said as she prepped her own hit. "But I thought the rule was never get high on your own supply," she said, laughing afterward. Sean was too high to even know what she was talking about. Sunny hit herself next and fell backward on the bed and enjoyed her temporary high. Life was good in Sunny's opinion. After all she still had her man and he was an endless supplier of the heroin in the whole city.

Sean rushed into the warehouse, late again. BG was sitting in a folding chair with her arms folded and her lips poked out. Beans, Ak and Ty were all there wearing looks of disgust too.

"What up!" Sean called out, his voice sounding a bit too cheery for his usually cool, calm and collected personality. Everyone turned toward him and then they all looked at one another and started shaking their heads. Once again their boss seemed to look and act out of character. BG and his crew had all been noticing a drastic change in Sean over the past year and a half. He was always late for meetings now, which used to be a pet peeve for him before. Sean was always usually well groomed to the point that even his fingernails were filed evenly. Now, his hair was overgrown, his nails were chipped and dirty underneath and his skin looked ashen. The most remarkable change though, was Sean's clothes. He was once the best dressed in the city, wearing only the finest designers and the sharpest styles. Now, he donned the same old clothes he'd been wearing for days, he hadn't purchased any new styles and the worst violation for a clean-cut dude like Sean, was the fact that now he wore his clothes so wrinkled and disheveled it was like he'd just rolled out of bed and come outside.

"You're mad late," BG gritted, standing up and scowling at Sean.

"Yo . . . I'm here right," Sean retorted, scratching his nose and flexing his neck like something was biting him on it. He was sweating like he had just come from the gym. BG squinted her eyes at him and looked at him carefully. The drastic changes with Sean were glaring now, but BG didn't say anything.

"A'ight, so let's get down to business," Sean said, clapping his hands together and rubbing them against one another real fast.

"What's up with this nigga lately? He be acting real jittery," Ak whispered to Beans. Just then Sean started scratching his nose again and shifting his weight from one foot to the other like he couldn't keep still. He had the dope itch and jitters worse than any other time he could remember.

"Acting like a fiend if you ask me," Ak whispered again. "I ain't never see this nigga look so dirty and he scratching like a corner fiend."

"Everything is already ready to go to the distributors . . . no thanks to you. You took an advance on your cut last time so here is the balance of what's left of your share. You need to pay your people out of that," BG said sternly, pushing a small stack of cash toward Sean. He looked down at the money like it was a pile of garbage or poison.

"Nah . . . this stack look mighty small," he complained, backhanding the sweat off his forehead. "This ain't even half the take off that shipment. Once I pay these niggas that's gon' leave me with shit."

"Yeah, because you took an advance on your take or did you forget that too?" BG snapped, glaring at Sean in disgust. Sean couldn't remember what he did the day before aside from getting high, much less remember how much money he'd taken in advance.

"I don't remember . . . but you know what, I take your word for it BG. Also . . . I need to take a brick for a private deal I got going on. I'll bring you the cash after the trans-action is made," Sean lied, reaching down for one of the neatly wrapped bricks of heroin. He had been taking a lot of their supply lately and BG had definitely taken notice. BG stepped over and put her hand on top of his to halt his motion. Sean paused and looked at her evilly.

"What private deal? We makin' private side deals now?" she asked through her teeth. Sean flicked her hand off of his.

"Yo, BG. You better know your place. You better remember who the king is," Sean warned her, sniffling back the snot threatening to fall from his nose. It was already time for another hit and his body was letting him know. Sean felt like little bugs were crawling on him and he knew it was that urge to get high coming back. He needed to get out of there as fast as he could with the drugs.

"Nah, Sean . . . you better know your place. A lot of shit with you ain't adding up these days, but the one thing you're not going to do is fuck up the business," BG replied, snatching the heroin from under his grasp. "All these bricks are accounted for. If you want to work side deals you need to find side supply. Ain't no more walking away with unaccounted for bricks because that's like walking away with half of my money," she said authoritatively. Her security team moved in around her.

"A'ight . . . that's how we playin' it? A'ight," Sean said, flexing his shoulders and neck and then scratching his nose.

"This nigga definitely gettin' high," Beans grumbled under his breath. "That's fucked up. The king let his bitch take him down."

Sunny jumped up out of her sleep to the sound of loud banging on the condo door. Sean was in a dopefiend sleep, which meant the entire place could've collapsed around him and he would've stayed asleep.

"Sean! Sean!" Sunny shook him vigorously. "Sean! Somebody at the door," Sunny urged.

"What?" Sean growled at her, barely able to move his arms to push her away.

Just then, the loud banging turned into loud crashes. Sunny jumped up.

"Sean, somebody in the house!" Sunny screamed, trembling. She had been attacked one too many times to just sit there and let it happen again. Sean finally got a little of his bearings, but before he could even sit up, he was staring down the barrel of a gun.

"Police and sheriff's department. We came to remove you from the premises for failure to pay mortgage on this property. Your lender sent notices and now there is a court order to vacate . . . today," the fat white policeman said with a Southern drawl.

"Y'all niggas need to come up in here like y'all raiding and shit," Sean grumbled, covering his naked body with the comforter.

"Give us a minute," Sunny pleaded. "We have to put on some clothes."

"One minute," the officer mumbled. When he was gone Sunny turned toward Sean.

"What the fuck, Sean? You haven't paid the bills?" she asked in a harsh tone. "All that money you been making and now we gotta leave all of our shit behind with no notice?" she scolded.

"Pay the mortgage? Pay the fuckin' mortgage? How? We been spending every fuckin' dollar getting high!" Sean snapped at her as he slid into his pants. His tone was accusatory.

"You just collected money three days ago! It can't all be gone," Sunny screamed.

"Shut the fuck up, Sunny! You don't know shit. I wasn't able to get the H from BG that night, so I have to buy the shit . . . You think the money gon' last the way you fuckin' suck me dry to get high every ten fuckin' minutes?" Sean shot back. He grabbed some of his designer clothes and shoved them into his Louis Vuitton duffel bags and suitcases. He grabbed his watches and jewelry too. He had been maintaining their habits off of his cash reserves so he still owned a lot of precious jewelry and clothing items . . . for now.

"Where we gonna go?" Sunny asked on the brink of tears.

"To a hotel until I can figure shit out. I'll fix it. I'll get us another place or I'll make a deal with the bank on this one. We ain't gon' be in the streets that's for sure," Sean promised as he slid his last pack of heroin and his works into his jacket pocket. Sunny twisted her lips like she didn't believe him.

After a month of being holed up in a four-star hotel room with Sunny, Sean was finally out of cash and drugs. He had already pawned all but one of his Rolex watches and had sold his furniture from the condo. The money from those transactions was gone too.

Sean showed up at BG's newly opened restaurant looking for her, his appearance so disheveled and dirty that BG's security team didn't even recognize him.

"I need to see BG! I'm King Sean! Don't fuckin' act like you don't know who the fuck I am!" Sean boomed. His words weren't swaying BG's team of muscular, wrestler-type goons.

"Listen, dirty nigga . . . get from round here before you come up missing," one of her goons growled in Sean's face.

"What nigga? You know who I am? Huh! I'm the king!" Sean barked loudly.

BG heard the commotion outside and came out to see what was going on.

"Hey . . . hey . . . what's happening here?" BG asked, fighting her way through the huddle of huge, muscular security guards.

"I'm her fuckin' partner! I made her! I'm the king!" Sean was still screaming as he tried to fight the big dudes off. BG finally made her way to the middle where the men had Sean hemmed up by the collar of his dirty shirt. BG clasped her hand over her mouth. She almost cried when she laid eyes on Sean.

"King?" BG whispered almost breathlessly. Sean's appearance had literally taken her breath away and sent a wave of cramps trampling through her gut. Gone was the well-groomed, well-dressed, sharp as a tack businessman BG had partnered with so many years ago. Sean stood before her in jeans that were almost falling off of him, sneakers that had been in style two years ago, with a face so gaunt and drawn it looked like he hadn't eaten in months. His hair and facial hair were all overgrown and in serious need of a cut. He was sweating profusely and his eyes were almost bugged out of his head. Sean noticed her and cracked a dirty-tooth smile.

"BG . . . yeah, it's me. Tell these niggas to back off. I needed to come see you," Sean called out to her when he noticed her. BG couldn't stop staring at him. She wanted to cry, but all she could do was shake her head.

"Where have you been?" BG asked with her face crumpled like she smelled something stink. "Why you look like this?

"That's what I need to talk to you about," Sean said, scratching his nose and rubbing his arms like they itched real bad.

"It's all good," BG said raising her hand and calling off her security. They opened up a small path so that Sean could follow BG inside.

Once inside, Sean looked around the posh restaurant in amazement. "This shit is tight," he complimented. "You been investing I see," he said, his words sounding a little salty as jealousy crept up on him like a ghost.

"Let's go upstairs to my office," BG replied, ignoring his snide comment. They entered her office and BG took her seat behind her grand, mahogany desk. Sean stood in front of the desk feeling small compared to her and like a failure. He looked at how well dressed BG was in her designer blazer, jeans and pumps and he immediately regretted coming to her looking like he did.

"I know I have been missing meetings and shit, BG," Sean started, sniffling like his nose was running. BG leaned forward on her elbows and squinted her eyes at him. She didn't want to believe it before, but it had been confirmed for her now . . . Sean was on drugs heavy.

"I don't want to hear any more of your fuckin' excuses, Sean. You haven't run this business in months. All you want to do is collect money and get your hands on product, but you ain't putting in no work. Your boys are all going their separate ways, but you didn't know that did you? Ty . . . that nigga works for God now. Beans, he's interested in partnering with me on a half-and-half basis like me and you used to do. Ak and Bo, they are finding their way out there in the streets. You ain't got no more business with me. I don't owe you nothing because you haven't invested nothing back into the business. Our dealings are done," BG said through clenched teeth. Sean felt smaller and smaller with every sentence that came out of her mouth. He slumped down in one of the chairs in front of her desk and put his head in his hands.

"I'm fucked up, B," he lamented. "I'm real fucked up right now," Sean said, shaking his head pitifully.

"What the fuck happened to you?" BG asked seriously. "I don't even know you anymore."

Sean looked up at her with red-rimmed eyes and snot at the tip of his left nostril. He couldn't believe how fast the tables of his life had turned.

"I fucked myself out of the game, B," Sean said, raising his sleeve and extending his arm to show her the track marks that ran up and down his arm. BG's mouth hung open for a few seconds as Sean's revelation settled in her mind. She had suspected it and probably knew it in her heart, but seeing it firsthand and knowing for sure was literally killing her inside. She closed her eyes for a few seconds to let it settle in her mind. Then, as if a bolt of electricity had hit her BG jumped to her feet.

"You're fuckin' weak! You let that bitch drag you down to the lowest place on fuckin' earth! I loved you! We could've been good together, but no . . . you was in love with a fiend! Now look at you!" BG spat cruelly, fighting to keep the tears welling up in her eyes from falling. Sean's chest rose and fell rapidly and his eyes went wide. He wasn't expecting her reaction, nor was he expecting her to say that she had loved him.

"You disgust me! You came here to beg for money? Or H? Is that why you came to see me after a whole fuckin' month?" BG gritted, her heart breaking with every cruel word. Sean looked at her pitifully at a loss for words. She had figured him out from the door, but was hopeful that she had been wrong.

"Here! This is your exit cut! I'm doing this out of mercy, not because I owe you shit. You ain't got nothing left around here!" BG growled as she went behind her desk and pulled out three rubber banded stacks of money. "This is what you came to beg for so here it is. Take it back to your fiend bitch and get high," BG screamed, tossing the cash in Sean's face. He scrambled out of the chair and picked up the money. He needed it more than ever right now.

"Yeah, that's what I thought," BG snarled, looking at him with disgust. "Now get the fuck out of my office! Don't come back around until you're ready to get some help! You disgust me . . . you ain't no fuckin' king!" BG yelled at him, her voice cracking. Sean looked at her one last time before he turned to leave. Her tears had finally started to run down her face.

"B . . . once you start you can't stop," Sean said sadly. "No matter how much you want to, you can't fuckin' stop." With that he was gone.

BG slammed the door behind him and fell to her knees sobbing. She still loved Sean, but now it was apparent that he could never love her back. He had chosen Sunny and drugs over her.

In the months after her encounter with Sean, BG took the helm of the business and it soared to new heights. She invested in a chain of high-class restaurants, lounges and even bought into a D-league basketball team to make her dirty money clean. BG was the new king of the city with Beans and Ak at her side.

Chapter Eighteen

Back to Present Day

After what seemed like an eternity, the graffiti-covered door creaked open. Sean got to his feet swiftly, his jaw was rocking feverishly and he clenched his fists at his side. Sean watched the young dope boy bop out of the room smiling with sweat glistening on his face and chest. His pants were still unbuttoned and halfway off his waist where the butt of his gun peeked out. He eyed Sean up and down with a smirk and then laughed at him. Sean looked at the kid with his thick gold Cuban link chains dangling around his neck and his slick True Religion jeans and Louboutin sneakers fitting him perfectly. Sean remembered when he was on that side of the game, wearing nothing but the best clothes, shoes and jewels. He felt ashamed now, standing there in his dirty, faded jeans, beat-down Nike Air Force Ones and a fitted cap so dirty the team name was barely visible anymore.

"That's a sweet piece of pussy you got there. I can only imagine how much sweeter it was before the whole town ran up in those guts," the young boy said to Sean snidely. Sean lifted his fists, but quickly but them back down when he thought about what would happen to him if he bucked on the young kid. Sean was once one of the most feared men on the streets but that had changed too.

"I guess you ain't king no more, huh? King Sean," the kid taunted, waiting for Sean to react so he could clap on him and make a name for himself.

Sean's chest rose and fell rapidly. His radio went crashing to the floor and he bit down into his jaw. The young boy stopped in front of him and pulled his weapon. He sat it on Sean's shoulder in a bold show of bravado.

"Remember when I worked for you and you beat my ass within a inch of my life that time?" the kid asked, then he lifted his gun and cracked it across Sean's head.

"Ahh." Sean winced crumpling to the floor in a heap. The kid stood over him and laughed.

"Damn, now I got your bitch working her jaws for me and ain't shit you can do . . . fucking fiend-ass nigga. You wasn't never no king in my eyes," the kid said viciously. Then he bopped away, leaving Sean scrambling up off of the floor with his pride and manhood crushed.

Sunny stumbled out of the room with her lipstick smeared, her hair an untamed mess and her cat green eyes wild. She refused to hold eye contact with Sean as she dug into her purse for the tiny bottle of mouthwash she had stolen from the drugstore earlier. Finally locating the bottle, she popped it open, took a swig of the mouthwash, gargled it and spit it right on the floor of the dilapidated house. It was all she could do to wash the taste of another man from her lips.

"You ready? I got a twenty for that and I'm hitting more than half for all of my hard work," Sunny smacked her lips and said with a disrespectful tone. It had been hard for her to maintain her respect for Sean and even harder for her to hide it. Sean got to his feet and pushed her back into the room. He snatched the bundle of heroin from her.

"You ain't doing shit unless I say you doing it," he growled, grabbing her collar forcefully. "You enjoyed that shit right? Right?" Sean barked in Sunny's face.

"Don't do that, Sean! Give it back to me! I worked for that!" Sunny whined like a baby, being real careful with her words. She knew how he could get when it came to sharing the drugs and with his already-bruised ego rearing its ugly head, Sunny knew Sean could be violently unpredictable.

"You get what the fuck I give you," Sean spat, squeezing the packs in his hand like he never wanted to let them go. Sunny burst into tears, something she knew would tug at Sean's heart. She had been working that trick on him since they were kids.

"But since you worked for it like you like to remind me, I'ma let you hit first," he relented, softening his tone.

Sunny hurriedly pulled out her works and with shaky hands she tied the belt around her arm. Sean pulled it for her so she could feel the best vein since the room was too dimly lit to see that well. He tossed one of the little black balls of heroin into the spoon and lit the bottom of it. Sunny was salivating as she watched him cook the drugs with a hawk's eye.

When it was ready Sean loaded Sunny's needle and touched the fattest vein in her arm. She looked at him, her once-flawless face finally showing the signs of her addiction. Sean turned his eyes away from her face, it was too painful to see her looking like she did now.

"Do it, baby, hurry up," Sunny whispered in her deepest sex kitten voice. Sean sniffled back the snot threatening to drip from his nose and plunged the needle into her arm easing the poison into her vein.

"Ssss." Sunny winced, her body relaxing against the chair. Her head fell back and her eyes rolled up into her head until only the whites were visible. Sean pulled the belt loose so the drugs could move through her system with ease.

"That shit must be real good," he said as he watched her head roll back forward and her chin fall to her chest.

"Yo, I'm next so c'mon," he demanded anxiously. Sean started cooking his portion of the heroin as his mouth watered waiting for the hit.

"A'ight you ready to hit me?" he asked without looking at Sunny. All of a sudden Sunny's legs did something funny that startled him.

"What the fuck?" he whispered. "You almost made me drop my shit. Stop the shit and get up and help me hit this shit. Don't be so fucking selfish all of the time," Sean growled at her. Then Sunny's body jerked like she had been hit with a bolt of lightning and she fell off the chair. Sean dropped the drugs, let go of the belt around his arm and fell down at Sunny's side.

"Baby! Sunny! Wake up!" Sean yelled, grabbing her into his arms. Sunny's body began convulsing and her eyes were completely white. Her legs flopped around like she was being electrocuted.

"Sunny! No! C'mon!" he yelled, slapping her face vigorously. White foam was spilling from her mouth and her body bucked so wildly even he couldn't hold on to her.

"Help me! Somebody, help me! Help me!" Sean screamed frantically. But there was no one in that house that would care enough to call an ambulance. No one would dare call 911 and risk having the cops bust up in there and break up their getting high.

"Help me . . . God, help me," Sean whispered through tears as he held Sunny's face up against his. He could feel her starting to get cold.

Finally Sunny's body went still. Sean laid her head down and looked down into her face. He couldn't stop the tears from falling as his body jerked with sobs. He hadn't cried like that since his mother had died.

"Sunny!!" he screamed at the top of his lungs. "You can't leave me! I need you!" he hollered some more. He lay his head on her chest and there was no sound. The heart he had fallen in love with so many years earlier was no longer beating.

"I did this to you. I did this to you," Sean said, his voice trailing off and his mind reeling backward.

Sean finally got his bearings enough to stumble out of the shooting gallery onto the street. He could barely walk; he was so dope sick and so shaken up by Sunny's death that his legs felt like two lead pipes. Sean was at rock bottom now and he knew it. He had no friends, no family, no woman, no money and nowhere to go. He stopped at a corner to see if there were any dope boys out that might front him something just to keep him from getting sick. The corners were empty but for a few fiends that were on the hunt, just like him.

Sean leaned over and dry heaved a few times as his body began giving in to the need for a hit. He fought hard to keeps thoughts of Sunny from his mind, but it was killing him that he'd just left her body in that disgusting, abandoned building like a piece of trash. Sean didn't have a choice, he was too messed up in the game to do anything else. He couldn't afford to bury Sunny now even if he wanted to.

As Sean started walking, he started thinking back on his life and the one person who had always seemed to have his back . . . BG. Sean had heard BG was doing big things, but the last time he'd seen her their meeting hadn't ended well.

"I'm ready for the help," Sean whispered out loud thinking of BG's last warning to him. Pain was starting to take over his entire body and Sean knew it wasn't going to be long before he couldn't walk at all. "BG, I hope you still keep your word. I'm coming for the help," Sean groaned, dragging his feet forward.

***

It took Sean two hours to walk to one of BG's spots, the one he knew she kept her office inside of. His legs and back ached and he was dizzy by the time he got there. His entire body was soaked with sweat and his mouth was dry as a cotton ball. He was severely dope sick by the time he weakly tugged on the door to BG's restaurant.

"No . . . fuck," Sean huffed feebly, barely able to get enough breath out to say it. It wasn't opening time yet so the door to the restaurant was locked. Sean was too sick to stand any longer. He put his back up against the door and slid down to the ground. Shivering with the beginning of withdrawal, Sean lay in front of the door so long his body gave out and he fell into a fitful sleep.

"Yo, nigga, get up!" a man barked, nudging Sean in the chest with his foot.

"This ain't no fuckin' homeless shelter," the man continued, kicking Sean with a little more force this time. Sean could barely open his eyes with the pain that was pounding behind them. His stomach was doing somersaults and he felt acidy vomit creeping up his throat. Sean rubbed his hands over his face and could feel the dried crust around his eyes and mouth as he forced himself awake.

"I said get the fuck from 'round here," the man growled, this time hoisting Sean up by his dirty shirt. Once Sean was up, BG squinted and cocked her head to the side. She had been standing there waiting for her security to clear the homeless man from in front of her place of business.

"King . . . Sean?" BG whispered, her eyes going wide with recognition. Although Sean looked like he had aged twenty years over night, he was dirty and had so much facial hair covering his face his features were hardly recognizable, BG could never forget his familiar eyes. As she stood there, she had a flash of their night together in Miami years ago when she'd stared directly into Sean's beautiful chestnut eyes.

"BG . . . BG . . . yeah . . . yeah, it's me," Sean said pitifully, silently praying that she didn't dismiss him. "I . . . I . . . came for the help. Remember you . . . you . . . said come back when I was ready for the help," Sean pleaded, on the brink of collapsing. BG's security team was looking at her as if to say "you know this bum?"

"Open the door. Get him inside before he falls over," BG demanded of her team. They looked at her reluctantly, but they didn't dare question her request.

Two of BG's men helped Sean up to her office and put him down on the leather couch she had inside. BG told them to leave so she could have a minute with Sean.

She stepped over to the couch and stood over him. "Are you really ready for help?" BG asked Sean. He was rocking back and forth wracked with pain all over his body. His teeth were chattering, although it wasn't cold in the room.

"Yes. I'm ready," Sean huffed out, barely able to speak. "But . . . but I need something right now to set me straight until . . ." Sean practically begged. It broke her heart to see him like this.

"Sean, you're a boss. You don't need to live like this. You're the smartest m'fucker I know and look at you right now. I'm going to help you, but only because I know that the king still lives inside of you," BG said with sincerity. Sean kept rocking; tears drained from the sides of his eyes as he listened to her words. He was a boss and he still knew it, but at that moment, he didn't feel like it.

BG walked out of her office for a minute and returned with a small bundle to set Sean straight.

"This is the first and last time I will give you this poison. I'm not going to help you kill yourself with this shit. You

came to me for help and that's what I intend to provide,"
BG said firmly, tossing the bundle at Sean. He snatched it
up like a starving man being given food for the first time
in years. BG looked at him and shook her head with a
combination of pity and disgust. For the first time since
she'd met him, she felt sorry for him. "Hit that and I'll be
right back. We need to talk," BG said seriously. She left her
office and when the door closed, Sean went about getting
high for what he hoped was the last time.

Chapter Nineteen

Sean leaned over the side of the bed in BG's guest room and threw up into the bucket on the floor for the sixth time in a row. "Agh!" Sean screamed out as another wave of pain shot through his lower back and abdomen. He was drenched in sweat and his legs stiffened to the point he was wracked with Charlie horses and severe cramps.

"Cold turkey is no joke, but it's the only way to do this shit," BG said as she sat a big cup of ice chips down on the nightstand next to the bed and picked up the vomit bucket so she could empty it.

"B . . . just give me one pack. Just one more," Sean begged, barely able to speak. "I swear . . . it will be the last one. I can't do this, B. I ain't built for this shit."

"No. It's been three days and you've made it this far. In a few more days you'll be well enough to go to a place I set up for you," BG told him. "If I give you a pack you'll be starting from the door and that ain't about to happen, King."

"Fuck!!" Sean screamed at her. "You don't fuckin' understand!" he cried out, kicking his aching legs like a toddler throwing a tantrum.

"You can do all of that but I'm not getting you no H. The man I know you to be can kick this shit straight cold turkey," BG said. "You're doing just fine. Just trust me."

Sean wanted to jump up and punch her in the face, but he was too weak.

"Fuck you! Fuck you!" Sean growled at her as he leaned over and dry heaved this time.

"I know. I know. But you'll thank me later when you get well enough to take the streets back," BG said with confidence.

After another three days of cold turkey withdrawals, Sean finally felt strong enough to sit up in the bed and put his feet on the floor. The sunlight was streaming though the blinds of BG's guest room and for the first time in years Sean appreciated the sun, the trees and the blue sky outside. He didn't feel 100 percent, but well enough to get up.

Sean stood up for the first time and almost fell because his legs were so weak from not using them for so many days. He knocked a glass off of the nightstand and sent it crashing to the floor.

"Damn," Sean hissed, bending over to pick up the shards of glass.

"Sean?" BG huffed rushing into the room. "You all right?"

"Yeah . . . yeah, I'm good. I just hit the glass by accident," Sean explained, finally looking up at her. Sean stared at her for a few minutes and he immediately felt ashamed of himself. BG was still gorgeous and flawless, standing there in her designer threads with her diamonds sparkling from her wrist, ears and hands. Time had been kind to her and she didn't look like she had aged a day. Sean lowered his eyes, unable to hold eye contact with her, realizing he could barely stand, dressed in pajamas she bought for him with not one piece of jewelry of his own.

"Leave that . . . the cleaning lady will get it up," BG told Sean. "I'm so glad to see you up and about," BG told him.

"Yeah, I need a shower like nobody's business," he said with a halfhearted chuckle trying to take the focus off of his raggedy appearance.

"That's what I like to hear," BG said smiling brightly. She was starting to see hints of her old partner shining through.

BG provided Sean with toiletries, razor and a brand new plush Ralph Lauren bathrobe. When he first stepped into the shower, the water stung his skin like thousands of needles were stabbing him. Sean allowed the hot water to run over his battered and abused body, which seemed to revive him. As he stood under the shower stream, Sean couldn't help but think about the last time he'd taken a shower with Sunny.

"Wash my back," Sunny said, giggling as Sean moved his naked body close to hers. The hot water rained down on them causing a steamy mist to develop between them. The entire scene was sexy as hell and made Sunny feel like a sex kitten.

"I'ma wash ya front first," Sean replied jokingly, reaching around from behind her so he could fiddle with her clitoris. Sunny leaned her back against his chest as the shower water washed over her breasts and face.

"Didn't I say no fucking this time? Huh? Huh?" Sunny chided playfully, lifting her arms, reaching back and cradling his head. "That's all you wanna do lately."

"What you say don't matter. This my shit and I take it when I want. Plus ain't nobody tell you to be so fuckin' sexy," Sean said softly, kissing the back of her neck while his ever growing manhood pressed against her ass. "C'mere," Sean instructed, gently turning her around.

"Damn you so sexy when you're dripping wet," he whispered pushing Sunny against the shower wall. She lifted her legs so he could take her.

"Mmmm," she moaned as Sean entered her wet center. Their wet bodies slipped against each other making a loud, slick noise as their skin slapped together.

"Ahh. Yes. Yes." Sunny panted as Sean took her while the powerful shower water pelted them like a warm rainstorm.

"I love you," Sunny whispered, holding on to Sean like she never wanted to let him go.

"I love you too," Sean said for the first time since Sunny had been with him. Sunny opened her eyes wide and stopped his motion. She looked him in the eye in disbelief that he had finally said the three words she thought she'd never hear him say.

"Yeah, I said it and I mean it, Sunny," Sean assured her, finally letting his guard down and giving himself to her emotionally.

"Aye! Sean! You a'ight in there!" BG banged on the bathroom door and called out from the other side. Sean jumped fiercely and looked around the steamy bathroom dazed as he snapped out of his reverie. He swallowed hard, realizing that he was alone in the shower without Sunny.

"Yeah! I'm good," Sean responded as BG knocked again. He put his hands up against the shower wall and let the water beat down on his head for a few minutes as he tried hard to get Sunny out of his mind. Sean was glad that the water streaming from the showerhead had washed his tears away.

"Damn, nigga. I was scared for a minute. I thought you fell in," BG was saying with her back turned as Sean stepped out of the bathroom.

"I almost fell in," he replied sarcastically, wrapping the plush bathrobe around his body. When BG finally turned around and laid eyes on him, her mouth involuntarily dropped open like she'd seen a ghost.

"Damn all that? What? I still look that bad?" Sean asked, noticing her wide-eyed stare and agape mouth.

"Um . . . no . . . um," BG stammered at a loss for words as she stared at his newly shaven face and clear skin. They shared a long gaze until BG finally lowered her eyes. She felt something suddenly start throbbing in her pants. Sean looked like his old self and she was love struck by his gorgeous face all over again.

"Damn . . . that bad," he joked. "Shit I thought a nigga was looking better 'n' shit."

"No. That good," she whispered, too scared to let him know how she was really feeling.

BG didn't trust the at home cold turkey detox that Sean had gone through at her house. She didn't think he would be able to fully kick his heroin addiction staying in the city, so she arranged for him to get a full detox at an exclusive holistic drug cleansing center in Los Angeles that most celebrities frequented when they were trying to kick the habit. There was a hefty price tag attached to the place, but BG didn't care if it meant the old King Sean would be back at her side.

"You know I ain't with this shit, right?" Sean griped as he slowly walked up the steps of the private jet BG had chartered to fly them to L.A. "I don't let nobody tell me where I gotta go, when I gotta go. I don't give a fuck you chartered a jet or not," Sean went on complaining like a grumpy old man.

"I can tell the old you is almost back. Always tryin'a run shit. Well this time, I got this and you going where I say you go . . . chartered jet and all," BG went back at him with a sassy tone.

"Yeah, a'ight. If them niggas at this place start chanting or some other ill white people shit voodoo 'drink a pig's blood' type shit, I'm straight out that bitch on the next thing smoking," Sean told her flat out. BG shook her head at him, but she was smiling at the same time. This complaining, demanding, overbearing annoyance was the King Sean she remembered from back in the days.

"Nigga, get on the jet and shut the fuck up," BG said chuckling. "Damn you complaining more than a bitch right now."

Sean couldn't front, when he walked inside of the spacious interior of the private G4 he felt like a king again. The inside was luxury at its best, but he also felt slightly ashamed that his first trip in a private plane was because BG set it up and not because he had moved up to that level on his own accord. This was what his life was supposed to be like before it got sidetracked with a heroin addiction.

"Damn, cashmere blankets, personal Bose headphones and reclining seats . . . this shit boss," Sean said admiring his surroundings. BG shook her head proudly. She still thrived off of Sean's acceptance and approval, she just didn't let him know it.

"Help yourself to the food, too," she said invitingly. "Shit I'm paying for it, might was well eat as much as possible." There were trays and trays of gourmet cheeses, freshly baked breads and crackers and colorful assortments of fruit. There was also an assortment of high-priced liquors that Sean was eyeing.

"Don't even look at these shits," BG scolded him, moving the liquor tray out of his reach. She wasn't taking any chances with any substances and his recovery. Not until she was sure he could handle being clean and sober. Sean just shook his head, amused at how protective she was being over him.

"This is how you are supposed to live, King," BG said winking at him. Sean nodded his head up and down. He didn't need her to remind him.

"I'll be back soon. Real soon, B," he told her with confidence.

They rode in silence for a few minutes before BG broke it. She looked over at Sean seriously, the scene so familiar that it gave her chills.

"I just want to let you know that I took care of everything for her," BG blurted out, finding no other way to ease into the conversation.

"Who? What?" Sean asked, crinkling his eyebrows and nose as he stuffed a cube of watermelon in his mouth

"Your lady. Sunny," BG said softly. "I made sure she was put away with dignity for you. I knew it was what you would've done if you were good. No matter what I felt about her, I wasn't going to let you live with leaving her in that fuckin' trap house to get stepped over like yesterday's trash," BG continued. Sean lowered his head in shame and he suddenly felt a wave of nausea roll through his gut.

"When you came to my office that day, after you hit that last bag and that H got into your system you were crying like a baby. That's when you told me that she was dead off some bad dope and you had to leave her behind. I could feel the pain behind your words. I knew you were too sick to do anything, so I had my dudes pick her body up and I gave her a proper sendoff. Believe me, now, Sunny is finally resting in peace, King," BG told Sean. She passed a sheet of legal sized paper to him. Fighting back tears, Sean looked at the paper. It was the itemized bill for Sunny's service and burial. He looked up at BG with love in his eyes. He was grateful.

"Thank you," he said, his bottom lip trembling. It was all he could get to come out without shedding his hard exterior and letting the tears run. BG had love for him and that was real.

Sean wasn't feeling the holistic cleansing center in L.A., but he knew it was his only way back to his place as king of the streets. The real cold turkey process at the cleansing center was no joke, but Sean fought through it like a champ.

BG came by and checked on him daily for the entire month he was there. Some days Sean gave BG his ass to kiss rudely, but other days, he was happy to see that he still had her in his corner. By the end of the program, Sean felt like his old self again and he was anxious to make some connections to build his empire back up.

On the day of his release, BG pulled up in a brand new smoke gray Mercedes-Benz S550 and Sean's heart jerked in his chest. It was the newer version to the Benz Fox had drove Sean around in so many times when he was younger.

"Why you look like you seen a ghost?" BG asked Sean as he got into the car.

"If you only knew," he replied, almost whispering.

"Damn you clean up nicely," BG said, reaching over and rubbing her hand over Sean's fresh low haircut. Sean flexed his head away from her.

"C'mon, man . . . don't be fuckin' up my waves rubbing my head like I'm ya son 'n' shit," Sean said jokingly. They both shared a laugh. It had been ages since they'd done that. BG was feeling nostalgic, but she wasn't ready to let her guard down with Sean again, just yet.

"So what we gon' do to celebrate your accomplishment, man?" BG asked.

"Get our ass back on the G4 and get home. I got connections to make. I'm sure a lot of niggas gon' be surprised to see that I've arisen from the dead," he said, rearing back in the car seat. "I got a bunch of niggas I wanna see . . . personally."

"Nah. You don't need to worry with all that revenge bullshit right now. We gotta celebrate while we out here in Hollywood, man. It's all-star weekend and I got these,"

BG said, reaching down into the middle console and pulling out two floor seat tickets to the NBA All-Star game.

"C'mon, B, I think I just wanna kick back and chill . . . no crowds 'n' shit," Sean said reluctantly. "I really got my mind on rebuilding myself. First I had to do the body, but now that it's done, I need to rebuild the name . . . the man."

"Nigga, please. You know you wanna see all those groupie chicks that be slithering around at the games and events looking for rich come-up dick. I bet it's been a minute since you had some ass, too," BG quipped, laughing. Sean looked at her strangely, then he busted out laughing too. He forgot how she could sometimes act as cool as one of his dudes.

"Yo, one hun'ed I ain't had none in a minute for real. At least some head from a bird would set me straight. I'll probably come so hard the bitch's head will blow off," Sean joked backed. BG laughed raucously and put on an act, but inside, she wanted Sean for herself.

"A'ight, I'm game to go, since you enticed a nigga like that," Sean said. "As long as you front me some ends so I can get some threads. A nigga can't catch flies without being the shit," Sean said laughing.

"Damn that line was corny as fuck!" BG yelled playfully. More laughter filled the car. It seemed like life was on its way to being good again.

"This that premium shit right here," Sean yelled to BG over the noise of the Staples Center crowd. "A nigga on the floor right up on the bench and shit," Sean said referring to their floors seat tickets she had gotten. BG had been pulling out all of the stops to show Sean what he had been missing out on getting high. She was hopeful that the difference would make him never want to use drugs again.

"You know how I do," BG joked. The Laker girls were performing their dance as a part of the pre-game show and as Sean watched the beautiful women move on the court, a small raucous group in the crowd across from him caught his attention. Sean stared for a few minutes, then squinted to get a better look. He could've sworn he saw a few familiar faces and just like that it hit him.

"Yo, is that . . ." Sean started but before he could finish . . .

"God . . ." BG completed his sentence. "Damn it's been years since I've seen that nigga. I didn't think he even left his compound out in Canada to get out 'n' shit." Sean said as he watched God and about eight goons. After a few minutes, God headed in Sean and BG's direction. God and Sean locked eyes from a distance and neither man would turn away.

"He's headed over here, but he better not buck. I got people," BG said to Sean.

"God ain't about shit," Sean said. "He's too big in the game to make noise at an event like this. That nigga ain't about bringing heat to himself."

Within a few minutes God was at Sean's side wearing a half grin, half sneer on his face. Sean stood up; he wasn't going to let no man stand over him.

"If it isn't King Sean back from the dead," God said, extending his hand for a gentlemanly shake.

"What up, God? You good?" Sean said, nodding at his old connect respectfully.

"I'm fantastic," God replied. "I hope the same for you. I heard you been suffering from a lot of . . . how do we say . . . *personal* tragedies," God said calmly feigning concern. Sean bit down into his jaw and his hands curled into fists at his side. Sean didn't like to speak about the string of deaths that had shrouded his life lately. BG touched him in a show of her support.

"I am really sorry for everything. I heard how they gutted and hung your poor grandmother, and how they shot up the car and caused your baby to die. And what happened to your old lady . . . her getting a bad bag of dope that took her out? All a shame," God relayed calmly. Sean's eyebrows went into arches on his face. He was kind of surprised God knew so much about his life, especially some intricate details other people didn't know.

"Surprised? I hear everything, Sean, you should know that. I'm God," God said cracking a slight grin. Sean bit down on his bottom lip, but kept his cool.

"Thanks for your words of sympathy," Sean said, trying real hard to hold it together as pieces to the puzzle started coming together in his head. BG held on to him, but at that moment Sean's insides were on fire. His chest heaved and his nostrils flared like a bull ready to charge and he had to will himself to stay straight. Sean knew he had been the only person to know that his grandmother had been hung; he had cut her down before the cops got there, which told Sean that God had to be responsible and not Faheem's people. Sean bit down into his jaw so hard he drew his own blood. God had sent that hit that had killed his son, too.

"Well, Sean, I hope the streets stay kind to you." God winked at him tauntingly. Then Ty and Freddie stepped over to Sean and eyed him slyly.

"He wasn't never no king in my eyes," Freddie whispered to Ty, hiding behind God and eye screwing Sean. Sean didn't hear him, but seeing Freddie's face now had taken him back to that day in the shooting gallery with Sunny. Something else hit Sean like a bolt of lightning; that day before Sunny had died, Freddie said he worked for God and the dope was a gift from God. Right there on the spot, Sean had figured out that God had not only killed his grandmother, he had also set Sunny up to get a bad bag of dope that was meant for Sunny and Sean.

Sean nodded and kept a grin on his lips. He knew it didn't pay to buck in a public forum like the Staples Center, but the gears of his mind were already calculating things. BG was squeezing his arm because she could tell he was trying his best to keep his cool.

"A'ight, God . . . you and your people take care. Like you said, I'm just back from the dead. A nigga back on the come up but I guess it'll be a long way back to the top," Sean conceded, his insides burning up. God chuckled in Sean's face.

"Good, so long as you know your place," God said coolly. "Let's go," God told his flunkies. He turned and walked away as cool and calm as he'd walked over. Before God was fully gone, Sean turned to BG with that old King Sean look in his eyes and said, "Yo, call the team. Fly them out here now. It's time to put in that work." BG's shoulders relaxed with relief and she let a sly grin move slowly across her face. Her heart sped up with excitement, because at that moment she knew, the old King Sean was back.

Chapter Twenty

After the game, BG and Sean returned to the suite she had booked on Hollywood Boulevard. Sean's mind couldn't really rest after his interaction with God and BG could sense the tension emanating from him.

"Why don't you sit and relax," BG told Sean as he paced passed her for the tenth time. He looked over at her, his eyes apologetic. He knew she didn't understand his restlessness because he had never shared with her how his grandmother died or who had given Sunny the bad dope.

"I'm so proud of how you handled yourself in front of that prick God tonight. I love when a man can keep it together like that," BG commended.

"Ah that's nothing. I'll see that man another time . . . not with a lady around." Sean smiled at her. BG walked over to him holding two champagne flutes filled halfway with Ace of Spades she had just removed from the chiller.

"Aye, aye . . . that shit looks good, but remember what your white people at the cleansing center said . . . alcohol is a gateway back to that boy," Sean warned her, waving her away with the liquor. BG smiled and set both flutes on the glass top bar and started clapping.

"Yes! That was a test and your ass passed that shit with flying colors," she cheered. She picked up a regular glass of grape juice for herself and Sean.

"To the new and improved stronger King Sean," BG toasted.

"Damn you corny," Sean joked, clinking his glass against hers. BG set her glass down and Sean did too. They stared at each other for a long minute and that old Miami lust feeling came back to both of them. Sean was the first to break the heated eye exchange.

"Yo, I never told you this, B, but you remind me so much of my mother. They called her Mook on the streets and she was a top of the game H dealer when I was a kid. She ran blocks and she ain't take no shit. You showed me in so many ways that you have the same heart that she had. My mother would feed a nigga, care for him, loan him money, but if that same nigga crossed her, she wouldn't hesitate to blow him out of his fuckin' shoes. I get that from you, B. You walked with me from day fuckin' one and there's a reason. Don't you ever let no nigga tell you that you ain't worthy of being that top bitch. I think that's the only thing I could say about my mother that I wish was different, she put business before her own heart and she let the love of her life slip away," Sean poured his heart out to BG.

BG was fighting hard to hold back the tears welling up behind her eyes. She had never gotten compliments like that from a man. She knew how hard Sean could be sometimes, so his words meant a lot to her. She looked him in the eye and then mindlessly, she leaned in and forced her mouth on top of his. Sean opened his lips and accepted her tongue into his mouth. They were both breathing heavily and touching each other in places that neither of them had been touched in forever. Before she could protest, BG's satin pants were pulled down around her hips and her panties were off within seconds. Sean pulled his pants down, his legs shaking with anticipation. He hadn't touched a woman since his last experience with Sunny and that was a hazy memory now.

"Ahhh!" BG yelled out as Sean entered her with so much force she felt like he was in her intestines. Sean was going crazy, pounding into BG's pelvis with the force of a jackhammer. He was grunting and breathing hard like an animal. It had been so long for him he couldn't control himself now.

"Agggh!" BG screamed out because he was kind of hurting her. She didn't want to tell him to stop though. Sean leaned up on one hand and looked down at her. "I'm sorry," he huffed, he was climaxing already.

"Oh, Sunny. I'm sorry," he huffed as he pushed farther inside of BG and bust his nut. When the name left his lips the air in the room seemed to all dissipate and both Sean and BG felt like they were suddenly suffocating. Sean caught himself right away, but he couldn't take it back.

"What, nigga? What the fuck did you call me?" BG screamed, using her hands to forcefully push him up off of her. "How fuckin' dare you!" BG hollered, punching him in the face before she scrambled to put her panties back on. She was so embarrassed and angry that she couldn't fight the tears back and they started falling freely from her eyes. She felt stupid for putting herself in this position again.

"B . . . wait . . . listen," Sean tried to plead with her, but his attempts were to no avail. BG stormed like they eye of a tornado toward the bedroom of the suite.

"I knew I should've never thought that Miami was more than just a fucking fling to you. Even in death that bitch still got you by the balls. I can never come close to that, Sean . . . never! And you know what? I will never try to fuckin' do it again!" BG screamed through a stream of tears. Sean felt like someone had stabbed him in the heart listening to the hurt in BG's voice.

"I'm sorry. No . . . wait . . . let me talk to you, B," Sean apologized trying to go after her. He wasn't fast enough. BG went into the room and slammed and locked the door before he could get to her.

"BG, I'm sorry! You're the only family I have. I should've never gone there and complicated things between us. I crossed the line and I'm sorry!" Sean yelled through the door, slamming his hand on it in defeat.

"Fuck you, Sean! Let's just make it all business from this day forward. I'm done! I'm fucking done!" BG replied. Sean could tell she was fighting hard to sound like she wasn't crying.

"A'ight, all business," Sean agreed, shaking his head like he had messed up real bad. "Let's start with taking care of that plan for God. That's still on no matter what we going through with it," he said.

On the other side of the door BG shook her head in disbelief, but she was pulling herself together. If all business is what he wanted, all business was what he was going to get.

"This nigga just fucked me, came in my pussy, and called me his dead bitch's name now he's talking about going ahead with a plan for God? He is so fucked up. I should've never let my guard down again . . . never," BG whispered harshly, scolding herself.

Sean flopped down on the couch and held his head in his hands. He couldn't afford to lose BG's support right now. Sean wasn't sure how things would be after this, but he felt horrible about what he'd done to her heart.

After a few minutes Sean heard the door to the suite bedroom click open. He jumped to his feet ready to throw himself at BG's mercy. BG stepped out of the room dressed like star. Her clothes, hair and makeup were all flawlessly put together. She didn't even look like she'd just been crying a little while earlier. Sean's mouth hung slightly open. He couldn't front, Sunny had always had his heart, but BG was a close second with her beauty and brains.

"Don't wait up," BG said dryly without looking at Sean. She grabbed her car keys and headed toward the suite door, moving her hips seductively. Sean could smell her perfume from a distance.

"Wait . . . wait . . . B," Sean was saying, but BG kept walking and slammed the door behind her, practically right in his face.

"Ain't this about a bitch," Sean huffed standing all alone in the suite like he had just lost his best friend and he probably had.

Club Lure in downtown L.A. was crawling with Hollywood's hottest celebrities and moneymakers. The hotspot was one of God's favorite places to party whenever he came to the U.S. from Canada. The waitresses being suspended from glass orbs especially thrilled God was there and he always took up the VIP section, which was set up like a secret garden, at the back of the club. God sat on one a plush black chaise longue surrounded by his goons and some of his own imported beauties. God lifted his fourth bottle of Ace of Spades to his lips and took it to the head. A lazy grin and sleepy eyes were the order of the night for God, but he was very alert. He watched as top model beauties tried their best to get into the VIP section just to be in his company. The ones that were lucky enough to get in hitched their already-tight dresses up a little higher and exposed more cleavage than their outfits called for. The VIP section was crawling with some of the most beautiful women L.A. had to offer, God was especially amused by the blond-haired, blue-eyed statuesque runway models that seemed totally enamored with his presence.

"Aye! Aye!" God waved his hand at Freddie and Ty. They were partying so hard that had seemingly forgotten they were always working when God was around. Freddie rushed over to God, barely able to stay steady on his feet. The liquor had taken a toll on Freddie's skinny frame.

"What up, God?" Freddie slurred and hiccupped.

"Get those two bitches over there to give me a show," God demanded, pointing to two well-known Victoria's Secret models. Freddie busted out laughing.

"I look like I'm fucking joking?" God said calmly, but stern enough that Freddie got the message. Freddie walked over, whispered to the two women and pointed over at God. Both of the models giggled and pointed, but within a few seconds they were both sauntering toward God.

"Ladies . . . welcome," God said with a sinister smile on his face. They just didn't know God was about to turn them out right there in the club.

After about an hour of watching the models kiss and finger one another, God grew bored. He dismissed them rudely and turned his attention out toward the club. God was drunk out of his mind, so when he saw the gorgeous vision in front of him, he squinted, opened his eyes wide and then squinted again, thinking that his eyes were deceiving him. God looked around behind him and found all of his hired goons standing, strapped like the Secret Service so he knew it would be impossible for him to just get up and casually walk to the bar without them following him and making a scene in the club.

"Freddie!" God called out. "Freddie, c'mere now!" God slurred. Freddie was at God's side so God didn't really need to scream again.

"What up, God? What's good?" Freddie answered, pushing a gorgeous, big titty girl off his arm.

"Look out there by the bar. Tell me my eyes are deceiving me," God told Freddie as he pointed. Freddie craned his neck, ducked, and came back up trying to spot what his boss was pointing out.

"Is that who I think it is?" God asked. Freddie looked on dumbfounded. He had no idea what God was talking about.

"Black dress! Fat ass, big tits," God described who he had his eye on. Freddie scanned a little longer and finally he spotted the mark.

"Oh shit! Yeah . . . yeah! That's BG! Yo, and she's by herself!" Freddie exclaimed excitedly, touching his waistband.

"Calm down. Calm down. I don't want anything to happen to her, I might just want to speak to her . . . or something more," God told Freddie. God kept his eyes trained on BG. He licked his lips as she moved her long slender athletic-build legs in a tight-fitting black dress that hugged her body so tight God could see the roundness of her hips and the plumpness of her high ass cheeks from a distance. BG wore her hair pulled up into a high-class bun with a few tendrils at the sides of her face. Even from where he sat, God could see BG's smooth deep cocoa skin gleaming.

"You want me go over there and call her over to you?" Freddie asked.

"Nah. This is a special one, I'll do it myself. Shit, I have never seen that sexy bitch in a dress. She always tries to act like a man in the streets . . . jeans and slacks and shit every time I run into her or have pictures taken of her, but from where I stand now, I see a feminine pretty bitch that needs some God in her life," God said snidely, a sly grin creasing his lips. He tried to stand up, but he slid back down when his wobbly legs didn't cooperate.

"Whoa, nigga . . . you good?" Freddie said, grabbing God's arm for support.

"Fuck off me, little boy," God growled. "I been drinking before you could pee straight," God said, wrestling his arm away from Freddie. A few of God's hired security guards rushed over to his side to help him too.

"It's all good. I'm good. Nothing to see here," God joked, slurring his words and holding his hand up in a halting motion.

"All I need you dumb m'fuckers to do is watch me while I go over there and speak to that pretty bitch sitting right there," God garbled his words as he pointed in BG's direction. "She looking like she came out here to find some dick in that 'come fuck me' dress with those chocolate stick legs calling out to me 'n' shit," God continued. He was finally stable enough on his legs to walk out of VIP and head toward where BG was sitting at the bar. God had told his security to just watch him, but a few of them fanned out around the club to make sure they were in close striking distance if anything popped off with their boss.

BG threw back her fifth shot of Patrón and crinkled her face when it burned going down. She had too much on her mind right now. BG could not stop thinking about the moment Sean called her Sunny's name during sex.

"Motherfucker. Bitch-ass nigga," BG whispered as she lifted a Coco Loso to her lips.

"Harsh words," a voice came from her left side. BG whirled around on her bar stool with a scowl on her face that could've scared away an opposing army.

"Get the fuck . . ." BG started, but her words were immediately clipped short when she saw who the voice was. BG eased the look on her face and touched her Chanel bag to make sure her .27 Glock Special was handy.

"Looking beautiful tonight, Black Girl . . . or should I call you BG?" God said politely, trying hard to keep his words straight as drunk as he was.

"God . . . thanks . . ." BG nodded.

"I never thought I'd see you in a dress, but I'll tell you, you should wear them more often. You are fucking simply gorgeous," God complimented, laying his game down. BG blushed even though she didn't want to. She was feeling lonely and vulnerable and with the liquor easing her defenses, God was right on time.

"Where's all of your security?" God asked, looking around and then back at BG.

"I needed a night out on my own. You know . . . to clear my head," she said.

"I know the feeling," God lied. He could care less about her clearing her mind, he was just making sure she was really alone.

BG finished her Coco Loso and before she could order another drink, God held up his hand to the bartender.

"Bring her three of whatever she's been drinking . . . on God's tab, VIP," God told him. The bartender nodded and within a few minutes he placed two more shots of Patrón and two Coco Losos in front of BG. She chuckled.

"There's no way I can drink all of this," she said.

"Nonsense. We got all night, beauty," God said smoothly.

BG was really feeling his compliments, it was easing the pain she was still feeling from the mishap with Sean. BG picked up the first of the shots and took it straight back. God started clapping and laughing.

"I knew you were my kind of woman," God said. He picked up his drink and did the same. BG laughed at him. The liquor definitely had her on another level tonight. BG was usually very guarded and defensive, but tonight she was easy going and open. God noticed the change and he planned on making the best of it. After another shot, BG's head started to lull side to side and she was winding her waist in her chair from the music. God was watching her through hazy eyes, but that didn't keep him from becoming turned on.

God stepped closer to her, smiling. He extended his hand and ran it up her leg. BG stopped moving for a second. God thought she was going to slap him and throw a drink in his face, but instead, she winked at him, licked her lips and smiled. God moved his hand farther up her leg.

"So where's your partner in crime at . . . the king?" God whispered seductively in her ear while he moved his hand farther and farther up her dress. BG giggled, but that quickly changed.

"Don't even bring that nigga up to me right now. I ain't fucking with his fiend-ass. After all I did for that nigga, he's shitted on me for the last time," BG said seriously, looking at God pitifully.

God could see the pain in her eyes. He used his other hand to stroke her face.

"Baby, you're too beautiful to let any nigga mistreat you. I would treat you like the queen that you are," God said. The hand that was under BG's dress had finally reached its goal. God fiddled with BG's dripping wet middle until his pointer finger slipped inside of her. BG closed her eyes and licked her lips. She opened her legs a little more so God could get a better feel.

"Sisss. Ahh," BG moaned into God's ear. "I bet if I fucked you tonight that would show that nigga Sean who the real boss is," BG panted. God's left eyebrow went up on his face and his dick was hard as a roll of quarters.

"Let's go back to my suite. Let me show you how God puts it down," he said. God was suddenly a little more sober. It was like the real heavenly God had opened up the sky and poured him out a blessing. God saw the opportunity to get BG into his clutches so that he could use her against Sean, plus, she was so gorgeous, God didn't mind adding her to the notches in his belt.

"You ready to go, baby girl," God asked BG as he pulled his fingers from under her dress and put them in his mouth.

"Damn that was sexy as fuck," BG slurred, throwing her arm around God's neck.

"You got me ready to fuck the shit out of you, gorgeous. Let's get the fuck out of her," God told BG, helping her down from the stool. BG stumbled the first time she stood on her legs after all the time she spent drinking.

"Slow and steady, beautiful," God told her, holding on to her waist. He waved a few of his henchmen over along with Freddie.

"What up, God?" Freddie said all the while smiling sinisterly at BG.

God leaned in to Freddie's ear so BG wouldn't hear what he was saying.

"I'm about to slide off with this beauty. You bring the truck around and tell the rest to fall back. I'll be in my suite. I'll be good," God told Freddie.

Freddie was smiling and giggling like a goofy little boy. He was excited that his boss was going to finally get BG after all of the years she acted like she was such a tough nut to crack.

"A'ight, God, I'll be around back with the truck," Freddie said excitedly.

BG was hanging all over God's neck. She was laughing although no one had told any jokes.

"You smell so fuckin' good," BG giggled, putting her nose up against God's neck taking a big sniff.

"C'mon so I can show you just how good I smell," God said, moving forward. BG stumbled and almost hit the floor. God grabbed onto her just before she fell forward.

"I'm ... I'm ... sorry, sexy. I ... I ... had too much to ... dri ... drink," BG mumbled, her words garbled and choppy. God was laughing inside. He was sure he had her right where he wanted her.

Freddie pulled the Benz G-wagon to the back door of Club Lure. BG was so drunk she had pulled her dress up around her hips and started doing a seductive dance in front of God while they waited. God was amused as he watched BG get totally out of character.

"C'mon because I can't wait to have you," God said as they entered the back seat of the truck. BG climbed inside and immediately removed her thongs. She put them up to God's nose, teasing him with her scent.

"Taste it," BG whispered, sliding down in the seat and opening her legs wide. God laughed as he lowered his head between BG's beautiful, toned legs.

"You are so fucking beautiful," God said. Then he extended his tongue and pressed it into BG's creamy center.

"Shit!" she huffed, clutching the top of God's head. God moved his mouth over her steamy box like a starving refugee. He licked and sucked and licked again.

"I'm about to cum," BG growled as she grinded her hips toward God's face.

"We're here!" Freddie called out from the front seat. God stopped licking and lifted his wet face.

"No, don't stop," BG whined, trying to grab for God to come back between her legs.

"I'll finish when we get upstairs. I got a lot more shit to show your pretty ass," God told her as he wiped her moisture off his lips and chin. Reluctantly, BG closed her legs and slid her dress down over her ample backside.

"Hurry up because I'm fuckin' horny as shit right now," she demanded.

She looked at Freddie through the rearview mirror and winked at him. Freddie tried to avert his eyes after getting caught watching, but it was too late, BG had already saw him and she let him know it too.

"Wait here and I'll call when I'm done," God told Freddie. Freddie nodded; he was too busy watching BG's ass to watch out for his and God's well-being.

God held on to BG's hand and led her into his five-star hotel. BG was giggling and cooing like a silly schoolgirl. She was so drunk, she couldn't keep her hands off of God, which was causing a scene.

"Let me see it. Let me suck it," BG demanded loudly as they walked to the elevators. God smiled awkwardly at all of the stuffy rich people watching them. He still had a reputation to uphold amongst his legitimate business connections so he was trying his best to keep BG at bay.

"Wait until we get upstairs, baby," God said calmly, trying his best to hold on to his composure.

"I just can't keep my hands off of you. You sexy fuck!" BG called out loudly. God was relieved when the elevator doors finally dinged opened. Once inside, BG watched him press 10. Then he turned toward her and pushed BG up against the wall. God ran his hands over her breasts and roughly hitched her dress up around her hips.

"Yeah . . . that's what the fuck I like," BG huffed. But, before God could do anything else the elevator was opening on their floor.

"Shit!" he grumbled. God grabbed BG and pulled her toward his suite. BG looked on the door.

"Mmm, lucky number 1050," she repeated. "1050 is my new lucky number," she said again.

"Yeah, it's the number of strokes it's going to take to make you cum all over yourself," God laughed. He slid his cardkey into the slot and led BG inside. Once they crossed the doorsill, God moved toward BG like she was his prey.

"Now you can have me . . . all of me," God told her as he crushed his mouth over hers. BG pulled away from him and laughed like a valley girl.

"I gotta tell you something," she giggled and then bit down hard on his bottom lip.

"What! Ow! Fuck!" God growled, pulling away from her.

"Sean . . . um . . . Sean knows you killed his grand-mother and his woman and his baby," BG slurred with a drunken drawl. God crinkled his eyebrows and took a few steps back from her.

"What? What did you just say to me?" God grumbled. Just then, BG reached into her Chanel bag and pulled out her Glock. God's eyes went wide, but his jaw went square.

"What the fuck you think you doing, bitch?" God said angrily.

"Shut the fuck up, you old-ass m'fucker," BG snarled with suddenly clear speech as she leveled her gun at him.

"You dumb bitch. Do you think I'd be dumb enough to bring you here without my men watching me?" God scoffed at her.

"Nah, you the dumb m'fucker. Do you think I'd be dumb enough to be drinking with you all night and letting my fucking guard down around my enemy? You think I would really fuck your old ass?" BG shot back.

"What? I saw you?" God said dumbfounded.

"You saw me drinking pineapple juice and water. Already paid the bartender off. Oh and this dress . . . specially made just for your eyes, bitch," BG said.

There was a faint knock at the door. God whirled around and stumbled a little because he was still tipsy himself.

With her gun aiming right at God's head, BG stepped backward and twisted the doorknob. She smiled at God when the person knocking walked into the room.

"Thanks, baby. I was getting a little tired of listening on the phone," Sean said, holding his cell phone up so God could see it.

"Oh I was hoping you could hear everything clearly," BG said with a wicked smile as she lifted her cell phone out of her purse. "Gotta keep that call going. Lucky num-ber 1050," BG said, winking at God. Then she laughed.

"So what the fuck you gon' do, fiend?" God spat at Sean. "You ain't shit and neither was your grandmother when my men fucked her old ass then gutted her like a fucking pig," God said maliciously.

Sean looked at God like he was bored. Sean was calm, he wasn't going to give God the satisfaction of letting him get under his skin and make him act up.

"You know, God . . . when you've been through all the shit I've been through in life there ain't much more that can fuck you up. Your words don't mean shit to me, but sending you to hell is what I've been living for," Sean said. With that, he rushed into God with a long hunter's knife in his hand.

God threw his hands up, but he had no wins. Sean swiftly brought the knife across God's neck with the precision of a first-class surgeon. The first slice hit a major artery in God's neck and deep, dark red arterial blood spilled from God's flesh with every pump of his heart. God's eyes bulged and his tongue came out of his lips as he gasped for air. He reached one arm out toward Sean and BG while he used the other to try to put pressure on his bleeding artery.

Without a word, Sean stepped closer to God and whipped his knife again. This time it cut so deep God's head was almost severed. BG turned her face away and dry heaved from the smell of fresh blood.

Sean turned toward her and smiled. "You good?" Sean asked her. BG nodded. Sean moved close to her and kissed her on the cheek before she could protest. BG jumped, but it was too late. He had already done it.

"No matter what our differences are, one thing is for sure, B . . . we work damn good as a team. You my family and I'm yours and that's real nigga shit," Sean proclaimed. BG didn't want to crack a smile and make him think she had forgiven him fully, but she couldn't help it. Sean was her family and she couldn't deny that no matter what.

Sean quickly changed his clothes and they exited the hotel as if they were a loving couple. Outside, BG smirked when she passed the G-wagon and saw Freddie slumped forward over the wheel. She looked at Sean with questions in her eyes.

"I had them boys you called in take care of that bitch-ass nigga. They said that nigga pleaded and cried like the bitch that he is," Sean said with a evil chuckle.

"Well what goes around . . ." BG said as she slid into her Benz, which Sean had driven to the hotel.

"Let's get the fuck out of L.A. and back to our city. We got streets to claim," Sean said. BG smiled and nodded her agreement. King Sean was officially back in business. At least, she hoped so.

Chapter Twenty-one

Two months after they returned to their city, Sean and BG had reclaimed their spot at the top of the heroin and meth business. Sean had reunited with Beans and Ak and partied until he was too tired to move. BG had hooked him up with a low-key spot to live that overlooked the water, but when Sean was alone in the apartment, he was overwhelmed with thoughts of Sunny so he tried to keep busy and stay on the streets making moves. It had been a little difficult for him to be around all of that heroin when the shipments came in, but Sean was handling himself as well as could be expected.

BG hadn't done much partying with Sean and his dudes because she had been feeling slightly under the weather the past few weeks. Now, BG lit the end of a fat blunt and took a long toke. She swung her legs in and out as she paced up and down on the cold marble floor of her bathroom.

"Come the fuck on. This shit says results in less than two minutes," BG grumbled out loud, taking another long drag. Even the powerful purple haze she was puffing on wasn't easing her nerves.

"I hope this shit says negative. I can't afford another complicated fucking situation with this nigga," BG spoke to herself as if another person was in the room. One last long toke and an even longer exhale of the smoke and BG was finally ready to read her results. She flopped down on the lid of her toilet seat and grabbed the little test. BG had purchased the high tech ones that read "pregnant" or "not pregnant." She didn't have time for the two lines or one line tests.

BG took a good ten seconds before she had the heart to look down at the test. Finally she inhaled and looked at it. She read it and let the results settle in her mind, but instead of settling, the words sounded off in her head like small bombs exploding.

"Fucking pregnant!" BG yelled out. "Can't believe this shit! Pregnant from a night of passion where a nigga called me the dead bitch name," BG relayed out loud to herself. She stood up and looked at herself in the full body mirror hanging on the back of her bathroom door. She touched her stomach, but it was still flat as a board. BG's shoulders slumped and she sat back down on the toilet. She was contemplating whether or not to tell Sean. BG had to weigh her options. If she told him and he reacted negatively, she would never forgive herself, but if she told him and he realized that the baby was going to be the only family he had he would be extremely happy. BG closed her eyes and cradled her head in her hands. After a few seconds of mulling things over, BG jumped to her feet with a smile on her face.

"Fuck it! You know what , you're going to tell him and he's going to be happy. He doesn't have family and he could use this news. Finally, you will take a spot in his heart as the one who gives him a piece of himself to carry on his name," BG pep talked herself. Feeling confident, BG rushed around her house getting dressed in an outfit she thought Sean would like.

BG held several different blouses, jeans and pumps up against herself until she was finally satisfied with her look. When she picked up her cell phone, she looked down at the screen and noticed the calendar. BG's heart sank and her stomach immediately went into knots.

"Fuck! The anniversary of her death," BG whispered, realizing it was a year to the day that Sunny had over-dosed and died. Suddenly, BG wasn't feeling as confident about relaying her news to Sean. BG paced a few seconds trying to get her nerves up.

"You know what . . . fuck this. I'm not going to continue to live in the shadow of a dead bitch. I'm carrying his baby and even if he is having a hard time with today, this me and this news will trump all of that," BG mumbled.

"Fuck you, Sunny! Fuck you! I got the upper hand now! Rot in hell and stop fucking haunting him and stop fucking haunting me! Die forever, bitch! As soon as I tell him about *our* baby he will forget about you! He will fucking forget about you!" BG screamed as if Sunny were standing right in front of her.

Sean sat on the floor of his bathroom rocking back and forth. Next to him on his left was the gram of heroin he had lifted from the last shipment, on his right was a needle and a rubber arm tie and in his hand was a picture of Sunny. In the picture, Sunny wore a orange, flowing Gucci blouse that brought the striking green out in her eyes and played up her caramel skin. Sunny was smiling like a model and her hair danced around her face perfectly. Sean remembered the day she'd taken the picture and his heart broke into pieces.

"I fuckin' miss you, Sun. This life ain't shit without you," he whispered, using his thumb to wipe his own tear off the glass part of the frame that covered the picture.

"I can't do this shit. On everything, I ain't really got shit without you, my moms, Fox, Big Mama . . . y'all the only ones I cared about," Sean said, his voice rising and falling with grief. "I ain't built to be the nigga to live without no family."

Sean's shoulders quaked with a round of sobs as he thought about how he had the opportunity to save Sunny, but he blew it.

"Arggg!" Sean growled, throwing the picture across the bathroom. The frame smashed and cracked making Sunny's image seem like it had been cut to pieces.

"I was supposed to always protect you! I promised you that I would! I failed you, Sunny! I fuckin' failed you! Instead of saving you, I joined you in this hell! I fed you drugs every day! I did . . . me! Instead of saving you!" Sean cried out. He felt like a 1,000-pound boulder of guilt was sitting on his chest and he couldn't breathe. Sean couldn't live with himself for what had happened to the only woman, beside his mother and grandmother, that he had ever really loved from the heart.

"I don't deserve to live," Sean growled, picking up the pack of dope at his side. He squeezed the packet in his hand for a long few minutes, while he rocked back and forth sobbing.

"I can't do this shit . . . not alone! Not without my Sun!" Sean cried. Then, as if he was possessed, Sean jumped to his feet. He grabbed his works and laid them out on the back of his toilet seat. He placed a little ball of heroin into a spoon, dropped a few drips of water on it, and flicked his lighter on. Sean eyed the spoon carefully as he heated up the dope. Suddenly he could hear Sunny's voice in his ear as if she was standing next to him.

"Sean, don't cook it too long. That's how you get that half-ass high. It only takes a few minutes, baby. Put it down carefully and tie your arm before you get that stem. Loading your stem is the last step when you doing this shit by yourself. Remember to tie that shit above the elbow or else you only gon' get them little tiny weak veins that will collapse before you can hit it. Pull tighter. As tight as you can stand it. You got it . . . just like that,

baby. Now it's time to load your stem. When you load your stem, pull the plunger back slowly so no air don't get trapped in between the dope. If air hits your vein that shit can rush to your heart and take you right out of here, nigga. Yeah, you got all this shit down pact now. Like a pro, I'm so proud of you, baby. I knew you could get high without my help, nigga . . . you been faking all along." Sunny's voice played in his ears.

Sean had everything done just like Sunny had taught him the first time he ever hit his vein himself. He took one last look at himself in the mirror, the veins in his arms bulging under the tight grip of the rubber tie. He lifted the needle, his hands shaking fiercely. Sean took a deep breath as one more tear slid down his face.

"I can't do this without you, Sunny," Sean said sadly. With that, he put the needle to his arm, closed his eyes and blindly hit his vein. Sean eased the heroin into his vein. When the needle was empty, his legs gave out and Sean hit the floor. For a few minutes, his body stiffened and he could hear the music that his mother used to play at her parties when he was a kid.

"Urggg," Sean growled, as his jaw tightened causing him to bite down into his own tongue. Blood filled his mouth within seconds. Then, his body involuntarily bucked like he'd been hit with the electric paddles they use to shock dead people back to life. Another low gurgle escaped Sean's mouth, this time a mixture of blood and white foam spilled from his lips. His body jolted again, but this time it happened several times in a row. Sean's bladder and sphincter muscle released urine and feces from his body and now vomit erupted up his esophagus.

"I love you more than anything in this world," Sean's mother said.

"Little man, I had love for your mother so I'll always have love for you," Fox said.

"Aww, baby boy. I love you so much," Big Mama said.
Sean could see all of his loved ones talking to him.
Then a little boy who reminded Sean of himself came
toward him and gave him a pound. Sean was asking the
little boy who he was, but the boy didn't say anything
and he just kept walking. When the little boy was gone,
so was everyone else and then blackness engulfed Sean.

BG laid on the bell again, looking at her watch with crumpled eyebrows.

"I know Beans told me this nigga was at home. Why the fuck he ain't answering his door?" BG huffed impatiently. She went from ringing the bell to all out pounding her fist on the door. "Sean! It's me . . . BG, open the damn door!" she hollered. BG didn't care about his neighbors; she was starting to grow concerned. BG banged for a few more minutes and then she called Beans. He told her to wait until he got there.

When Beans arrived, he used a spare key Sean had given him to get inside. BG and Beans almost killed each other trying to be the first to get through the door.

"King?" Beans hollered.

"Sean!" BG called out. They both rushed around the apartment.

Finally, Beans came upon the locked bathroom door. His heart immediately started pounding against his chest bone and he wanted to keep BG away just in case his suspicions proved true. BG was on Beans's heels.

"Is he in there?" she asked frantically, an ominous feeling coming over her like a dark cloud. Beans turned toward her with pain in his eyes.

"I don't know, B . . . Why don't you go call 911 just in case and let me handle this," Beans said sadly.

"No! I won't leave him! No!" BG screamed. "Open the door! Open the fucking door!" BG screeched through newly falling tears. Beans thrust his shoulder into the bathroom door four times before it finally gave.

"Sean! No!" BG screamed, falling to her knees as she looked down at Sean's lifeless body. His eyes were opened, staring up at the ceiling and he had what looked like a smile on his face. Sean was finally at peace with people who loved him the most.

Sean snapped out of his daydream as he heard the banging on his front door, followed by the bell being rang several times. The thoughts of BG finding him dead was heartbreaking. Tears in his eyes, he shook his head, disappointed in himself for almost falling to the allure of the drug. He heard BG hollering his name and at that very moment, he remembered that through it all he still had his ride or die bitch, BG. He tossed the needle across the room and looked up to the sky as if he was looking into the heavens at Fox, Big Mama, and Sunny. He smiled and vowed to never pick up a needle again. At that point, he knew that he had beaten his addiction. He would never go back to that dark place that he once was. The pounds on the door were getting louder. He unwrapped his arm and smiled. "Here I come BG. . . . here I come." he said with a smirk.

THE END

ORDER FORM
URBAN BOOKS, LLC
97 N18th Street
Wyandanch, NY 11798

Name (please print):_____

Address: _____

City/State: _____

Zip: _____

QTY	TITLES	PRICE
	16 On The Block	$14.95
	A Girl From Flint	$14.95
	A Pimp's Life	$14.95
	Baltimore Chronicles	$14.95
	Baltimore Chronicles 2	$14.95
	Betrayal	$14.95
	Bi-Curious	$14.95
	Bi-Curious 2: Life After Sadie	$14.95
	Bi-Curious 3: Trapped	$14.95
	Both Sides Of The Fence	$14.95
	Both Sides Of The Fence 2	$14.95
	California Connection	$14.95

Shipping and handling: add $3.50 for 1st book, then $1.75 for each additional book.

Please send a check payable to:
Urban Books, LLC
Please allow 4-6 weeks for delivery

ORDER FORM
URBAN BOOKS, LLC
97 N18th Street
Wyandanch, NY 11798

Name (please print):_____

Address: _____

City/State: _____

Zip: _____

QTY	TITLES	PRICE
	California Connection 2	$14.95
	Cheesecake And Teardrops	$14.95
	Congratulations	$14.95
	Crazy In Love	$14.95
	Cyber Case	$14.95
	Denim Diaries	$14.95
	Diary Of A Mad First Lady	$14.95
	Diary Of A Stalker	$14.95
	Diary Of A Street Diva	$14.95
	Diary Of A Young Girl	$14.95
	Dirty Money	$14.95
	Dirty To The Grave	$14.95

Shipping and handling: add $3.50 for 1st book, then $1.75 for each additional book.

Please send a check payable to:

Urban Books, LLC

Please allow 4-6 weeks for delivery

ORDER FORM
URBAN BOOKS, LLC
97 N18th Street
Wyandanch, NY 11798

Name (please print):_____

Address: _____

City/State: _____

Zip: _____

QTY	TITLES	PRICE
	Gunz And Roses	$14.95
	Happily Ever Now	$14.95
	Hell Has No Fury	$14.95
	Hush	$14.95
	If It Isn't love	$14.95
	Kiss Kiss Bang Bang	$14.95
	Last Breath	$14.95
	Little Black Girl Lost	$14.95
	Little Black Girl Lost 2	$14.95
	Little Black Girl Lost 3	$14.95
	Little Black Girl Lost 4	$14.95
	Little Black Girl Lost 5	$14.95

Shipping and handling: add $3.50 for 1st book, then $1.75 for each additional book.
Please send a check payable to:
Urban Books, LLC
Please allow 4-6 weeks for delivery

ORDER FORM
URBAN BOOKS, LLC
97 N18th Street
Wyandanch, NY 11798

Name (please print):_____

Address: _____

City/State: _____

Zip: _____

QTY	TITLES	PRICE
	Loving Dasia	$14.95
	Material Girl	$14.95
	Moth To A Flame	$14.95
	Mr. High Maintenance	$14.95
	My Little Secret	$14.95
	Naughty	$14.95
	Naughty 2	$14.95
	Naughty 3	$14.95
	Queen Bee	$14.95
	Say It Ain't So	$14.95
	Snapped	$14.95
	Snow White	$14.95

Shipping and handling: add $3.50 for 1st book, then $1.75 for each additional book.

Please send a check payable to:

Urban Books, LLC

Please allow 4-6 weeks for delivery

ORDER FORM
URBAN BOOKS, LLC
97 N18th Street
Wyandanch, NY 11798

Name (please print):_____

Address: _____

City/State: _____

Zip: _____

QTY	TITLES	PRICE
	Spoil Rotten	$14.95
	Supreme Clientele	$14.95
	The Cartel	$14.95
	The Cartel 2	$14.95
	The Cartel 3	$14.95
	The Dopefiend	$14.95
	The Dopeman Wife	$14.95
	The Prada Plan	$14.95
	The Prada Plan 2	$14.95
	Where There Is Smoke	$14.95
	Where There Is Smoke 2	$14.95

Shipping and handling: add $3.50 for 1st book, then $1.75 for each additional book.
Please send a check payable to:
Urban Books, LLC
Please allow 4-6 weeks for delivery